THE
DEAD SEEKERS

BY BARB AND J. C. HENDEE

The Noble Dead Saga–Series One

Dhampir
Thief of Lives
Sister of the Dead
Traitor to the Blood
Rebel Fay
Child of a Dead God

The Noble Dead Saga–Series Two

In Shade and Shadow
Through Stone and Sea
Of Truth and Beasts

The Noble Dead Saga–Series Three

Between Their Worlds
The Dog in the Dark
A Wind in the Night
First and Last Sorcerer
The Night Voice

ALSO BY BARB HENDEE

The Vampire Memories Series

Blood Memories
Hunting Memories
Memories of Envy
In Memories We Fear
Ghost of Memories

The Mist-Torn Witches Series

The Mist-Torn Witches
Witches in Red
Witches with the Enemy
To Kill a Kettle Witch

THE
DEAD SEEKERS

Barb & J. C. Hendee

ACE   *New York*

ACE
Published by Berkley
An imprint of Penguin Random House LLC
375 Hudson Street, New York, New York 10014

Copyright © 2017 by Barb Hendee and J. C. Hendee
Penguin Random House supports copyright. Copyright fuels creativity, encourages diverse
voices, promotes free speech, and creates a vibrant culture. Thank you for buying an authorized
edition of this book and for complying with copyright laws by not reproducing, scanning, or
distributing any part of it in any form without permission. You are supporting writers and
allowing Penguin Random House to continue to publish books for every reader.

ACE is a registered trademark and the A colophon is a trademark of
Penguin Random House LLC.

Library of Congress Cataloging-in-Publication Data

Names: Hendee, Barb, author. | Hendee, J. C., author.
Title: The dead seekers/Barb and J. C. Hendee.
Description: First edition. | New York: Ace, 2017.
Identifiers: LCCN 2016025986 (print) | LCCN 2016034496 (ebook) |
ISBN 9780451469342 (hardback) | ISBN 9780698154469 (ebook)
Subjects: LCSH: Dead—Fiction. | Man-woman relationships—Fiction. | BISAC: FICTION/
Fantasy/Epic. | FICTION/Fantasy/General. | GSAFD: Fantasy fiction. | Horror fiction.
Classification: LCC PS3608.E525 D43 2017 (print) | LCC PS3608.E525 (ebook) |
DDC 813/.6—dc23
LC record available at https://lccn.loc.gov/2016025986

First Edition: January 2017

Printed in the United States of America
1   3   5   7   9   10   8   6   4   2

Jacket art by Steve Stone
Book design by Kelly Lipovich

THE
DEAD SEEKERS

PROLOGUE

"**O**ne more, my lady," the midwife urged a woman before her on a bed. "Bear down!"

The room was lavishly decorated with tapestries, cushions, and polished furniture, but the sheets of the great bed were soaked in blood. The dim chamber was thick with the smell of perspiration, amid sounds of panting and pained cries.

"Now!" the midwife ordered.

Baroness Reagan Vishal drew a deep breath, and her sweat-sheened features twisted with agony in a final effort.

"I have him, my lady!" cried the midwife.

Reagan fell back in exhaustion against sweat-drenched pillows.

The midwife smiled as she straightened, holding something small wrapped in cloth. "It's a boy. A moment, while I cut the cord."

"A boy," Reagan whispered in relief, not even lifting her head.

As the small knife slit through the infant's umbilical, the midwife's smile faded. She froze for an instant and then rushed to a side table, laying the bundle there and unwrapping it.

Eyes closed, the newborn did not move.

The midwife breathed lightly into the infant's mouth, then waited, watched, and tried again—and again. Nothing changed.

The young baroness struggled to sit up in the bed, watching them. Stricken, the midwife barely glanced aside.

"My lady . . ."

"No!" Reagan cried out.

The great door to the manor bedchamber slammed open.

As a wide-shouldered man in a blue tunic strode in, the midwife spun to intercept him.

"My—my lord, you cannot be in here."

"Out of my way," he ordered without slowing.

"Gerold!" Reagan called. "Help him. Tell me he's not . . . that he's not . . ."

Baron Gerold Vishal stopped at the side table and looked down at the unmoving infant for a long moment. His hard features twitched, perhaps with grief, as his wife began weeping in silence.

The son they had longed for was stillborn.

The baron didn't look at the midwife. He whispered, "Take him away from here. Prepare him for immediate burial."

With a short nod, the midwife stepped in and rewrapped the tiny body, even covering his face. The child had been out of the womb too long with no breath and would not recover. Holding him close, she fled the great bedchamber, intending to go down to the kitchens below to clean the tiny corpse. Out in the upper passage, she couldn't help stopping.

"Poor little mite," she whispered to the born-dead. "Not even a moment in this world before you are off to the next."

The blanket moved slightly, and the midwife tensed. With a gasp, she shifted the bundle to one arm and drew back the blanket's corner.

The infant boy's eyes were open.

Those eyes were so dark, seemingly without color, as they stared up at her in the dim passage without blinking. Then they began turning light blue. The bloodstained blanket rose and fell just barely with his small breaths.

"My lord! My lady!" the midwife called out, running for the bed-chamber. "He lives."

As she burst into the room, both noble parents were already staring toward the door. She held out the child, at a loss for which parent to rush to first. Baron Gerold strode toward her in disbelief and looked down. Reaching out, he took his son and hurried back to the bed and his wife.

"He lives?" he said, his voice trembling.

Reagan's flushed cheeks were still coated in tears as she reached for the child.

"Let me hold him," she pleaded, and took her newborn son gently— carefully—as if afraid he might die again.

"We'll call him Tris," she whispered, "after my father, if you agree?"

The baron didn't answer and instead looked to the midwife. "He is so quiet. Should he not cry?"

The midwife stepped near, perhaps now puzzled as well.

The infant made not a sound and looked at no one present. Instead, he stared off to the right of the bed, where the one lantern's light barely reached. In a glance into the room's dark corner, the midwife saw noth-ing, and yet when she turned back, the boy's gaze had not wavered from . . . whatever he saw.

Thirteen Years Later

At the proud age of ten, Mari Kaleja had no fear of entering the Wicker Woods, or so she would've said. She sat safely between her papa and mama on the high front bench of her family's rolling wagon home. Everything around her was a comfort she knew well, from the crunch of wheels on a hardened road to the creak of the old, worn wooden bench and the dank smell of moss on a wet night.

Two other wagons followed behind, filled with aunts, uncles, and cousins in this family of the wandering people—the Móndyalítko. Known to themselves as "the world's little children," they were too often thought of by others as vagabond thieves and tricksters.

When Papa had announced they would camp in the Wicker Woods, a thrill had run through Mari. Common folk nearby shunned this place, for all knew the story. Before she was even born, a captured murderer named Wicker escaped his execution and hid in these woods. He caught passersby and killed them for what they had—or maybe just because he could.

Mari looked up at Papa, holding the wagon's reins. "Aren't you afraid?"

He was a big man with a mustache like a bushy hedge under a wide nose.

"No, my little kitten, not a bit!" And Papa chuckled. "That Wicker is long dead, though he'd done us a good turn without knowing. We'll camp without being bothered by locals, too scared to follow us in, even if they knew we'd come here."

If Papa wasn't afraid, then Mari wasn't afraid. Still, she couldn't help a shivering thrill. Whenever they camped in this place, it did scare her a little. But she was loved, protected, and even more. Now and then, some Móndyalítko were born special—like her.

They rolled deeper into the Wicker Woods. Being tucked in between Mama and Papa on the wagon's bench made her feel brave. She liked feeling brave, especially when she wasn't.

"Over there," Papa said, leaning out to call back to the family's other two wagons. "Near the stream, but not too close."

Before long, all their wagons stopped, brakes and wheel braces were set, and everyone busied setting up "home" for the night. Above, the near-full moon lit the clear sky, though little light reached through the branches into the woods.

Mari crouched by the fire lit in a ring of gathered stones as her mama cut up potatoes, carrots, and dry-cured jerky into an iron pot hung over the low flames. It had been another long day on the road, and Mari yawned.

"Don't fall asleep," Mama said. "Not until you've eaten."

Mama was younger than Papa, with green-flecked brown eyes and long hair like dark chocolate—like Mari's. And she was special too, in a different way. Mama sometimes saw things that others didn't: things far away or that hadn't happened yet. Not always, but sometimes. Mari's eyes were a shade of brown so light they could be called amber.

"I'm too hungry to sleep," she answered.

Mama smiled. "Not long now."

Mari's eyelids began to droop just the same. She hugged her knees where she crouched, scrunching the wrapped quilt-work skirt, with its shiny little garnishes sewn into the pattern. Those little disks cut from inside seashells sparkled in the firelight. Her head began to nod just as she heard Papa's voice.

"Should I carry her to bed?"

"No, wake her," Mama answered. "She needs to eat."

Suddenly a scream made Mari's eyes pop wide.

"Look out, Tisia!"

That was her mama's name; that was Auntie Esmeralda who'd screamed it. Mama cried out in pain as something white that resembled a hand came through her chest. Then something struck the fire. Smoke and sparks scattered everywhere. Everything turned so dark, and Mari couldn't see anyone else by the ring of stones.

Two more screams from across the camp drove shudders through her.

"Mama?" she cried, and then screamed herself. "Mama!"

Smoke in darkness swirled as someone ran through it.

Mari tumbled backward in trying to get away and then saw Papa. He ran for their wagon, though she didn't see why until he spun about. In his hand was his long-handled woodsman's ax, taken from where he kept it beneath the bench. He stalled at spotting her.

"Run!" he shouted in the dark. "Hide in the woods. Don't come back till I get you!"

Fear wouldn't her let move.

"Run—now!"

Terrified, Mari turned and scrambled away, but she didn't go far. More screams and shouts rose from back where she had left her home. Moss-wet branches and thorny bushes snagged and pulled her skirt again and again until she rounded a crooked but ancient tree trunk to peer toward camp.

There were glimmers like white wisps in the night among the trees. Shapes that moved, walked, and seemed to fly. She heard another shout, from her uncle Gustav, and then a shout from Papa as well, though she couldn't see them. One glimmering wisp slipped right through an oak near her wagon home, and Mari leaned in, hugging the wet tree trunk, trying for a clearer look.

It was a woman, white like chalk dust in water. Trees and the wagon showed through her as she rushed toward other shouts. A darkness flickered by in the woman's passing.

Mari shuddered and then whimpered even more.

That pure black shape was like the silhouette of a slender boy. It stopped, perhaps turned in a pause toward—or away from—where the ghost woman had gone. Mari couldn't be certain which way the silhouette turned, for it was nothing but pure blackness. No eyes, no white teeth in a mouth, nothing at all but black deeper than night.

More screams sounded, from her cousins this time. Someone ran at the black thing, and an ax-head suddenly appeared as it cut through it.

That ax-head slammed down into the earth as if it had touched nothing.

Papa came stumbling through the black thing, losing his grip on the ax, and his mouth and eyes gaped. His face twisted like he was choking.

Mari stepped out around the tree. Before she could run or call to him, he saw her.

Papa mouthed only one word before his knees hit the ground.

—Run—

A black hand sprouted through his face.

He fell forward, as if that hand wasn't there. It had slipped out through the back of his head. He flopped face-first on the wet ground and didn't move.

There was the black boy-shape opposite her through the trees.

Mari heard a whimper somewhere far-off. It cut short in a choke before silence. More glimmering white figures came through the woods—through the trees—nearing on the black one as if it had called to them. And that one took a silent step toward her.

She twisted away and ran deeper into the Wicker Woods, panting too hard to even scream. Branches tore at her clothing, caught in the quilt-work skirt, and she fell.

Mari ripped at the skirt and thrashed to get free, scrambling and then running . . . on all fours.

CHAPTER
ONE

N ightfall came and went. The chill air smelled of autumn leaves, decay, and dank earth around the quiet town of Strîbrov, hidden in the thick forest of southern Stravina.

Tris Vishal walked the main road through town, the place he now called "home." Time had passed slowly since he'd left his first home, his birthplace, and he felt older than his twenty-five years.

The pack slung over his left shoulder was heavy. His soggy black cloak hung well below his knees, weighed down by the recent rain. So was the cloak's hood, though he kept it pulled forward and low over cropped dark hair shadowing blue eyes so pale that some thought them colorless.

Tris had no wish to greet or be greeted by anyone. Thankfully, townsfolk here retired early, as this was not a region to be out late after dark. Side streets along the way were little more than mud-packed paths. When he reached a squarely built, three-story building of weather-stained pine planks at the far end of town, he paused about a stick's toss before its front door.

The bottom level was used as an herb and apothecary shop, owned and run by his landlord, Heilman Tavakovich. Tris lived on the second floor. The top floor remained unoccupied, its spare rooms used for storage, and he paid extra in rent to see that it stayed that way. All the windows were dark, including the shop's, which had glass panes behind their outer shutters.

He rounded to the building's back side and dug for his key. An actual lock in a door wasn't common, but Heilman wasn't a common proprietor or landlord.

After letting himself in, Tris climbed the back stairs to his second-floor door. Once inside, he dropped his pack and stepped through the chaos of his main chamber. Even in the dark, he didn't trip over anything, as clear paths were always kept amid the mess. He unlatched and raised the front window—the only one of his with glass—and pushed open the outer shutters.

Scant moonlight passed him, likely illuminating the room's clutter and shelves of books—parchments, tomes, and odd objects and knick-knacks everywhere—though he didn't look back.

Tris stood there staring over the silent town and the still forest, and into the darkness. Perhaps the span of twenty slow breaths passed before he finally turned around. By then, the room had turned cold from the night air.

Three faded tables were cluttered with small urns, bottles, and mortar and pestle, leaving little room for more than a cup. A single bed and a small chest stood near the back, though to the south was a door to a bedroom that he never used. He preferred one room for himself, with his possessions always kept within sight.

Tris had been gone four days and returned feeling more hollow than usual. Of late, the trade he had chosen—no, had chosen him—offered few tasks and no relief.

He'd gone seeking the truth of a rumor of a wandering spirit haunting the main stream of a not-too-distant village. The people there had become so frightened that they had taken to collecting rainwater in pots and buckets rather than venturing to the stream in the forest.

The haunting had been false—a neighboring village's ruse to seize water rights to the stream. There had been nothing for Tris to do. With no spirit to eject or mystery of its demise to solve, he had returned again with nothing to sate his own need.

How many times had he stood here, his back to the window, surveying this silent place, this dark room, this home that was not the home he had left years ago? That choice had been better for everyone. Still, he hated having too much time to think—to dwell.

But there was nothing else to occupy him when he had nothing to hunt.

No fence or wall surrounded Stríbrov—only the thick, dank forest—and Mari Kaleja easily avoided the main road. She slipped through trees and undergrowth to enter the town's northern back side and crouched near the front corner of an aging stable attached to a smithy.

The place stank of dung and char even in the cold, even after the day's chill rain.

Her thick chocolate-colored hair was pulled back into a tail held by a leather thong darkened by years. Even so, her head was masked by a cloak's hood pulled forward to shadow her face, masking as well any glint from a street lantern that might catch her amber eyes, which were oddly colored enough to be noticed and remembered.

Both her narrow hands were covered with worn-out gloves, stolen and then stained with oil to darken them. Her snug canvas pants were now damp from the knees down, and her shabby soft boots no longer kept water from seeping in.

She didn't even care about or feel the night's chill.

Dark hope brought back the heat of long hate and pain.

Was this town really where she'd finally catch "the Dead's Man"?

Vengeance had turned to a knot like a stone in her gut. How many hints, stories, and rumors had she tracked about a man who wore black, who called spirits to himself and commanded them?

Mari reached under the front of her scarred leather jerkin, felt for the hilt of the long, narrow dagger hidden there, but she didn't pull it just yet. Even though she'd darkened it with char from her last fire, there was too much risk that the well-tended steel might catch any light in the dark. Gripping the hilt was just a reflex after so many times of getting close, so many false leads, so many things she'd done—that others wouldn't—just to buy the kind of blade she couldn't steal.

It was her one treasure, waiting to be bloodied with one man's life.

"Papa . . . Mama . . . ," she whispered.

The pain was as fresh as the night she'd fled in the Wicker Woods.

Mari tried to let go of such thoughts in remembering the last words— the last hint—gained ten days ago from a traveling merchant:

The Dead's Man? Yes, I heard someone mention him. He's in Strîbrov, living over some herb shop. Not much else like it in a timber town, so you couldn't miss it.

Releasing the hilt, she gripped the stable's post, leaned forward in her crouch, and peered both ways. The main street was clear, so she rose and stepped out along the drier side of the road. She passed dwellings and shops, turning her head a little, though her eyes turned more in watching every side path, door, and shuttered window.

Mari paused two side paths away from the town's far end. She veered into the deeper shadows beneath one structure's slanted awning. There it was at the last corner ahead—the three-story building of rain-darkened planks. A sign sticking out from the dark bottom shop had one word, which she couldn't read. That didn't matter, for it held a carved symbol of a garlic bulb surrounded with leaves. Others might not have seen that in the dark.

The herb shop was shuttered up for the night, and she wavered. After coming this far, she hadn't given any thought to how to get in, which floor housed her prey, or whether he was in there this night. She knew nothing about him other than his black attire and that he had power over the spirits of the dead.

Rushing in to attack blindly within his territory was stupid. Only a fool would think cunning and stealth were enough, and she'd become too cunning for that. Glancing around, she spotted a decaying shed in a side path farther on. The place just beyond it might be a candle-and-oil shop; that could be useful, if needed. She scurried for the shack, found its door had only a rope-pull latch, and tugged slowly to open it a thumb's width.

Then she froze, listening for the sounds of movement or breathing, as the shack was too dark within for even her eyes. It wouldn't be the first time—or twelfth—that she'd found some drunk, thief, or runaway in such a place. She'd hidden and slept in a few herself over the years.

Sniffing twice, she caught nothing of the living and slipped in with one hand under the jerkin around the dagger's hilt. The shack was as empty as her senses had told her, other than piled crates and bulging burlap sacks. She pulled the door closed halfway and peeked out through the crack around its rope hinges toward the herb shop.

Her best option was to wait for her prey to come out. She could follow and catch him unaware in the wilderness.

Slipping a leather satchel off her shoulder, she dug in it with one hand while still watching that three-story building through the door's crack. Her fingers found a raw carrot stolen from a garden on the edge of town.

Such food brought strength but not relief. It too often tended to bring a memory of warm food cooked by her mother, images of being half-asleep while waiting for supper beside yet another fire. Every time she was about to eat, the same memories rose again.

Those woods, that night, after she'd watched her papa die and then run away, came back to her. Half-naked, for she'd found only part of her clothing stripped away in flight, she'd crept into her family's last camp while watching the trees all around. She saw no one and nothing, not one glimmer of those white spirits in the woods. And not the black silhouette she'd seen kill her papa.

Only a few sparks from the cook fire's scattered coals guided her at first. Then came the dark shapes of the family's silent wagon homes as she closed on the camp. She already knew the first body she'd find and never tripped over it.

Papa lay facedown on the wet ground and dark weeds, his woodsman's ax lying just out of reach beyond his head.

Mari sobbed once and, in sharpened terror, quickly clamped a hand over her mouth. She twisted frantically, looking everywhere through the trees. She saw no spirits but kept looking with wide eyes that never blinked.

And how could she even see that black one—if he was still there, here—in the dark?

She collapsed next to her papa's body, sobbing in great gasps, but no matter how she tried, she couldn't roll him over. She never saw his face again.

As she knelt there listening and looking, and not wanting to look for anyone else, she already knew she'd never find any of them alive. There might be food to find. There might be clean, dry clothes, or at least a blanket in the wagon. But all she did was curl on the ground, with her papa's shoulder for a pillow.

She dreamed of a boy's shape, blacker than moonless night, of ghosts white as wisps, and a hand erupting from her papa's face. If she screamed—more than once—she still didn't awaken until the sun came again.

On the third following day, a gamekeeper and his lad who didn't fear the Wicker Woods shook her awake at dawn. She lashed out instinctively and screeched at them like an animal—her papa's little "kitten" turned savage and feral.

Mari crouched atop her papa and wouldn't let them touch him or her.

The lad ran off at the gamekeeper's instruction. Soldiers from the nearby keep arrived. Though they looked all over, draped scavenged blankets over the collected dead, it took three of them to remove Mari. She was hauled off eventually, was later questioned but had never answered.

What could she tell them, even if that would bring back her mama and papa?

The gamekeeper tried to take her in after that, but she ran off into the dark the following night . . . to seek out more of her own people.

Mari froze in the shack, no longer chewing the raw carrot, fighting to push the memories away. The rest was useless to remember now. All that mattered now, after so many years alone in searching for vengeance, was blood on her blade. She stared at the dwelling where he lived.

Perhaps she shouldn't wait for him to come out.

Tris turned toward the window, seeing only the rooftops of the silent and dark town. He knew he should try to sleep but dreaded the thought of closing his eyes. Some people believed a long and sharp memory was a blessing. He knew better.

He remembered everything from the night he was born, though that should have been impossible. So many things set him apart, made him different, but this was the thing he minded most. He remembered his mother's love, how she doted on him and coddled him as his father looked on. If Tris's mother had refused to see that he was different, not right, his father did not.

Father's eyes soon clouded with mistrust—later with open dislike, maybe revulsion and fear as well. When Tris was only a year old, and his mother happily cradled him in a rocking chair, his father had burst in and walked over to stare down at them.

"Have you ever wondered," Baron Vishal began, "if the midwife tricked us?"

Baroness Reagan stopped rocking. "Tricked?"

The baron took only one more step and halted with a glance at his son.

"She left the room with a dead child," he said, "and suddenly returned with a living one. How do we know they were . . . are . . . one and the same?"

Baroness Reagan said nothing.

"How do we even know that is our son?" Gerold whispered.

"Get out," Reagan said quietly, and then said with greater force, "Get out! Don't touch him!"

Turning, the baron left in silence.

It was not the first time, but it was the last.

Tris's mother held him close and sang to him softly, though her voice shook. And all of this he remembered now, though then he had yet to understand all the words. When language was later fully understood, so were those words.

Tris had driven a wedge between his parents merely by being born.

By the time he could walk, his father left the manor more and more, and stayed away longer. His mother did not appear to care, though her love for Tris became smothering.

One evening of relief came when he was three years old. He'd been left alone to play with toys in his room, and a movement caught his eye. White wisps rose out of the shadows to fly and whirl all about the room—all around him. He could see right through them, and he smiled at such a wondrous sight.

They felt so familiar to him, almost more real than anyone within the manor.

He was much too young to know they didn't belong.

And then he saw the black one, so much like himself in shape, but it was so black that he could not even see its eyes. It was his size, his shape, and even sat on the room's floor in its darkest corner away from the hearth's light. When it rose, teetering like he still did sometimes, it walked out of the shadows but remained just as pure black.

It was like him . . . exactly like him.

The door opened and his father stepped in quickly, as if come for some urgent purpose.

Baron Vishal stopped at the sight of Tris-in-black, now halted halfway out of the shadows. His eyes widened—first in shock and then fear. He turned in terror upon his son.

The Tris-in-black did not want Father here. Somehow Tris knew this. It wanted Father gone, though it did not move. When it did . . .

Tris did not mean to make a sound, but his mouth opened with a shriek, loud and long and savage. It was like no sound he had ever heard, and yet it had come from him. Like all that he had ever seen, heard, or felt, he would never forget it.

His father backstepped but did not leave.

The black shape and the wisps vanished.

Baron Vishal stared at his son—at Tris—with the same terror on his face.

Yes, Tris had done something wrong that night, though he had not known it then.

Now, in his room above the herb shop, he stiffened at hearing a knock through the open window at the building's lower front door. Who would come here to a closed-up shop?

Perhaps someone with a sick relative seeking help from Heil?

Thankfully, it was not Tris's place to answer the front door, but the knock came again—and again—and again. When he stepped toward the open window, he stalled as he heard the door open. An annoyed voice was too soft to hear clearly, and so were the whispers of whoever had come.

Tris turned away, for after another empty foray into another village, he was too weary to care about whoever had come. Then he heard the footsteps coming up the inner front stairs of the building. Two pairs halted outside his door.

"Tris, open up."

Tris exhaled—in hope and dread—at Heil's voice outside his door. Without hesitation, he walked over and opened it.

There stood Heil in nothing but canvas trousers too hurriedly pulled on and only partly belted. His long silver hair and silver-gray eyes were starkly visible in the dark. So was a thick silver earring in his left earlobe as Tris lit a nearby oil lantern.

Somewhere past fifty years old, Heil was lean and wiry, though it was easy to tell he had been muscular in youth. He had no trouble attracting female company—even half his age—when the need struck him. He never settled on any particular one.

Tris still thanked whatever fate had brought him to Heil, who, unlike superstitious peasants, was unafraid of even the most terrifying truths. And he was the only one who had ever assisted Tris in seeking his own truths.

"How did you know I was home?" Tris asked.

Heil rolled his eyes and cocked one eyebrow. That was answer enough, but he jutted his chin over his right shoulder at someone half-hiding behind him on the landing.

"This one is persistent," Heil said. "Though I tried to ignore the pounding."

Tris turned his eyes toward someone shorter in the back shadows beyond the landlord. He could not make out much of the visitor, who was cloaked and hooded.

"You wish to speak with me?" Tris asked, dreading but knowing the answer. "At this time of night?"

"Are you the Dead's Man?" the shorter figure asked, barely above a whisper. He spoke with a northern dialect and accent, but Tris followed the question well enough.

Tris's left eye twitched. He did not know where or when that unwanted title had been placed upon him. There was no point in trying to change it, as in some ways it served what he sought for himself in serving those who came to him.

"Yes," Tris answered, and then, "Why have you come?"

Mari had frozen in place as she watched from within the shack as a shabby peasant boy in a dark hooded cloak approached the herb shop. He knocked softly at first, peering around at the noise, though his face was hidden in the depths of the hood. When no one came, he knocked again.

As the knocking grew to pounding, Mari pressed her face into the door's hinge-side crack, watching, wondering if anyone would answer, if she would get a first glimpse of her prey.

Finally, the door jerked inward, and an irritated man with silver hair stood glaring out and then stepped halfway through the opened doorway.

Was that him? He wasn't what she'd expected, though she'd not known what to expect. He looked too old, or at least older than she'd imagined. A short argument ensued in soft voices, but the visitor was finally ushered inside. And the door shut quietly.

Mari remained crouched with her face pressed to the door's hinge crack and waited.

And waited.

It wasn't long, though it felt so, until the door opened again, shutting quickly after the shabby youth hurried out and scurried down the street and the north side of town. That was odd as well, since most in this region wouldn't come—or go—alone at night.

Mari finally released a slow breath, realizing she'd held it. What did this mean? What had changed, if anything? What should she do now?

A short while later, the front door opened again.

Mari tensed, dropping the last of the carrot and reaching for her blade.

Someone else stepped out of the herb shop.

A figure walked slowly through the town's main way, seeming not to care about his surroundings.

Though slender and of medium height, he was obviously a man. His gait gave him away as younger than the old one who'd answered the boy's knock. Covered in a low cloak and a deep hood, both black, both hanging heavily as if wet, he carried a pack slung over one shoulder by its worn straps. He was little more than a black silhouette, even before he passed out of the first lantern's light.

Mari began to tremble as the figure walked slowly north the same direction as the peasant boy had gone. And she watched in stillness until he reached the far edge of town and went on without pause.

After so many years, could she really be this lucky?

Was it this easy after all this time?

As the last of him faded in the dark up the road beyond the town, Mari slipped silently out of the shack to follow. Her hand grew sweaty inside her glove where her grip tightened on the narrow-bladed dagger.

CHAPTER TWO

Mari kept hidden among the north-side trees as she tracked her quarry out on the road. The figure in a damp black cloak kept a steady pace, though she didn't need to hear his soft footfalls to follow him. The main road was exposed to a three-quarter moon's light, enough for her to see, if not for others.

She couldn't guess the connection he had to the peasant boy who'd visited the herb shop. But the visit had somehow served to draw the Dead's Man out of town, into the open, and alone, and that was all that mattered to her.

Twice he slowed and turned; twice she ducked low among the brush while reaching for her dagger, but she didn't draw the narrow blade.

Mari grew even colder the farther she followed. Her pant legs were damp to the knees, and her boots were wet all the way through. She couldn't remember the exact count of nights since she'd last bathed or at least rinsed out her clothing.

Mama wouldn't have approved. Then again, she couldn't disapprove of anything anymore . . . because of *him*.

In his pauses, the Dead's Man never looked her way. He only stared back down the road, though there wasn't anything there that she could see. Strîbrov was well beyond sight, and then he turned back to move on.

Mari had been living alone on the run for so long, shunned and driven out by even her own kind. Sometimes at night, she couldn't push out memories of what they'd said about her. Were any such Móndyalítko right in driving her out, when they learned what had happened?

Was something wrong with—about—her?

Had surviving that night left her "cursed"?

If so, then that was *his* fault as well.

Someone—some*thing*—had murdered her family. A black shadow of a youth—now grown to a man—had called spirits of the dead to serve it. Once, she'd questioned that, for after what he'd done to her papa why would he have needed such servants at all? That didn't matter anymore either.

If she killed him, it might end her curse, and she'd find a place in this world, if not some peace.

The black-cloaked figure stopped again on the road.

Mari dropped low and froze, peering through a scraggly fern. Had he sensed her? Had she misstepped or made a sound in being too lost in the past? Could he sense the living as well as the dead?

She drew air deep through her nose and could smell him: *sweat . . . herbs . . . too much fennel and lavender . . . garlic . . . pungent mud from the road.*

Could he smell her? No, he wasn't like her in that—few were—and even if so, he would've done something by now. A soft sigh in the dark cleared her thoughts.

The Dead's Man turned his back to her in facing the road's far side.

She rose a little, hand tightening on the dagger's handle. The moment had come.

Suddenly he strode off the road into the southern trees, and Mari's breath caught as she stalled in place.

She didn't dare step into the open without knowing if he could see her. Panic took hold. What if he was watching from hiding, even now, waiting to see something—someone—he might have sensed? Did he have some invisible spirit serving and watching over him, warning him?

Even so, she couldn't lose her prey now. Tearing out of the brush, she scurried low enough across the road that she might have dropped to all fours. When she neared the far tree line, she dropped when she heard . . .

Not footsteps—something metal clicking harshly on stone, over and over.

Mari flattened in the wet weeds and silently crawled under a wilting heather bush just far enough to see beyond it.

He was crouched on the ground beside a pile of twigs, and striking a piece of flint with the back of a knife. He was making camp? It was late, so perhaps he'd grown weary of walking and needed heat as opposed to light.

After all, what would a man who commanded the dead have to fear in the dark?

Once the fire was lit, he pulled back his hood and shrugged off his cloak. It was not the same man who'd answered the shop door. He was younger, perhaps mid-twenties, with a pale, narrow face. His hair was dark and cropped short. His clothing was nothing special: a long-sleeved black wool shirt and black pants. The only weapon he appeared to have was the small knife.

As firelight grew, she could see his strange eyes. Were they blue? There was so little color in them that she couldn't tell under the flicker of flames reflecting in them, like beacons in the dark that called her.

Aside from this, nothing about him struck her as special, powerful, forbidding. Then again, why betray himself in any way for what he could do? After spreading his cloak for a blanket upon the ground, he dug into his pack and pulled out a small leather-bound flask and what looked— smelled—like a bit of fresh cheese.

Mari felt a pang of hunger, as she couldn't remember the last time she'd tasted fresh, clean cheese.

She watched and decided she would wait for him to settle for the night. Once he lay down, and then slipped into sleep, she would wake him suddenly before her strike. She wanted him awake for what she'd do to him. She wanted to tell him who she was and what he'd done to her before he died. Let him call his spirits with his last scream; she wouldn't care what they did, once he was dead . . . truly dead.

More unwanted memories pushed themselves up from where she kept them buried and hidden in her mind, and she saw herself as a child, alone, desperate for help. After leaving the Wicker Woods—and the bodies of her parents—she'd walked for three days.

Finally, to her relief, she stumbled upon a quartet of traveling wagons, another family of Móndyalítko, from the line of Taragoš, and she ran to them. At first, the people were concerned, welcoming her, taking her to fire for warmth.

But one woman kept staring and finally said, "It's her. She is the one."

Everyone tensed. A man with graying hair had asked her, "Where is your family?"

"Dead," she answered.

"All of them?"

She nodded, fighting tears at the images she'd seen.

"In the Wicker Woods?" he asked.

She nodded.

Gasps sounded, and an argument ensued among the family, frightening her. She heard the angry word "cursed" several times.

Finally, the man with gray hair said, "We'll have to find her a place in one of the wagons. She cannot be left here. It is not our way."

Mari was given a blanket and a place beneath a bunk in the second wagon. That night, she was given dinner, but no one talked to her.

Later, she learned that the gamekeeper and the lad had spoken of what they'd found in the Wicker Woods. The soldiers had spoken. Word spread of at least twenty people found dead without a mark on them . . . their skin white . . . purple circles beneath their open eyes. Only one person had not died.

A young girl found walking among the bodies.

This story had spread quickly and far, and it was even whispered that Mari had brought about these terrible deaths herself. She didn't want to stay with this Taragoš family, not with people who didn't want her, but she had no choice. She was too young to survive on her own.

They fed her. They gave her a place to sleep. But they watched her night and day, and no one offered a kind word. Finally, in her loneliness, she found that she could weep. Alone, hiding beneath the bunk, she wept for her papa and mama, and she never stopped trying to better remember the black silhouette she'd seen on the edge of camp who seemed to command white flying spirits. She didn't bother trying to explain what she had seen that night. No one would believe her. They thought she was cursed.

Six moons later, she was passed off to a family from the line of Klempá. Money changed hands as the Taragoš paid the Klempá to take her.

Mari found herself still among the Móndyalítko, with a new family, but nothing had changed. If anything, things were worse, as this family was poorer and food was scarcer. No one spoke to her more than was necessary, and she often slept outside.

This became the pattern of her childhood, passed from one family to the next.

Every night, she longed for her papa and mama.

And now, she had their murderer in her sight.

Trembling from the effort required to hold herself back, she watched him.

He took his time eating some of the cheese and sipping from the flask. When he appeared finished and prepared to settle for the night, she readied herself, dagger in hand.

Then came a soft rustle . . . then two more . . . no, three more.

Mari's eyes tracked those soft sounds in the night. She fixed on the trees at the clearing's far side, and then quickly looked back to the Dead's Man. He was still preparing to bed down, tucking away his flask and wiping off his knife. Didn't he hear those sounds, even as soft as they were?

Not a small animal—something bigger and more than one—but she tensed in uncertainty.

A stocky man boiled out of the far brush, wielding a heavy club. Two more followed to either side: one with a short sword, and the other with a flanged mace. All three charged in.

Their clothing was filthy and tattered. She'd seen their kind too many times; they'd kill for a single coin or whatever they could take. Panic resurged harder than ever, and then rage.

The Dead's Man thrashed over, reaching for a small branch still aflame in the fire.

What if he died by someone else's hand? No, not when she was this close—not *her* prey!

As shouting broke out in the clearing, Mari ripped off her cloak and dropped low . . . and let go of the dagger.

Tris snatched a burning branch from the campfire as the root-knot of a crude club came down at his head. He dove and then rolled away. He was not a warrior, but this was not the first time he'd had to defend himself. Now and then, those who hired him were not thoroughly satisfied with his "service."

This time he had not rendered any service. Perhaps these men were part of the village that had tried to seize water rights from another. Perhaps they were only thieves.

Tris whipped the burning branch upward, forcing his attacker to reel back. He had barely gained his feet when he saw two more closing on him, better weapons in their hands. His gaze shifted back to the bulky one with the thick-stubbled jaw and neck, and that one came at him as well.

He sidestepped the other way with another swish of his brand, driving the first big one off into the path of the other two. It did not work. One of that pair with a bladed mace ducked around the big one and came at him.

Tris evaded a hard swing and felt the swish of air on his cheek as the mace's head passed by.

"Mihkt!" the mace man shouted.

Perhaps that was a name, but the rest Tris could not catch. He had never mastered the local dialect of Belaskian spoken near his birthplace; he was no better with any other variation. Born into an old-world noble line, he was fluent only in traditional Stravinan, the original tongue of those who had conquered and settled this nation more than two centuries past.

Footsteps closed behind him—he had lost sight of one of the assailants.

Something hard and sharp cut through his jerkin's sleeve into his right arm.

Tris spun away from the impact before the sword cut deeper. As he wheeled, he lashed the burning branch all around, ignoring the pain. The stocky man with the club recovered and shouted as he rushed in.

"Three sides!"

That Tris did understand. He could not afford to let anyone get behind him, outnumbered as he was. All he could do was whirl and swing the brand in trying to keep all of them back until he saw a way out. The one with the short sword, perhaps Mihkt, shot around to the left as he thrust the branch at the big leader's face. Again, Tris had to spin away from that blade, and he barely saw his mistake.

The one with the mace rushed him, a heavy dagger in the other hand.

Tris spun the other way and stumbled right through the remains of his campfire. As he tripped on half-charred branches, sparks and smoke whirled up around him in the darkness. Even his burning brand did not provide enough light for an instant, and something slammed off his right calf.

He teetered in a spin as whatever rushed onward. He heard a snarl, a scream, and shouts as he fell and tumbled. And then he stopped rolling and raised his head.

The man with the sword backpedaled from a dark, shadowy tangle of two forms fighting wildly on the ground to the right. With the fire scattered and nearly snuffed out, Tris was uncertain of what he saw, other than that some wild beast had put down the big stocky one.

The man was screaming and struggling beneath an animal that yowled and screeched as it clawed at him. The only part of the beast Tris made out was a stub of a tail on something the size of a dog, though its noise sounded more like a cat.

"Reese!"

That shout pulled Tris's focus to the right; he spotted the one with the mace and the dagger and rolled quickly to his feet. The other two were distracted, too stunned or afraid to aid their leader. The one with the sword backed away from the screams and snarls and yowls.

Tris had no wish to attract the beast's attention, but he took a chance.

He rushed the closer man, swung his branch, and caught the would-be swordsman in the face. The branch's flames were out, but at the crack of impact, the man teetered backward in flailing and dropped his sword. Before Tris could press again—

An inhuman shriek made him spin sharply around and then stiffen.

Two eyes were locked on Tris, and they were somehow a reddish yellow. Or was that just because of the stained muzzle below them? Open jaws hissed at him, the teeth and fangs stained as well. And tufted, tall ears flattened back as those eyes narrowed on him.

One wide, clawed paw rose in a first slow step toward Tris.

"Run!"

Again, one word that Tris could understand, but he did not dare turn his back. He kept his eyes on the hound-sized cat—a lynx from what little he'd heard of such. It seemed larger than what he knew of such beasts. He heard two sets of feet pounding away in the dark amid thrashing brush and crackling leaves and twigs on soft earth. But he remained fixed on the animal.

That one paw came down, flattened, and spread. Extended claws bit into the soft earth. The lynx was now completely silent. Stranger than this, its head suddenly swiveled, looking quickly after the two who had run away.

The stocky man lay unmoving on the ground behind the beast. Tris thought to run before he too ended up dead. For now he was the only target in sight. The feline's head swiveled sharply back toward him.

He kept as still as he could but prepared to dodge and run. It only stared him down, as if it could not decide if he was worth any effort. Those red-yellow eyes narrowed slightly in the silence. Again it glanced quickly toward the men who had run away. It turned back even quicker this time.

After another long stare, as if studying him as something it no longer wanted, the lynx spun and raced off, crashing through bushes. It was gone in the dark.

Tris heaved out a breath he hadn't realized he had held. He began to shake as if the night's cold had sunk into his bones. He stared after the lynx that had spared him—saved him—and a strange sensation took him.

He could sense the dead when they roused—but he could also sense the living for what they were. A foolish notion he might soon regret seized him then.

Slowly at first and then faster, Tris took off after the lynx . . . which was not a lynx.

The lynx heard someone following and veered through every bush, shrub, and other obscuring barrier in its path. The sound of hard footfalls faded farther behind, and it circled back toward the clearing's edge closest to the road. When it came upon a dark cloak and a narrow dagger left on the ground, it pulled up short.

A ripple began, first in its furred face. This spread through its body as it collapsed upon the wet forest mulch in shuddering convulsions.

Wide paws elongated. Narrowed as claws shortened and paled. Fingers sprouted as fur receded across its body, as if growing inward to reveal skin the color of pale caramel. The head and face changed last, until the muzzle became a distinct nose and jaw . . . still blood-coated from a kill.

Mari lay naked upon the ground, shuddered only once more from the change-pain, and pushed up on all fours. As she scrambled to pull her clothes from beneath the heather bush, her thoughts—her hate and vengeance—were clouded by what she'd seen in the clearing.

It made no sense.

The Dead's Man had seemed so . . . helpless. Why hadn't he called his spirits—or something worse—to deal with those wish-to-be bandits? He'd just rolled on the ground and swung a stick, like a yokel waylaid behind a carnival tent when no one was watching.

Or had it been a ruse? She'd done worse to lure someone into too much self-confidence. Had she intervened too soon and now ruined her own plans? Shivering in the cold, wet night, she flipped her muslin shirt around, trying to pull it on first, and—

She heard a crunch of forest needles and leaves.

Twisting about, she grabbed up her dagger and then froze. Cold sank straight into her lungs with fright. Near the black silhouette of a fir tree's trunk stood a figure almost black in the night except for his pale-skinned face. His eyes were so wide, staring at a naked woman in the dark, that she could see the whites almost all the way around his pale irises.

At another time, in another place, she might've spit at a man, or worse, for daring to keep looking. Now all she could do was glare. He said nothing and looked away.

Had he seen her go through the change and knew she was

yai-morchi—"two-fleshed"—among the Móndyalítko, what outsiders called a "shifter"? She should kill him for that alone, but again, back in the fight, why hadn't he done any of the things she knew he could do in order to save himself?

Could she be wrong about him?

No, he had to be the Dead's Man.

"I . . . speak . . . not good," he started in broken Belaskian, face still averted, and then, "Get dressed. I will restart a fire farther off from the body that you left."

He had switched to Old Stravinan, the tongue of the nobles and other despots. No one else spoke that language by choice, and few even knew it. As one of the traveling people—and one who'd tracked him for so long—she'd learned well enough of it among other dialects.

Of all the questions he might've put to her, he asked nothing and stepped off around the fir tree. Not even a thank-you for saving him? Not that she should've had to save *him*—or wanted to. And now that he knew of her presence, the element of surprise was lost, and he'd be that much harder—more dangerous—to kill.

Mari listened to be sure he didn't circle back and then reached for her dropped cloak. She saw her hand still covered in blood, though the scent of it had already filled her head. Her face would be just as smeared. There was little to be done about it. Still, she grabbed wet leaves off bushes and tried to wipe herself off.

Doubt nagged at her again.

Before she killed him, she had to know—to be sure about *him*.

When she worked her way through the woods, following the noise he made, she didn't even glance at the one silent body in the clearing. She kept the narrow dagger in hand, its blade flattened against the inside of her forearm. Well beyond the clearing, he already sat on the ground before another small fire as he rummaged through his pack. She circled around the fire's far side, watching him carefully.

This time, his strange almost-blue eyes rose and fixed on her.

"I have food," he said. "Though I do not know all of what is in here as yet."

How could he not know what he carried? Up close, he was alluring, though too pale. His manners seemed almost childlike.

"I am Tris," he said.

He pulled a white cloth something out of the pack and looked up at her, perhaps expecting something. Did he want her name now? She rarely told that to anyone, so why him?

"Mari," she said, for all the good it would do a dead man.

"You are Móndyalítko," he said, unwrapping the bulky white cloth.

This was an easy guess by her dusky skin and the fact that he'd seen her go through the change. Though she wasn't really one of her people anymore, since they didn't want her.

Unwrapping the cloth, he held it out with both hands. Inside it were small wheat rolls.

"Most likely baked today," he said. "Heil is particular about bread."

Who was Heil? A man's name, so maybe the older one who'd answered the herb shop door. But she fixed on those rolls. She couldn't remember the last time she'd eaten fresh bread.

He sat there, holding them out. She rose out of her crouch, keeping her blade tightly gripped and hidden, as she reached out. She took one, backed a quick step, and crouched again. And she didn't take her eyes off him, even as she bit into the roll and tore it in half.

Tris?

What did that name mean? Hers meant "little one of the water." It was odd to even think of him as anything other than the Dead's Man.

He held out the flask, and she froze and stopped chewing. She wasn't about to drink anything she couldn't see.

"Water," he said, as if reading her face. "I do not care for wine, but it is clean . . . from a well."

She was only a little thirsty, and she had her own water. Again, he sounded more like a child than a man. On impulse, she reached out for the flask.

"Why did you help me?"

She froze with the flask near her mouth at his sudden question, the first thing he'd even asked of her. He hadn't said a word about what he'd seen her do. A normal person would be in shock, pelting her with nervous questions.

But not him.

"Why?" he repeated.

Mari rarely interacted with other people, but she could lie well enough—better than enough.

"I was traveling," she answered, speaking Old Stravinan, "too late at night and alone. Not wise. Heard shouts, and then saw . . ."

She shrugged slightly.

He nodded once and softly said, "Thank you."

She had no idea how to respond. He said nothing more about what he'd seen or about her. Anyone else would have. Something about him pulled at her, and she fought it off. He was still the one she'd been hunting for so many years. Maybe there was a reason he hadn't called upon any spirits tonight.

He drew a chunk of cheese and picked up a small knife.

"Why didn't you use that"—she jutted toward the blade—"instead of the stick?"

He shrugged. "It is too small. The branch was better."

They both fell silent as he sliced the cheese, holding out every other sliver to her. She ate in slow bites, savoring its rich flavor. Then a sudden guilt rushed in for accepting food from him. He ate a roll and drank from the flask.

When they'd both finished, he motioned to the ground where she sat.

"Sleep," he said. "There is little of the night left."

The thought of sleeping across the fire from him didn't sit well with her. Of course, she could just kill him in his sleep, and there'd be two bodies to be found later. But she wondered, where was he going and what was he going to do now? How was it connected to that peasant who'd knocked on the shop's door? Why was he helping anyone—or was he?

Mari scooted back another step in her crouch. She settled slowly, pulling half of her long cloak under herself before lying down. Slowly closing her eyes, she kept her ears locked on every little sound.

And he said, "If anyone comes—"

"I'll hear them," she finished for him.

It wasn't to reassure him; it was a warning.

After a long pause, he added, "No one will likely come. They were probably passing thieves, and most people near here know who I am."

Mari waited two breaths. "And who are you?"

Another pause passed before he answered, "Sleep now."

Tris awakened early next morning well before the sun lit up even a small portion of the sky above the trees. He lay there studying the strange young woman lying across the smoking fire's remains as if asleep. Some of her thick, dark brown hair had fallen across the lower half of her pretty face, covering her mouth.

Her clothing was faded and travel-worn, and she was long in need of a bath. She lay there so perfectly still with her eyes closed.

He had never allowed anyone to sleep at his fire. He did not belong with other people—and they did not belong with him. There was something about this woman—threatening as she was—that did not make him want to disappear.

She was most certainly not asleep.

And he did not believe her story.

Rolling over on his back, he studied the lightening sky. No one would be simply passing by at night in this isolated area—no one with any sanity, no one except perhaps for him. That part of her story was an obvious lie.

He had also not missed the hatred in her eyes last night; that at least was familiar, though he did not know her reason for it. Even those who came seeking his aid were more relieved when he left than when he agreed to help. Horses and dogs did not let him near; hence, he always walked wherever he went. Strangely, cats were never bothered by his presence.

Tris grew tired of waiting for dawn to finish and rolled back on his side.

And there were those eyes watching him. Nothing else had changed; she had not moved even to brush hair off the upper side and lower half of her face. There were only those yellowish eyes, appearing more amber in the faint light, like those of the deadly cat the night before.

She studied him, perhaps searching for something.

Who was she? Did it matter?

Yet, there was more to his reaction to her than just her other self. She was alone in this world. She knew what it was to be surrounded by people and yet be completely alone. When she finally sat up, he had no idea what to say.

"There is safety in numbers," she finally said, as if that was a pure fact.

He took a slow breath. "True."

"Where are you going?"

"North."

She rose, swept back her cloak, brushed off clinging leaves and needles, and finally tucked away the blade she thought he had not seen. Sensible for a woman in the wild, even one with two shapes.

"North," she said, "so am I."

He should have told her to go her own way; instead, he rolled to his feet and hefted his pack.

When he began to walk, she fell into step beside him.

CHAPTER THREE

Mari traveled northward for three days with the Dead's Man—or "Tris," as he called himself. They spoke little, not that she wanted a chat with him, unless to ask a stealthy question, which he always evaded. Nothing new in that, since by the first nightfall after being caught, she knew he'd give nothing away through words.

They walked each day, all day, and made camp at night.

He asked her no questions in return, which was fine. So she waited, watched, and hoped to learn *why* before she saw *where* he was going. Maybe something in that would finally quell her small doubt and free her to kill him.

Though she hadn't seen him do anything to prove it on the night in the clearing, she believed he *was* the Dead's Man. She just needed to be absolutely certain it was he who'd murdered her family.

Stravina was heavily forested, especially inland from the gulf toward the east. Most major roads were maintained, and he stuck to those. Thankfully it hadn't rained along their journey, though it was as chill as the many rainy nights she'd spent alone in the wild. Normally, she found a hollow or old low-branched fir tree in which to huddle, but she wasn't about to do that with him.

Even being bedded down across the fire from him, or anyone, made sleep difficult. She hadn't truly slept—didn't dare to—in the last few nights.

His pack proved an endless source of basic provisions, though. When the rolls were gone, there were baked crackers instead. When the cheese was gone, he revealed jerked-and-dried beef, and she dug up a few root vegetables. She commented once about how well he'd packed for his journey, and he only frowned in thought, as if such a thing had not occurred to him.

"Heil always knows how much to pack," he'd finally replied.

Mari considered pressing for more about this mysterious older man she'd seen once in the dark doorway of the herb shop. Learning more about Heil might be of little use in finding the truth about Tris. Then again, it might be the roundabout way to end the doubts that still stalled her vengeance.

In the late afternoon on the third day, she was studying his finely cut black cloak, his well-made boots, and his pack. Her people were travelers, but by the look of him, she hadn't expected him to fare so well on a three-day trek.

She couldn't stop herself from asking, "Why aren't you riding a horse? You look like you could afford one."

He slowed, blinking rapidly, and looked at her as if he'd been lost elsewhere.

"A horse?" she repeated.

"Horses do not like me," he answered, and walked on.

She didn't bother asking why, since this was one of his wordiest answers so far. Not long after, he stopped again and looked around. For the first time since she'd joined him, he appeared uncertain, but of what?

"Where are you going?" she asked, hoping for something more than "north."

When he turned his head, his eyes had a bit more color in the waning sun than at night.

"Jesenik," he answered. "A village about two leagues east of Soladran and three south of the northern border."

It sounded as if he'd never been there.

Mari knew Soladran well, a teeming city built on the border to the Warlands. As an unwanted child driven from one family to another until she gave up, she'd traveled widely, even into that bloody land of warring free-lords and ever-changing borders. Up ahead, she saw a fork in the main road.

"Soladran is straight on," she said, "and it can't be much farther than three leagues, four at the most. If this village is two to the east, we should turn off now. The path might be narrower but will run closer than the main road."

He gazed ahead. "Yes . . . good."

Mari took the lead this time, now that Tris accepted her implied familiarity with the region. For her own needs, they'd come that much closer to her learning more about him. And whatever that peasant boy had come seeking back in Strîbrov, it might reveal a bit more about the Dead's Man.

Tris followed the wild young woman with no more idea why she had joined him than he had three days ago. She wanted something from him, though she had yet to say what. When she thought he was unaware, she still looked at him with an unexplained confusion and an even more mysterious hatred.

Perhaps he had banished the spirit of someone she loved and wanted still. There were always those who did not want him or the "services" he rendered to others.

No, it was something else with this "two-fleshed" woman.

For one, he did not know her and had never seen her before. He would have remembered her among all of those he had forgotten over the years. Even more, he had heard of "shifters" as well as "mockers" and "tweens" among the Móndyalítko, though he had never encountered one; to the best of his knowledge, few ever had, or, rather, known it when it happened. What puzzled him more was that she was alone—by choice, it seemed.

Móndyalítko were a communal people who traveled in extended family groups and larger ones. However, for him, the mere thought of them brought unwanted memories of the worst kind.

Mari turned off the main road onto the narrower path.

"We'll make it before dark," she called without looking back.

As he followed, panic welled up, signaling *the* memory would come again. He felt himself slipping back. Here and now ceased to have meaning . . .

At thirteen, he had been wandering the manor grounds, trying to be alone and away from anyone. His father rarely returned home anymore, preferring mistresses over Tris's mother, but the baron did come back sooner or later. Tonight was sooner.

Tris stopped atop a hillock overlooking the countryside and heard rolling wheels in the distance. Below along a distant side road, a procession of three Móndyalítko wagons rolled through the Vishal lands.

Thankfully, his father had not seen this and sent soldiers to run them off at sword's point.

Tris watched those wagons, built like small houses painted in wild colors. The one in front had red shutters, and a big man sat on the forward bench with a pretty woman on the other end and a little girl between them. All were dark-haired and dusky-skinned. Two more wagons followed, one with ivy green trimmings and the other in yellow.

Their horses were enormous, thick-legged beasts with clean coats that shimmered even at dusk. People on benches and two walking beside the last wagon were dressed in bright colors with the occasional glint of bangles, baubles, and other cheap adornments. Some had their hair covered in tied or lanyard-bound scarves and kerchiefs.

Tris felt a pained urge to run to them. Perhaps they could take him away with them, never to return. But he could not abandon his mother—not yet—and stood watching that colorful life he could not have roll into the woods and out of view. And still, he lingered.

Darkness fell.

When he forced himself to return home, passing between guards at the gates and the front doors, they all bowed their heads respectfully. It meant nothing compared with the dread of dinner with his parents.

Tris's first hint that something was wrong came with a white flicker.

It shot past him down the entryway toward the dining hall before he saw it clearly.

He did not need to see. Another rushed out of the hallway's sidewall.

Tris stopped and stared at a white, transparent man in a cleric's robe, whose feet did not touch the floor stones. As a child, he had seen similar mere wisps at night in the manor. They had not frightened him.

A scream of agony echoed through the stone manor, and then another.

Tris bolted down the passage for the dining hall.

When he slammed through the heavy double doors, neither of his parents was inside the hall. There were only two house guards and servants who would have been setting up for dinner. All were running, screaming, shouting amid a torrent of white wisps tearing about the high hall's air.

For an instant, he was too stunned by anyone else *seeing* those white forms.

One wisp slammed into a young serving girl's back.

Her mouth gaped in a silent scream. When that white blur shot out of her chest, she was already falling, and slammed face-first against the stone floor. At another pained cry, he saw an elder maid jerk in a convulsion and slump down against an oak chair into stillness, but her eyes and mouth never closed.

Tris shuddered at every impact of white he saw crashing into someone trying to escape.

This was his fault, though he did not know how or why.

And his mother was somewhere inside the manor.

He spun and ran for the manor's front doors. He had to get out of here and hope those white dead spirits followed, led to wherever he went. He had to go somewhere that anyone living would hesitate to follow. As he hit the front doors and shoved one wide-open, he paused and looked back.

That was a mistake.

There in the passage behind him came a black form as slender as himself and exactly the same height. Even the shape of its dangling hair looked like a silhouette of his own. He froze, somehow unable to move, waiting to hear a footfall, but none of its steps made a sound.

It kept coming . . .

"Tris!"

That cry jerked him from terror and . . .

Tris stood in the side road, staring ahead, the weight of his pack slung over one shoulder somehow feeling as if it had tripled. There was no hall, no screaming servants, and no guards rushing toward those sounds and to their own deaths. No black form in the mirror image of himself. There was only the thick and darkening Stravinan forest all around him.

Mari stood facing him from three paces ahead, her features flat except for the creasing of her brow over narrowed, amber eyes.

"What's wrong?" she asked. "Why did you stop and . . . You didn't hear me at first?"

She had called to him? If so, it would have been the first time she used his name. No one besides Heil had ever seen him sink that deep into his waking nightmares.

"Nothing is wrong," he finally answered. "Move on. It is getting late."

She still stood there watching him for a long moment and then finally turned onward. Her pace was slower now, and though she never halted, at times her head appeared to turn a little to one side—always to the left—as if she might look back.

She never did.

Tris followed, still unsettled that he had left himself completely undefended in her presence. She could have done anything while he had been trapped in his waking nightmares again.

Anything at all.

He could not let that happen again.

Neither of them spoke again as they walked; he kept three paces behind her, and she appeared to know where she was going. Although he eventually located any given destination, he found navigation a necessary annoyance. It was almost a relief to have her to follow.

After about two more leagues, the sun vanished and twilight began to fade. She stopped ahead of him and pointed.

"There," she said sharply.

Tris followed her nod to the left and ahead. Hanging lanterns glowing through the trees in the late evening illuminated the outskirts of a village. She stepped onward, he followed, and as they drew closer, the place proved to be larger than expected.

No wooden stockade surrounded Jesenik; by its location, most likely it did not need one. At least twenty wattle-and-daub huts were visible through the trees, though there could be even more beyond clear sight. Thick smoke from a smithy or a communal fire pit hazed the lantern-lit air between them. That good-sized central space was enough for an open-air market in summer and early autumn.

As Tris drew closer, people dressed in earthy browns and tans went about all ways. He halted short of the village's edge, and Mari must have heard him stop.

"Are we going in or not?" she asked.

He waited for someone to see them first.

A young woman with dark blond hair stopped, staring directly at them. Her gaze flicked quickly between the two strangers among the trees, expressing a mix of fear and hope.

Tris had seen this mix too many times.

The young woman's eyes finally locked on only Mari. Perhaps seeing two visitors, and one being a woman, somehow assured her. She half turned, calling out in general to others.

"Someone . . . get—get the zupan!"

He followed most of her words, and this at least saved him for the moment, since speaking their language versus Old Stravinan often wore him down. If nothing else, "zupan" was a common word in nearly all languages in the region.

Something less than noble as a village's prime elder.

When the young woman's eyes turned back to him, he nodded once, and she spun to run off deeper into the village.

Mari glanced back at him as well, her eyes somewhat questioning, but he had no wish to enlighten her. He never entered a village or a town without local leadership present. Doing otherwise led to panic if not open hysteria over strangers arriving after nightfall. Especially when something had driven one of them to come seeking someone like him.

The wait was not long.

The woman returned with two men: one young and one past middle age. Tris recognized the younger, almost a boy, as the villager who had come to the herb shop. He must have run half of the journey home but could not have been here long.

The other man was in his late forties, perhaps early fifties, with wiry muscles in his forearms below the rolled-up sleeves of his smudged canvas shirt. He had the start of fattening below straining wooden clasps of a leather vest. His peppered brown hair was long enough to pull back in a tail, exposing a lined, severe face not recently shaved.

Tris matched the elder's steps, closing the gap between them, but the elder spoke so quickly that Tris caught only the words "Dead's Man" and "zupan."

At that, he noticed Mari had stepped in as well, though she looked at him and not the villagers.

He knew what to expect, but it never got any easier. Most common people in northern Stravina spoke a dialect of Belaskian that borrowed words from the more contemporary lands of Belaski to the south. Only the old-blood nobles of this land spoke Stravinan anymore, or at least its traditional dialect. And that was what he had grown up speaking.

Heil had tried in vain to tutor him in other local languages, let alone dialects. As with navigation, it quickly became too tedious compared with other preoccupations. Not only did this zupan speak a local dialect, but his accent was so thick that Tris barely identified separate words.

Other villagers began to gather around with their fearful but hopeful gazes shifting between Tris and their elder. He remembered the youth who had come seeking him, and he was about to try speaking with that one when he noticed Mari was fixed only upon the zupan.

Whatever the man was saying, she understood it.

Tris whispered to her, "What is he saying?"

She blinked twice. "You don't know?"

When he did not answer, she frowned slightly.

"His name is Zupan Alexandre," she explained, causing the elder man to pause. "The other is his youngest son, Martin. Martin told his father of someone he'd heard of called 'the Dead's Man,' and that's why he came looking for you. The zupan wants to know if that's really who you are."

Tris took a long, slow breath and tried not to cringe or become angry. He was sick of that title. He eyed Mari for an instant, making her scowl back in renewed suspicion. At least she might be helpful here, though a large number of villagers had gathered around them.

"Tell the zupan I prefer to speak in private," he instructed quietly.

Mari looked about the gathering. Without word to him, she prattled off something to the zupan, who replied shortly, and turned away with his son.

"Come on," Mari added. "We're going to the village common house instead of his cottage. It'll do if we shut out everyone else."

She headed off after the zupan without waiting for him.

Tris followed in silence, ignoring the stares from everyone else around him.

Language had often been a problem over the years since he'd left home, particularly once he began rendering unique services in his hunt for more information to suit his own needs. That he was fluent in only one language—that of the land's nobles—set him apart as someone of higher rank and greater respect. But occasionally this worked against him among the more oppressed.

They headed deeper into the village, though too many other villagers followed behind, whispering among themselves. They stopped before a large, two-story, log-walled dwelling, and Zupan Alexandre opened the heavy front door. He waited, ushering in the "guests."

Mari did not move and stood waiting as well, so Tris entered first, though he had little chance to look around before he heard the door clunk shut. Mari was looking about, as if unsettled, as she joined him. Alexandre and his son followed, and the zupan gestured to a long, crude, and stained wooden table ahead.

Three long tables with benches or chairs filled the large room. Other smaller tables with chairs were arranged around the room nearer the timber walls with fully shuttered windows. Welcome heat radiated from a fire in a stone hearth set in the back wall. Two doorways at either end of the front wall led to somewhere else in the structure.

Zupan Alexandre waved all of them to the nearest long table as his son retrieved a taper from the fire and lit a lantern.

Tris rubbed his hands together and shifted the pack over his shoulder, though he did not take a seat.

"Ask him why they called for me," he told Mari.

Three nights back in Strîbrov, young Martin had told him little, only that his "skills" were desperately needed.

Again, Mari hesitated, and then came several exchanged words with the zupan that Tris could not follow. He was not concentrating on the words as much as on the strange Móndyalítko woman who had rescued him in the forest and then run away at the sight of him and then joined him.

He watched Mari's eyes grow wider with each exchange of words. When she further questioned the zupan, Alexandre cut her off with a wave of one hand and pointed at Tris.

Tris was careful not to react when she turned his way.

"He says they are plagued by a . . . ghost," she began. "The ghost of a girl from this village—named Brianne—went to Soladran and came home sick. She wasted away before morning and nothing helped her. She died half a moon ago, but—"

"But she reappears here at night," Tris finished.

Mari frowned.

"You do not believe in ghosts?" he asked.

"Yes, but—"

"Ask the zupan if there have been any other deaths."

Still, she stared at him before finally turning back to the elder. She spoke briefly, and at Alexandre's reply, she related, "No other deaths, but he says the visage is terrifying. His people are scared, just the same, and . . ."

"Problems with livestock," he finished for her.

She fell quiet for another breath.

"Hens have stopped laying," she said. "The cows have gone dry. He wants to know your price." She paused briefly. "What do they expect from you?"

He did not answer the last question. "Tell the zupan we will discuss the price later, once I know more."

Mari just kept watching him too much like that lynx in the clearing—as if she was not certain whether he was something to hunt or another predator and thereby competition for survival.

Not long after, Mari sat at one of the long tables in the common house. The zupan and his son had left after telling them food would be brought.

No one would've ever given just her a free meal.

Sitting across from her, Tris ignored her as he rummaged through his pack, likely checking for something, since he rarely pulled anything out besides food. She kept going over everything she'd heard since arriving here and translating for him.

And he seemed to have heard some of it before, perhaps more than once.

"So they're plagued by a ghost," she began, "or think so. And they hired you . . . to do what?"

He didn't answer her, though he stopped fiddling with the pack. His gaze drifted to the far hearth, and he watched the low flames. She waited for an answer, and then spun around at a creak of wood from behind.

An aging woman with a kind face and a drab dress entered the common room. She came through the room's far back, carrying two steaming clay mugs and a small loaf of dark bread on a wooden tray. Upon spotting Mari watching her intently, the woman slowed, glanced quickly at *him* and then back.

"Some hot, spiced tea," she explained, slightly raising the tray. "I'm sure you need it after walking so far."

Her voice was as kind as her face.

Mari didn't know how to respond to kindness—not anymore.

The woman didn't appear to expect thanks and set down the tray. "I'll be right back with your supper."

The scent of spiced tea quickly filled Mari's nostrils as the woman vanished back through the door. Mari eyed the mugs she hadn't asked or paid for. Tris hadn't even seemed to notice the woman's arrival or quick departure. Mari picked up one of the mugs.

Hot, spiced tea was a luxury—especially the spiced part—in a place like this. For a moment, she just let that scent fill her head, and then took a sip. It filled her mouth even better than her nose. And then there was the rich, dark bread. About to grab for it, she hesitated and looked across the table.

He still sat there, staring at the fire in the hearth. Though he appeared lost somewhere else, it wasn't the same as whatever had happened to him earlier on the road. He was thinking about . . . something.

As Mari took another long sip, the woman returned carrying two plates and set them on the table.

On each plate, potatoes and carrots and onions surrounded pieces of roasted chicken. Broth or drippings had filled the plates' hollows, and that bread was waiting to be used. A baked apple sprinkled with cinnamon also sat on the side of each plate.

"Will this do?" the woman asked.

Do? Mari couldn't remember having seen such a meal.

"Yes . . . it will be fine."

After a partial smile, the woman turned to leave.

"Oh," she said as if it was an afterthought, "if you go upstairs, you'll find padded mats with blankets on the floor." And again she glanced briefly at *him*. "There are hanging curtains between the mats, if you wish for privacy."

Sleeping indoors—with blankets—had become as rare for Mari as the meal in front of her.

"I'm Erath," said the woman, with a nod. "Leave the plates when you're done. I'll get them in the morning."

"Thank you," Mari called out.

The woman, Erath, glanced back, lingering in the doorway, suddenly looking frightened. She glanced at him, Tris, and then back.

"We are grateful for your coming . . . for *him* coming," Erath said. "I hope he works quickly."

She turned and left, and the door clunked quickly.

Mari was alone again with the Dead's Man. Everything on this table was because of—for—him, not her. She tore out a hunk of bread with one hand. Before shoving it in her mouth, she paused. He was still watching the fire.

"Will you stop staring at nothing," she said, "and eat something."

"Hmm?" He looked down and saw the food. "Oh . . . yes."

Digging in his pack again, he pulled out his small knife and used it to cut both his chicken and potato. Then he used the point to stab small pieces and lift them to his mouth.

Mari ate with her hands, thinking again on all she'd seen and heard. Apparently, these villagers wanted him to rid this place of a ghost. Though she knew his title as "the Dead's Man," she hadn't understood what that might mean to others, not fully, not until now. She'd been told that he called spirits and controlled them. What else could he do?

Maybe he'd been the one to raise the ghost girl, just as a way to gouge coins from peasants. He didn't seem to be playing a game with them, but maybe he wasn't going to reveal himself while she was watching. She'd have to wait and watch and see what exactly he did and how he did it.

And then she'd know for certain that she'd finally found . . . *him*.

The food was delicious. Saving the baked apple for last, she ate it slowly. It had been a long time since she'd eaten something sweet, a long time since she'd eaten anything that wasn't just for survival, to keep going, to keep hunting. Cinnamon dissolved on her tongue among the apple's juices, and she sat there as the taste drowned out all her other senses.

Then she realized he was watching her almost curiously. A small piece of chicken was stuck on the tip of his knife with the blade hovering halfway to his mouth.

"What?" she asked.

He dropped his gaze. "Nothing."

Once her dinner was gone, all she could think of was the padded mat, warm blanket, and curtained privacy waiting for her upstairs.

"I'm tired," she said.

He nodded and returned to staring toward the fire as he sipped his tea.

Mari pushed up off the bench and hefted her pack.

"You speak their dialect," he said, startling her.

This was a statement, not a question. She was still surprised that he didn't. She spoke four dialects of Belaskian as well as her people's tongue that had no name. This was not unusual for Móndyalítko, but he should at least know the one spoken here.

He turned his pale eyes on her. "And Old Stravinan. Do you speak any Droevinkan?"

"Yes. Why?"

"I have no gift for tongues," he returned, and then, "Good night."

For an instant, she wanted more, anything to give her one sliver of certainty that she'd found her prey. Instead, she walked away, though she stalled after stepping through the same door Erath had used.

What if he slipped off when she couldn't see him?

No, game or not, he wouldn't leave until he got whatever he'd really come for.

She headed onward for the crude steps at the hallway's far end, ignoring two side doors along the way. At the top of the stairs, she entered an open loft area, but Erath had spoken true.

Wool blankets stitched to cords hung as curtains that draped off four private spaces, two to each side of a center path to the common house's back wall. A chipped pitcher and basin sat on the floor to one side of the stairs' top.

Mari crouched, refilled her water flask from the pitcher, and then washed her hands and face. She went to the near right curtain and brushed it aside. The space around the padded mat and folded wool blanket wasn't large, but it offered more comfort than she'd had in a long while. She stowed her pack at the mat's head, where it couldn't be grabbed by anyone peeking in, and she undressed down to her long muslin shirt before settling behind the blanket. Most passing travelers probably had to pay a few coins for the pleasure of a meal and a bed here, but not Tris—and therefore not her.

Her thoughts churned with all of what might happen tomorrow, though she didn't know what to expect. Tris was supposed to now hunt a ghost. Or maybe he'd wait until no one was watching and simply command it to appear.

She closed her eyes, listening for his steps and even the creak of the far door to the common room, but she drifted off until . . .

Mari came awake in the dark and then started upright in panic that she'd fallen asleep. Whatever had awoken her, her first thought was to listen for Tris or sneak out to see if he had come up here yet. She never got that far.

The sound of weeping filled her ears, and she scrambled off the mat to the back of the curtained space.

The visage of a transparent girl stood at the foot of her mat.

Mari's breath caught as she rolled back over her mat to get away. She came up in a crouch before the blanket partition to the next loft space.

The girl's face was beyond pinched, with thin hair that hung down and over her shoulders. Her skin looked shriveled and shrunken to the bones of her face, and the same with her arms, as if she'd starved to death. With one exception, she was white all over, even to the peasant dress; there were purple half circles under her eyes.

She reached out with both arms and bony fingers to match as her mouth gaped. Maybe she tried to say something, but Mari was too shaken by all she saw.

A long, pained wail suddenly echoed through the rafters.

Since the night of death for Mari's family, she'd never cried out again. But the sound of fear tore from her in a feral shriek as she ripped through the side blanket for the path between the sleeping spaces. She remembered those white forms among the woods, and everywhere they went, those she'd loved had died.

Then the black one thrust a hand through her father's head and out of his face.

As Mari pushed through the blanket curtain into the path between the private spaces, she saw the white girl slip straight through wool material to block the path out of the loft. The ghost's arms were still outstretched, and it began to drift toward her.

How could she fight something she couldn't touch, or kill something already dead?

She glanced to both sides at the blanket curtains. Either way, she'd have to get through and then bolt out of the front curtain to get to the stairs. Her own space was the closet to the stairs. And the white girl was now only three strides away.

Terror began to force a change within her. Her sight widened, like that of her other flesh, until the dark lit up like twilight. And then the ghost looked too bright before her eyes.

Mari twisted back to dive under and into her own sleeping space. She stalled as she heard pounding footsteps from the direction of the stairs.

"Mari!"

That one word came from beyond the ghost, but it didn't turn.

A hand thrust through the white transparent form.

Mari felt a scream out of childhood trying to come out. But that hand wasn't black.

It had living flesh she saw more clearly than others would in the dark. Fingers curled as the hand ripped downward. The ghost girl came apart like vapors in the air. Those torn, white swirls like mist vanished in the dark.

In the path between the blanket curtains stood the Dead's Man.

Mari couldn't stop shaking. For that instant, she couldn't even think, and then she saw his eyes with her fully feral sight. His irises glowed in the dark like beacons, but they were as white as the ghost had been. The glow began to fade as he panted.

"Are you all right? Did it speak to you?"

Each of his questions was like a tossed stone's strike that made her flinch. More so when he took a step, and she quickly retreated. Where was her dagger? Glancing down at herself, she suddenly realized she wore no pants and was dressed only in her long muslin shirt.

"What did it look like?" Tris pressed. "Did it touch you? Are you all right?"

No, she wasn't—but he was. She'd never before faced a spirit, though she'd heard of others who had. One or two had claimed they'd been touched, and they hadn't been all right. Her own loved ones were dead because of that. But he had touched this spirit and it had suffered instead.

He *was* the Dead's Man.

Where was her dagger?

"Mari?"

She flinched, still frozen in place. Why couldn't she move? Had he done something to her? As he came closer, a bit more blue showed in his eyes, as if they continued changing. Looking at her—into her eyes—his own widened at what he saw. Fear in his face like concern confused her even more.

"Answer me," he said, barely above a whisper. "Are you all right?"

Where had he been? Why hadn't he come up to sleep?

"What did you do?" she hissed. "How did you do that . . . tear it apart?"

He flinched this time and dropped his gaze, but he didn't answer.

"How did you get rid of it?" she asked, inching toward him. "Why didn't you suffer . . . and die?"

He took a deep breath and let it out slowly, as if relieved she was angry.

"I did not 'get rid of it' yet, not so easily. It does not work that way," he said, "no matter what you have heard."

Now that the white girl was gone, she wanted him gone—dead—as well. So why not do it? Even without the dagger, she might tear him apart, if she could change flesh quickly enough.

"What are you?"

He winced. Still not looking at her, he asked, "What did it look like?"

Mari's heart still pounded in fear and rage. She tried to push down the memory of her parents' murder, of the white visages she'd seen that night.

"White," she answered, "even to her clothes."

"No." And he finally looked at her. "Her face, form, anything about *her*."

That question stalled her even more. What did it matter?

"Starved, or maybe withered," she said. "Her eyes had dark circles, maybe purplish, around them. Why?"

Tris went still, and his expression turned hard. "Starved to death? And purple-colored circles under her eyes? You could see that in the dark?"

His attention was so intense now. He closed his own eyes briefly and opened them again.

"It is gone for now," he said, in the flat tone he usually used. "It has no connection to this building." He pointed to her right. "I will take the space across from yours. It will not come back tonight, so you can sleep without fear."

She didn't move and waited until he slipped behind the blanket-curtain across the path. Only then did she back into her own space. She settled silently on her mat, then dug into her things, and pulled out the narrow dagger as she listened.

She heard him drop boots on the floor, maybe his cloak as well, and settle on the mat, and then came the rustle of a blanket. After a while, his breath grew long and soft with sleep. She could still smell him by the strong scent of spiced tea.

Mari sat awake into the night as sweat built beneath her grip on the dagger's leather-wrapped hilt. He'd gotten along before now without someone to stand in for his poor language skills. He didn't need her, even for that. She'd watched him tear apart a spirit. Someone—something like him—could've seized control of it instead, even used it against her, like on the night her family died.

So why hadn't he?

Tris lay on the mat facing the blanket-curtain of his space. Sleep did not come. He had forgotten his pack in the main room, where he had been lost again in the past. Then he had felt something manifest in the common house.

He had not see anything in the main room—but he had felt it here somewhere. And then he had run for those stairs, for Mari.

What would he fear for her?

She had easily dealt with three would-be bandits in the forest, even killing one of them. But she would not know how to deal with an opponent already dead. He had not taken the time to stop and completely vanquish the spirit—and he should have—but he'd shattered its visual manifestation without even thinking at the sight of Mari trapped in the back of the loft.

Again, why had he felt so much fear for her, the drive to protect her?

It was not safe, not rational for his life so far, and he did not need that extra responsibility.

Such a thing could not happen again.

Throwing one arm over his eyes, he tried to think on something—anything—else. There were only memories to take the place of his strange panic over this wild, feral young woman who had invaded his life.

There was only the black one—that other *him*—whom he had first seen clearly when he was a child and later as a youth . . . and then later, he began to hear its whispers and to gain hints of what it wanted.

In the summer he turned seventeen, he and his mother traveled into northern Belaski to visit his aunt, his mother's sister, Ellen de Pierres. Aunt Ellen was married to a wine merchant—not a noble—and so most people believed Reagan had made the better bargain in marriage.

Tris knew better.

The de Pierres were a merry family of six, all so strangely fond of one another, or at least strangely to Tris. His cousin Alaina had always tried to make him feel welcome, tugging him into card games, or playing at spinning tops, and chattering at him all through a noisy, happy, boisterous dinner. And while he did not accept or encourage her overtures, he did not avoid them. He had never met anyone so happy. She was slender with thick, chocolate brown hair.

Somewhat like Mari's hair.

On that visit, Alaina dragged him outside for an evening walk through the rose garden, holding up both her side and his missing side of the conversation. She never appeared to mind. They were well away from the manor and almost to the tree line when she stopped and looked up at the sky.

"Oh, it's getting late. I didn't even realize, and now look," she rattled on. "We should go back, before it's fully dark—no, I won't get lost, not here, but still—"

"Why?" he cut in, as she did not seem particularly worried.

He did not want to go back; he wanted to stay here with her.

Alaina hesitated, then smiled with obvious effort. "Nothing, not really, and it was . . . moons ago."

That was the first time all day and evening that she faltered in chatter.

"Some serving children were fighting near the well," she began again, more slowly. "And . . . a boy was pushed in. It was awful, and since then, people have spoken of seeing strange things at night or twilight, just not in the daylight."

He stopped, touching her lightly on the shoulder, and she tensed.

"What things?" he asked.

She never answered. She inhaled, eyes widening as they fixed on something beyond him. That breath did not come out.

Tris half turned.

There in the far reaches of the rose garden stood a boy—maybe twelve—but as white as steam. At the sight of them, his roundish face twisted in rage around eyes like black pits.

Tris whirled around, forgetting Alaina. He looked all ways but saw no other white wisps of spirits. And no black him—that other *him*—in the darkening twilight. When Tris spun back, the boy's lips curled in a silent snarl as he rushed forward.

Tris knew what would happen if a spirit touched the living.

This time he could not run, not leave Alaina alone—and his face grew warm.

The growing dark began lightening, as if twilight reversed.

He saw every detail of the boy down to the buttons of his shirt, his swollen flesh and bloated belly behind the untucked shirt. He did not care if the boy got to him—but he would not let it touch Alaina. He forgot everything but her. When he turned to grab her, she lurched away in even greater horror . . . at him.

"Your eyes!" she cried out.

Confused, he tried to grab for her again, even as he looked away.

The boy ghost was nearly upon them. Without knowing, Tris lashed out with a fist. It struck the boy, as if solid.

That swollen little spirit reeled and rippled backward, like a shred of linen in a wind.

Tris wanted it gone—not simply vanished but gone. He could not risk turning away to Alaina, not if he wanted to save her.

His need to make the ghost *gone* became overwhelming.

Then . . . behind the ghost, the night appeared to gather, swirling in upon itself. For an instant, Tris feared the black one was coming again. But this time was not the same as before.

Darkness behind the boy—in the spot Tris fixed on—appeared to solidify in the air, like a hole in this world. The boy's face twisted, this time in an anguished snarl that Tris heard. And the boy charged again.

Tris stepped in the way, grabbing for the boy, and his fingers closed halfway through the semitransparent chalk white arm. His first reaction was shock that he could not stop the spirit, but pressure on his fingers forced its way through the surprise. And the more shock faded, the more solid became his grip.

The ghost screeched and thrashed, clawing at his face.

Tris quickly took hold with his other hand as he ducked a swipe at his face. His eyes fixed on that whirling black void beyond the boy. And on instinct, he shoved.

He neither heard nor felt the savage spirit's small boots slide across grass and earth; he did feel it resist his effort to drive it back. One white hand latched on to his upper left arm in a matched grip for his own on the spirit's. He hunched in a half crouch and shoved all the more.

The whirling darkness beyond spread out closer behind the boy.

Tris made a final effort and shoved with his whole body, releasing his grip in the last instant. And then fear filled him again as the small white form began to swirl, as if ripped apart by that whirlpool of pure darkness.

It was gone in an instant.

He stood there, just staring at what he had done, not knowing how he had done it. And then came whispers. At first, he thought someone else had come or that Alaina had approached behind him. Before he could turn, he heard it again, coming from the swirling darkness, which began to fade.

. . . my Tris . . . me Tris . . . I Tris . . . not you . . . Tris . . .

Somehow, he knew it was the other *him* speaking through the portal. He felt its presence and its rage and its longing to *be* him.

Then the black void drained like swirling ink sucked into a hole in the world—and vanished.

The whispers were gone.

Tris began to shake. There was another sound now behind him in the darkening dusk.

Rapid panting breaths came so fast there was no room for a voice.

Tris turned too quickly and nearly lost his balance.

There next to the manor's stone wall, half-hidden beneath a rhododendron, Alaina sat on the ground. One hand half-shielded her face, hiding her mouth.

She was safe. How he had managed this, he still did not know. But she was safe. And he went for her.

Alaina uttered a gasp and scooted back deeper beneath the bush.

"What—what—," she stuttered in whimpers. "What . . . are *you?*"

A growing chill sank into Tris as he backed away from Alaina's terrified eyes. The answer to that question would come in little pieces over the following years. Until it drove him away from anyone who might hear those whispers from the black one—the other *him.*

. . . not you Tris . . . I Tris . . .

That first time in Alaina's eyes, when he lost her, would not be the last time he saw this in the eyes of others.

Tris lay in the dark listening to Mari's slow breaths at the loft's far side beyond the blanket. By their rhythm, he knew she was not sleeping yet. It had been years purposefully spent alone since he'd had thought of protecting anyone but himself. And now he had no wish to face such a complication again. He rolled toward the loft's wall and away from the sound of Mari's breaths, but that one question would not let him sleep. It had been asked too many times—first in terror by a girl and now in fear-fed rage by a young woman:

What are you?

CHAPTER
FOUR

When Mari awoke, it was still nearly dark in the loft without windows, and she didn't remembering falling asleep. In one blink, she knew Tris wasn't in the loft anymore.

She didn't smell or hear him.

That panicked her as much as what she'd seen last night. She wrestled into her pants, jerkin, and boots, left her pack behind, and only tucked the sheathed dagger under her jerkin as she rushed downstairs. Hurrying through the door into the main room, she skidded to a stop.

There he was, and he lurched upright off a bench, startled where he'd been staring at the fireplace again. There was no fire in the hearth now, just the charred blackness of the soot-covered stone hollow. He turned away from her, back toward the hearth.

She didn't see his cloak or his pullover—no socks or boots either. He wore only pants and a faded, untucked black shirt. Same as last night, and by its wrinkles, he'd slept in it.

Crouching before the blackened fireplace, he began shaving kindling to start a fire. She didn't say anything—but neither did he—and she felt more uncomfortable than on their journey here. Sleeping across the fire from him had been awkward, but at least then he couldn't slip away like he had this morning.

Mari stood eyeing his back until the tinder ignited by flint sparks sprouted a small flame. He blew gently upon them, not saying a word, with his back still turned to her. His bare feet were so pale. She suddenly wondered what the day would bring.

"How do you . . . ?" she started, and then stalled. "What's next?"

He pivoted halfway in his crouch. "Normally, I would find someone who speaks a little Old Stravinan or someone with an accent I can follow a bit to help me in questioning others. But now that you are here . . ."

What? Did he think she'd just do whatever he wanted? Be his mouth-piece?

"I will pay you one-quarter of my fee," he said, turning away to thread another piece of tinder into the fire. "If you will translate for me."

Mari hesitated. He wanted to *hire* his would-be killer, his onetime victim left alive? She'd rarely had the chance to earn her own money, and the prospect pulled at her more than she cared to admit. Aside from keeping him within sight, it was better than other things she'd done for coin.

She tensed at hearing soft steps outside, and in a count of three or four, the common house front door creaked open.

Erath entered, bearing a wooden tray with another small loaf of dark bread. There were also two more steaming clay mugs and a small dome of plain fired clay covering something on a matching small plate.

Mari eyed the bread most of all.

At a soft crackle echoing in the near-empty common house, she looked toward the fireplace.

Tris was sifting through the piled firewood for small pieces to place on the growing flames.

Erath approached the long table nearest the door rather than step all the way in. For a moment, she watched him at the fire, and worry—or just fear—kept away her slight smile of the night before. Glancing at Mari, she silently mouthed, *Can he help us?*

Mari stiffened, and her thoughts went blank. What a twist, that someone should ask her that about him!

Erath stood waiting and watching.

Tris ignored them both. Mari's own people had thrown or driven her out every time she'd tried to join with them, or done so once they learned she was the sole survivor of that cursed night in the Wicker Woods. Word of such things traveled quickly among a traveling people. Anyone who'd somehow lived—unmarked—through something like that was suspect, a threat, perhaps cursed.

Like a disease that might spread among them.

If these villagers learned the same about her, she'd fare even worse among them as an outsider, what some called a *Tzigan*—"vagabond thief"—and more so if they knew she was *yai-morchi*—"two-fleshed"— or what their kind called a "shifter."

She looked back to Erath, still waiting for an answer. The elder woman's eyes began to glisten; maybe tears were coming next.

"Yes," Mari whispered without thinking about it.

"Yes to what?"

This question from Tris caught her off guard.

He had risen and was now fixed on her. He glanced once toward Erath, though Mari quickly cut in with her answer.

"She wants to know if you can really help them."

A frown spread over his face. "Do not make promises for me. You are my translator now, and that is all."

Mari heated up, but she swallowed down a retort for now. She noticed Erath's worried attention shifting rapidly between her and him.

"I brought tea and some goat cheese," Erath offered, and then began digging into pockets somewhere beneath her cloak. "And one each of these."

She set two brown eggs on the table, likely boiled, as she stuttered out, "I'm . . . sorry if . . . if I caused a problem."

"Don't apologize about him," Mari countered in Belaskian, which he wouldn't understand. Her ire was aimed in his direction, and she quickly added, "You're not the one who's a problem."

This appeared to just increase Erath's worry.

Mari approached the far table across from Erath and looked on everything that had been brought for *him* without even being asked for. She took a slow breath, raised only her eyes to Erath.

"Thank you," she said lowly. "Maybe you should go now."

Erath took a quick look at Tris. "The zupan wants to know . . . what the Dead's Man will do."

Even Mari wanted to know that, and she translated the question into Stravinan for him.

"First, I need to see the body," Tris answered. "They must dig her up."

"What?" Mari asked, aghast.

"Tell her." He nodded toward Erath.

Mari hesitated at such desecration but finally passed on his instruction. Erath swallowed hard. She nodded understanding just once, and Mari waved her off. Erath quickly left, and the instant the front door clunked shut, Mari turned back to Tris.

"What are you doing here?"

"What I was called to do," he answered. "Put the dead that will not rest . . . to rest."

"How? Isn't that what you did last night, tearing that girl's spirit apart?"

He looked away, as if this shamed him. "No, I told you that I had not . . . I was only protecting you."

That was worse. The last thing she wanted was a life debt to someone she'd hunted for half of her cursed life.

"How?" she went on. "You touched it, so why didn't you die, or even be hurt?"

He let out a slow exhalation and closed his eyes. "That is not how it works, not precisely."

"I don't know of anyone who can do what you did. So *how*?"

Whether it was anger, pain, or frustration, she didn't know as he snapped at her.

"Because I am like the dead in being born dead!"

Confusion shut her up as much as anything else. She didn't know what that meant or if she wanted to know. He made to step past her toward the still-warm food, which he'd seemed to expect and for which he hadn't offered a word of thanks. Worse, a few moments ago, he'd treated her as if she were there merely to serve as his translator.

She grabbed his arm.

"Play the noble with peasants if you like," she warned, "but don't try it with me! I'm not your servant, and you couldn't pay me enough, and you haven't paid me anything as yet."

He stared down at her, as he was nearly a head taller. Then he dropped his gaze, averted his face in something like shame, and did something that confused her all the more.

"I am sorry," he whispered. "I apologize."

Mari drew back in suspicion. He pulled out of her loosened grip, stepped to the table, and picked up only a mug of tea. She was still watching as he turned away without touching any of the food.

Dropping onto the nearer bench, she grabbed for an egg.

By late morning, Mari stood quietly in the village graveyard, set off in the nearby woods. She shifted uncomfortably from one foot to the other, back and forth, as several men pulled a shrouded corpse from the ground after digging it up.

Zupan Alexandre stood nearby in silence. He frowned in disapproval, though he hadn't refused the request of the Dead's Man. It was unsettling how these people did anything he asked. She'd seen their kind's quiet desperation before, but tampering with the dead was a bad idea, no matter what.

As the men set the body on the ground and stepped away, Tris didn't hesitate. He stepped in and knelt down, as if unaffected, and pulled—or peeled—the shroud from the corpse.

"Brianne," Alexandre whispered, staring as if he couldn't look away if he wanted to. "She was a lovely girl."

She wasn't lovely now.

Mari didn't look away either, but only because she saw it was the same girl from the loft last night. Time in a damp, muddy grave couldn't hide that.

But she could be seen in color now. Her hair was a rich shade of red-blond and her dress was forest green. She looked starved to death, pale and sallow skin stretched over bones, though her lips were slightly darkened somehow.

Tris began searching the body. He pulled open the dress's collar, dug into the bodice, rolled up sleeves, and lifted the skirt. He pulled off her slippers to check her toes for something.

Sitting back, he stalled for a moment.

"What is he doing?" Alexandre asked in a low whisper.

Mari didn't know or even know what to lie.

Tris then moved up and started on the girl's hair, combing it through his fingers, pulling apart the lashing that held some of it back in a tail.

Alexandre's fast breaths became audible and grating, though Mari had heard them clearly from the moment they'd arrived. He took only one step toward Tris, obviously hesitant to interfere, even at this desecration.

But then Tris sat back on his knees again, still and silent for a moment. "Ask the zupan if she wore any jewelry, some gift that meant something to her."

Mari blinked, startled, for she'd been staring at the body again. When she realized that question was for her, he'd turned to look at her. She repeated the question to the zupan.

Alexandre couldn't speak and only shook his head.

"No . . . or nothing he knows about," she answered for him.

Tris turned back, leaned forward again, and peered at the girl's head or face. He reached out and turned her head, or rather press-push-twisted it toward himself.

The faces of the men around the open grave darkened.

Two men with shovels gripped the handles so tightly their knuckles whitened.

Alexandre took another angry step forward.

"Tris . . . ?" Mari said uncertainly.

He ignored her and leaned even closer to the body's head. Examining the hair on the far side, he pulled up a lock between his fingers.

"It has been cut here," he said, "near the left side of her face."

Alexandre wouldn't understand those words, but he looked down at Tris's hand.

"He says her hair's been cut, one side only," Mari translated.

"Ask him why and by whom," Tris said, "and if it was done before or after death."

Mari couldn't see that it mattered but translated the questions. Alexandre shook his head.

"He doesn't know," Mari passed on.

"Did they hold a wake?" Tris asked, still fingering that lock of severed hair. "Did they lay the girl out for people to pay last respects, perhaps privately?"

When Mari asked, Alexandre confirmed this.

"Who knew her best?" Tris asked. "Who spent the most time alone with her in mourning?"

Mari balked. This was becoming ghoulish.

"Ask him," Tris ordered.

Mari clenched her jaw, but she put the questions to Alexandre, word for word.

The zupan's brow furrowed. He seemed lost in confusion and then some deep thought. Looking aside at Mari, he hesitated for two more breaths.

"Her mother, Cecilia," he began. "Her sweetheart, Leif, and her close friend, Gena. Those spent more time than others in farewells." He looked back to Tris, and his face darkened again. "Why?"

While translating the names and relationships quickly, Mari stepped closer behind Tris, halfway between him and the zupan, a foolish, dangerous act.

"Why?" she echoed to Tris.

"Because I need to speak to those he mentioned."

She had no idea what he was after. So far, none of it was useful to her own purpose and likely put her in as much danger as him. Still, he was in charge here, and she had to let him continue.

"Which one first?" she asked.

He glanced down at the cut locks of hair, the section missing about a finger's length compared with the rest.

"The most removed by blood or love, but the most likely confidante," he answered. "The friend, Gena."

It didn't surprise Mari when the zupan insisted on being present while the Dead's Man spoke with any of his people. She'd have done the same in his place.

She found herself inside a small home facing a frightened young woman about sixteen or seventeen seated in a chair. Alexandre sent the rest of Gena's family outside, but he remained.

Gena was pleasant enough to look at, perhaps a little plain-faced. Stocky, with a full head of black curls, some escaping a knot at the back of her neck, she stared at Tris in open fright. He appeared to realize this—was perhaps accustomed to it—and dropped his head, stepping near and whispering next to Mari's ear, too close for her comfort.

"I want you to handle the questioning. It will be less difficult for her versus you pausing to translate each answer. But remember the answers, word for word. I need to know the depth of the friendship and why Brianne went to Soladran." He paused. "Can you tell when someone is lying?"

Mari thought on that. "Yes."

He nodded once and stepped back. Then she felt somewhat at a loss.

Directly questioning a frightened, grieving girl wasn't one of her skills—nor a part of the bargain with him.

On impulse, she picked up a nearby stool, slid in next to Gena, and sat down with a cock of her head toward him.

"He just needs to know a few things," she said to the girl. "Nothing to worry about, but he doesn't speak your tongue very well."

Gena looked from her to the zupan.

Alexandre nodded to the frightened girl. "You tell Miss Mari anything she wants to know."

Miss Mari.

Gena wrung her hands in her lap.

"You and Brianne were good friends?" Mari began.

Gena nodded slightly and then answered, hoarsely at first.

"Best friends. She was the prettiest of us, all the girls here. Everyone loved Brianne, for she was kind too. I was lucky to be her friend." Her lower lip quivered. "I still can't believe she's . . . I want her back."

Mari kept her eyes on the girl, though she caught half of Tris's face off to her right. He was watching and listening intently. Perhaps he couldn't follow all that the girl said, but there was no mistaking the intensity in Gena's voice.

"Have you seen her ghost?" Mari asked suddenly.

Gena shuddered and cringed away, and her gaze turned to the zupan. The answer was obvious, but Mari couldn't let Alexandre interrupt.

"How many times?" she asked.

Gena's breath caught as she looked back, and Mari waited.

"Twice," the girl whispered.

"Did she try to touch or hurt you?"

"No! Brianne wouldn't . . . she'd never hurt anyone. She just wants to go back to Cameron, that's all!"

Alexandre lunged one step in toward the girl, and Mari tensed, ready to act.

"Cameron?" the zupan asked. "Guardsman Bródy?"

Gena clamped a hand over her mouth.

Mari studied both of them in confusion.

"Is that why she went to Soladran?" Alexandre demanded. "To see him?"

"Who's Cameron?" Mari broke in, looking to Alexandre.

The zupan loomed over Gena in open anger and anguish, and Mari again worried what she'd been dragged into.

"A guard garrisoned at Soladran," Alexandre answered. "He comes through on patrol twice a season."

At Gena's whimpers, tears now falling, Mari rose and stepped between the girl and the zupan. Tris inched in on her right, but she shot him a sharp glance, and he halted. Fixing again on the zupan, she waited. If he tried to step around and get to the half-wit girl . . .

Instead, he turned his ire on Mari.

"Cameron's a 'pretty boy'!" Alexandre nearly spit. "He likes to make the girls swoon, though I didn't know he toyed with our Brianne. She was betrothed to Leif!" Again, he glared at the sobbing Gena. "You knew and said nothing?"

"He's not like that," Gena whispered, "and she loved him, hoped he would come back with her. He hates being a guard. He told her so, but she came back . . . alone . . . so sick . . ." Leaning forward, she began to weep. "At least, I still see her sometimes."

Mari turned to the girl. "As a spirit? You *like* seeing that?"

Gena continued weeping, hiding her face.

Tris stepped closer. "Ask her if she cut Brianne's hair."

Mari eyed him once and then asked the question.

Gena lifted her face from her hands and stared in confusion. "Cut her hair? No, I would never. She was proud of it."

Mari echoed this to Tris; without a word, he turned for the door.

"Come with me," he said as he pulled the door wide. "Give me any other details on the way. I need to speak with the dead girl's betrothed, so ask the zupan to lead the way."

He was out the door before Mari overcame his abrupt exit and rushed after him.

After following Alexandre to another village dwelling, Mari found herself standing in front of its large attached stable with the front doors opened wide.

"Why here?" she asked, taking one step through the opening.

Tris stopped in the doorway. "Because Leif and his family probably own this stable. It is morning, so time to clean out stalls, usually the task of sons and other family children."

Inside the dim stable, a large chestnut horse tied to the wall suddenly swung its head toward them. Its nostrils flared and its eyes widened, and it whinnied loudly in pulling against its bridle tether. When it couldn't get free, it swung its rump around deeper into the stable and blew air out its nostrils.

Mari backstepped as a young man rushed out of the black shadows of another stall.

"Whoa, Heta!" he called, grabbing the horse's rope. "Easy."

Mari kept backing and almost bumped into Tris. He didn't look at her—only at the young man or the horse—and then turned out of the stable to walk quickly away.

"Tell the zupan to bring Leif outside," he said without looking back.

Mari remembered something he'd said in passing: *Horses don't like me.*

She cocked her head toward Tris as she told Alexandre, "He wants Leif outside to talk." Without waiting for the zupan's answer, she followed Tris. So far, everyone here did whatever the Dead's Man asked, whether they wanted to or not.

Tris now stood next to another dwelling at the far side of a wide, half-mud, half-dirt path through the village. She'd barely joined him and turned when she saw Alexandre emerge from the stable with the young man following behind.

Mari studied the latter.

He wasn't quite what she'd expected. Tall and slender, nearly gangly, he had a pinched, long face that was pockmarked, but only on one side. He walked with a slight limp on the other side.

And he was the betrothed of the dead girl?

When the limping youth approached, he looked straight at Tris without a trace of fear.

Mari's estimation of him rose.

"What do you want?" Leif asked Tris.

Mari stepped between them. "He'll need to speak through me."

The young man's eyes shifted briefly to her before returning to Tris. They were a clear light brown.

"Ask whatever you want," he said. "None of it matters to me. Brianne is gone, and that white *thing* coming at night isn't her."

"Leif!" Alexandre admonished.

"I don't care if it goes or stays," Leif added.

Mari had no idea why Tris was questioning these people, but she waited on him just the same. Little he'd done seemed to matter—to them or to finish off her last doubts about him.

He just stood there staring back at Leif.

"Ask him if he knows why Brianne went to Soladran," he said suddenly. "If he knows the truth, question him about all that happened when she returned. And do so again until you get answers."

Mari sighed in frustration. This wasn't getting anywhere that she could see, but she turned to Leif.

"Do you know why Brianne went to Soladran?"

He scoffed at her. "Of course I know. She went to see that guardsman, the one who loves himself most of all."

At this, Alexandre's mouth gaped. Apparently, a good deal had happened that he didn't know about, though apparently others here did.

"You were angry about it," she claimed rather than asked.

"Angry?" Leif returned. He coughed one laugh at her. "I was glad! I wanted her to see him and how he lived, in those barracks. I'd heard all about him from other guards in the patrols. He had three or four women in Soladran!" He lowered both eyes and head. "I loved her. Once she saw what he was, I knew she'd come back to *me* . . . but he'd already killed her."

"Killed?" Mari asked, startled.

"Or let her die; what's the difference?" Leif answered. "She stumbled into the village near dawn, looking starved or wasted away. I saw her first—watching for her return—and caught her as she collapsed. She kept mumbling and whimpering bits and pieces, but I put it together. Something at the barracks—horrible and white—touched her. He did nothing about it, even when she started wasting away. When he abandoned her, it was all she could do to get home . . . just barely."

Mari's breaths turned short and shallow; lost in his words and slowly heating up, she felt her eyes begin to burn as her irises opened. She could feel a *shift* coming in anger, and then Tris nudged her from behind. She took a deep breath.

"What touched her?" she asked with effort. "What could make her starve to death in the time it took to come home from Soladran?"

He cocked his head to one side, and his voice was cold. "I told you what she told me, and then she died." He looked away. "She was the only thing that mattered in this mudhole."

"Watch your mouth," Alexandre warned.

Mari said nothing and began to want out of this place before she heard any more. It wasn't her problem, wasn't her place. It wasn't gaining her what she wanted after half a lifetime of hunting *him*.

"Ask him about the lock of hair."

Mari almost turned on him at that, but she eyed Leif instead. Her ire at Tris, at this village, at everything, made the question come out harshly.

"Did you cut a lock of her hair . . . after she was *dead*?"

Leif started slightly. "Cut her hair? No—why?"

She didn't look back at Tris as she shook her head, but then she rattled off everything for him before he could ask. He didn't say anything. Finally, she looked over and up at him.

"Now what?"

Tris looked to the zupan and said in Belaskian, "The mother."

Mari didn't want to question anyone anymore, especially not the dead girl's mother. It would be awful enough to lose a child, only to have the same come back to haunt its home. That would only add to a mother's raw wound. Mari understood this.

She had enough of her own wounds and didn't want to face someone else's. This reluctance grew worse when the zupan knocked on another dwelling door.

After a long silence, the door opened, revealing a haggard woman, heavyset and with gray streaks in dark blond hair. The elder woman's expression remained blank. Ignoring everyone else, she turned her vacant eyes on the zupan.

"What do you want?"

"To talk," Alexandre answered. "These two have questions, and you'll answer anything they ask."

Cecilia said nothing. Was that hate in her eyes? Finally, she looked over at Mari and then up a little, likely at Tris. Either hate or something else flashed by then, with a single twitch of one eye and the left corner of her mouth.

She had to have been told before now about digging up her daughter, why, and by whose order. Suddenly she turned and walked away into the dark of her home, leaving the door open.

Mari hesitated at following like an intruder, but Alexandre gestured inward, and Tris nudged her from behind. She entered with twice as much reluctance.

Strangely, the place had a homey feel, though it was chill and dark with thick curtains hung over shuttered windows without panes. The little blackened hearth was unlit. She'd expected to see black-dyed, draped cloth everywhere, usually just burlap or canvas among the poor. But a red cotton cloth covered a table surrounded by simple actual chairs—chairs instead of stools or benches. Wooden cupboards lined one wall, all filled with fine but old and chipped ceramic bowls and cups.

The whole of it looked well-to-do at some past time compared with other village homes, though it hadn't remained well-to-do in recent years. There stood Cecilia at a cutting block below the cupboard, her back turned to everyone.

Mari froze in the middle of the main room. Alexandre stepped past after closing the front door, and Tris nudged her inward again.

"Did you know Brianne was chasing after Guardsman Bródy?" the zupan asked.

Cecilia turned slowly.

"That preening pigeon?" she said without emotion. "Of course; my daughter tells me everything. Her father is long dead, and it's been just the two of us for years."

One thing stuck in Mari's awareness—"tells" rather than "told."

"You knew she'd gone to Soladran?" she asked Cecilia, anticipating what Tris might want to know.

At this, a flash of pain broke Cecilia's flat expression.

"No," she answered. "That I didn't know. I was out of my mind with worry when she went missing, not knowing until she'd returned and Leif carried her here. When I saw . . . my girl . . . starved . . ."

Whatever else she said lost all voice, and Mari couldn't read the woman's lips.

"It isn't fair," Cecilia whispered.

Alexandre silently dropped his gaze.

Tris stepped around into Mari's view.

At that, Cecilia backed against the counter and cupboard, like a cornered cat ready to strike. She glanced back once. Maybe she was looking for a butcher knife, a dough pin, or something else in the cupboard she could use as a weapon.

Mari tried to watch Cecilia as well as Tris, as he touched a pot or mug left here and there. Once, he put a hand flat against the wall and closed his eyes in stillness.

"What is *he* doing . . . here?" Cecilia demanded.

Mari turned back at the venom in the question. She had no idea what Tris was up to. Without warning, he waved Alexandre to follow as he abruptly left the hut, leaving Mari.

Cecilia was fixed on the men and not her.

"I . . . We thank you," Mari muttered. "Forgive us disturbing you in mourning."

She didn't wait for a reply and fled. Outside, Tris had walked off toward the common house with Alexandre following. She hurried to catch up.

"Why didn't you ask her about cut hair?"

"I do not need to ask her," he answered without slowing.

Alexandre overtook Tris, rounding to cut him off and make him stop.

"I asked you here through my son, but . . . ," the zupan began. "I—my people—have had enough of your—"

"Tell him I can banish the ghost," Tris said, still facing the zupan.

At this, Alexandre looked to Mari.

"Sixteen silver pennies is my fee," Tris added.

Mari tried not to react.

That was more than some landed peasants could earn at year's end, let alone anyone here. And Tris had promised her a quarter cut of his gains, four times what she'd ever had at once in her whole life.

Caught between desire and guilt, she hesitated at repeating the offer to Alexandre—but she did. He paused only briefly.

"Done," he rasped.

Upon reaching the common house, Tris announced that he was "going up to rest" and slipped through the far back door to the stairs. He shut it before Mari could follow.

She heard his boots on the steps down the hallway beyond the door and then nothing. Part of her wanted to sneak up to see what he really did; another part was relieved to be rid of him for a while and still know where he was.

A third part felt only guilt and misery. This had been a difficult day, and after a life of struggling for survival, she wasn't accustomed to noticing the suffering of others.

Walking across the room, she was about to stoke up the fire.

The place was empty of anyone; then again, these villagers wouldn't gather here with *him* present. She began mulling everything he'd had her ask and what she'd heard, trying to find anything she'd missed in the moments.

With a shiver, she remembered what she heard of Brianne being touched by something "horrible and white." She heated inside at the girl being abandoned by a man she'd thought loved her, who'd left her to walk five leagues home while she was already dying.

Then again, had she been abandoned? Mari only had the secondhand words of a bitter, jilted young man. By Gena's account, Brianne's ghost mouthed Cameron's name in wanting him still. So why hadn't she gone to him instead of haunting this place?

What would cause her to remain here after death instead of going to him?

Most people believed that ghosts remained for some unfulfilled desire. Mari had a different view by her own experience, but that didn't mean other beliefs weren't true. Brianne's ghost had not hurt anyone; hadn't even come at Mari herself last night.

Could she have unfinished business?

Tris promised he could banish that spirit, but what did that mean or involve?

Mari grew frustrated by ignorance and chucked a small log into the fireplace without even looking. The rear door of the main room suddenly opened, startling her, and Erath stepped in, carrying folded blankets.

"Oh, hello," Erath said. "Alexandre said you'd come back. I wondered if you wanted to bathe or wash clothing?"

Mari looked about the main room, uncertain she'd heard correctly.

"Back there." Erath pointed to the door behind her. "There's a private room with buckets of heated water and a box tub that will drain outside."

The thought of a bath—an actual bath—was almost incomprehensible.

Mari couldn't remember the last time she'd even been able to soak in a washtub full of warm, if not hot, water. The problem was that this sounded too much like a favor she hadn't asked for, and this was suspicious to her.

She glanced toward the upper level with the lofts. Of course, this offer had been made more because of him than because of her, maybe as part of the payment.

Mari didn't like being indebted to anyone.

"Come. It won't take long," Erath said. "You can use the tub first. I've got blankets for us to wear while we dry our clothes by the fire."

Erath wished to bathe and wash clothing too? At least this took some of the edge off. If Mari wasn't bathing alone, then the favor wouldn't be all due to *him*.

Erath reopened the door, and Mari followed her to a back room on the left, short of the stairs at the end leading upward.

By the time dusk had fallen, Mari was clean—cleaner than she'd been in years—and settled by a stoked fire in the main room. Her clothes were now dry and clean as well. She'd almost forgotten how good any of this felt, and that put her on guard again. Too many things, little comforts, kept coming her way because of Tris. She couldn't allow herself to enjoy this, not too much. Or that in being connected to him, these people showed her respect.

Earlier, Alexandre had called her "Miss Mari," as if she was someone who mattered.

At the sound of footsteps, she turned her head to see Tris coming through the doorway and entering the common room. Maybe he was hungry—like her—as they hadn't eaten anything since the morning.

"Erath's gone for food," she said. "Some kind of communal stew."

He settled quietly at the end of the nearest long table, and she waited for him to say something. He didn't.

"What have you been doing?" she finally asked.

"Preparing."

Not much of an answer, so again she'd have to wait and watch.

Erath soon returned with yet another loaded tray: this time with steaming bowls but not steaming mugs. Mari could smell ale in the mugs this time from halfway across the big room. As Erath set the tray on the table near Tris, he glanced aside.

"Tea," he said, and returned to staring at nothing.

"Pardon?" Erath asked.

Mari flushed with embarrassment. He continued to treat Erath like a servant.

"He's not fond of ale," she explained, remembering what he'd said about wine. "Could you bring him some tea?"

"Of course, and you? I'll bring bread as well, as it wasn't sliced yet when I left."

She swept out of the room, and Mari walked over to settle across the table from Tris. Carrots and potatoes in the stew made her think of her mother. She froze amid picking up her spoon, trying to push that thought away, and blew on the bowl's steaming food.

Even as the smell of food—hot food—filled her senses, something else did as well.

Something smelled . . . wrong, even though she wasn't in her other flesh.

She sat there with spoon in hand, frowning at the stew; just as she leaned down to sniff it closely, Tris dipped his spoon and raised it to his mouth.

"Stop!" she said.

Slapping the spoon from his hand, she sent it spinning along the tabletop, spattering its contents.

"What?" he asked in open surprise.

She lowered her head over her bowl and sniffed deeply. Beneath that tempting aroma was something else, just barely there—musty, pungent, and rank. She couldn't stop a cat's grating hiss.

"Kwo'an!" she whispered in her people's tongue.

"What does that mean?"

Mari had learned some things about herbs and other plants from her aunt; even poisons had their uses in healing—some of them. Without lifting her head, she raised her eyes to him.

"Dropwort, numb-tongue . . . *hemlock*! Someone poisoned our food."

One more time, she'd just saved her prey.

Tris's eyes half closed as he leaned over his own bowl to smell the food. Then he sat back and shook his head slightly. Maybe only an animal or a *yai-morchi*—shifter—could've caught that under-scent.

Rising up, Mari shouted, "Erath!"

Almost instantly, the elder woman rushed back in, but before she could say a word—

"Who made this stew?" Mari demanded.

Erath flinched. "I . . . don't . . . It was different people, at times, more than one."

Mari was about to demand more answers, when a hand clamped on her wrist. She turned on Tris.

"Wait," he whispered. "Is this from a communal meal, something for the village together or for workers?"

Mari hesitated, wondering how much he had understood.

"Yes," she answered.

"Then only our portions were laced, or perhaps the bowls themselves."

She didn't quite understand how he'd reasoned that.

"Do not alarm her further," Tris warned. "Ask her who prepared our servings, her or someone else."

Mari had already done, but she asked again.

Erath frowned, looking between the two guests. "As I said, I don't know. The servings were ready and waiting by the time I returned from filling the mugs with ale."

Mari tried to remain calm, not that she fully believed anything at this point. She wondered how Tris had reasoned what had really happened. Erath was still looking between them in frightened confusion. Mari related the stew had been poisoned, but that it was likely only their bowls. Erath went pale.

"Tell her I still want tea," Tris instructed. "And bread cut from a loaf already being served."

And again Mari did so, and again Erath rushed off. Mari settled down, watching as he slid the bowls away, down the table.

"You're lucky I was here," she said.

"It is not the first time," he replied.

She stalled for an instant. "And you still eat what they give you?"

"Such a thing has been attempted when I have been called to render service," he said. "But not often, and I must eat."

She almost didn't believe what she was hearing, either that someone here would risk trying to kill him or that he took it so calmly.

"I am sorry you were targeted as well," he added.

Just the same, this village was willing to pay a hefty fee for whatever he could supposedly do.

"So who *here* would want you dead?" she asked.

"Someone who wants Brianne to remain."

CHAPTER FIVE

Tris remained in the main room that night after Mari went up to the loft. Beneath all her anger, he could see she had been shaken by an attempt on their lives, though he guessed that she'd faced worse. And he neither cared if Erath believed their food had been poisoned nor sought out the culprit.

Yet he could not stop thinking on Mari, the mystery of her, or why he had not sent her away.

She had proved herself useful during the questioning in the village, more so than even Heil on the times the apothecary had come with him. People were cautious around Heil, regardless that he spoke the local dialects. He was too learned and skilled for villagers to see him as one of their own.

They were far more open in Mari's presence.

Tris had followed enough of the verbal exchanges to see this. Not having to struggle with the language barrier had been a relief and an advantage with her presence. Without knowing what she sought, she had exposed much concerning those who were connected to Brianne.

Soon enough, he'd pieced together what had happened with Brianne—or at least most of it—and he knew what to do as soon as enough time had passed tonight.

Yet, his thoughts remained on Mari. Who was she and why had she agreed to remain with him, especially after that first visitation in the loft the night before? When he had offered her a quarter of the fee, her expression and demeanor had grown so intense he thought he'd somehow insulted her.

Then he realized the truth.

Regardless of her clear longing to accept, something else had been pushing her to refuse, perhaps vehemently. She was a creature of extremes, and he had more than once ignorantly stepped in between those. For him, the fees from these hunts meant little to nothing.

He charged people only because they expected it and would be suspicious otherwise. That, and because he would take no money from his family. With the exception of a few coins he kept for his own needs, anything else he earned went to Heil for food and rent.

Other than fluency in multiple dialects, Mari seemed to possess limited skills to offer, though this evening had been different. He would have sensed he had been poisoned soon enough to go after the remedies and antitoxins he always carried from Heil. Still, she had saved him from that suffering and being left vulnerable.

She wanted neither help nor charity nor friendship. That much was clear, and companionship was not something he could risk anyway. She served herself and her own needs first, but she was capable. However, for the rest of the task at hand tonight, he was better off without her presence.

And so he waited.

He watched the fire burn lower and lower. When only a faint flame remained, he headed for the front door, leaving his heavy cloak behind. The night was nearly frigid, but he needed to be unencumbered for his coming task.

Mari lay awake and fully clothed on her mat as she listened to every little sound. She heard the common house's timbers and the tree limbs outside creaking softly as the temperature dropped lower and lower. For a long while, that and the distant crackle of the fire in the main room below at the building's far end were all that she heard.

And *he* still hadn't come up to bed.

The longer she waited, the more she knew he wouldn't tonight. She'd prepared for that. The soft squeal of a half-frozen metal hinge carried faintly through the common house. And only a *mäth'ka*—one of the "cat-kind" among the *yai-morchi*—could've heard that.

Mari rolled onto all fours without a sound and crept under the blanket curtains. After rising, she went to where the roof's slant met a shin's length of front wall rising above the loft's timber floor. Before lying down to *not* sleep, she'd bored a tiny hole between two wall planks with the tip of her blade. Pressing her face to the wall, she peered out through that tiny hole.

The Dead's Man was already slipping away through the dark village.

He didn't skulk very well, though he kept to deeper darkness near any dwelling. She watched long enough to gauge his direction and speed. Just before he slipped from her sight, she spun, rose, and passed through the curtains toward her belongings.

Mari picked up her blade. She pulled it from the sheath to see that it slid freely, and then shoved it, sheath and all, into her belt and rushed downstairs to follow him.

Tris made his way quietly but directly to the dwelling of Brianne's mother, Cecilia. He had known within moments of meeting her that she was the one who had cut the girl's hair before burial. Not by grief's madness in her eyes; not by sorrow and loss greater than that of Gena or Leif; and not even for the angry, desperate edge in her voice.

During all the questioning, most of which Tris had not understood in the moment, Cecilia had never moved from her place before the cupboard. When Mari had asked if Cecilia knew of Guardsman Bródy from her daughter, the woman had answered with "tells" rather than "told me everything." Perhaps this was just a slip in a quick answer, maybe revealing or not.

She'd remained before the cupboard, even backing nearer to it when he surveyed the hut's interior, as if guarding something precious hidden away. And then had come that glance back at the cupboard.

He had not seen a worthwhile weapon there, let alone any reason for her to glance away from the intruders in her home. In that same moment, with his own hand flattened against the wall, he had felt the permutations of something other than the living.

Something dead had entered that place recently—and not a corpse.

This awareness was one thing on a long list involving his own nature that he had never been able to explain. In the beginning, it had been unnatural, frightening . . . revolting. Only later, upon meeting Heil, had he learned to accept it.

Tris reached Cecilia's home, slipped around back, and closed his eyes to listen.

Upon hearing nothing, he crouched down in stillness. The window at the hut's front would be the most accessible place, but timing was everything when hunting the dead, especially one held in bondage by a loved one. This situation was even more complicated, but all that mattered was freeing the living from the dead. That was why he had been called.

One of Heil's earliest rebukes came to mind: *Your ability is natural, so don't waste it . . . or my time in assisting you!*

The first encounter with the alchemist masquerading as an apothecary had forever altered Tris's life. Ironically, he had his cousin Alaina to thank in an indirect manner. After what she had seen in the rose garden—of the boy ghost and him—she never again let him near enough to touch her. But she must have told her mother what had happened, what she had seen, though Aunt Ellen had said nothing then.

In the following summer, when Tris turned eighteen, a letter addressed to him arrived. It was unsettling to see that it came from his aunt.

My Dear Tris,

I hope this missive finds you well. I am sorry that you and Alaina never became as close as I had hoped, but I have wanted for too long to thank you for my daughter's life.

It comes too late, I know.

I hope you do not find my request below odd.

But years past, my maid Patera left to wed the owner of a candle shop in Ceskú, about four leagues east of Bela. We still correspond once per moon, and her last letter disturbed me. Ceskú faces a similar horror to the one you faced for my dear Alaina.

A murderer who was beheaded there last moon now plagues that place as a vengeful spirit. Apples rot upon trees, milk drawn from cattle sours instantly, and two people have been paralyzed by the spirit's touch. The mayor hired an herbalist who is said to have knowledge of such unnatural blights, but so far, this man has been unsuccessful.

I have no right to ask anything of you.

But I beg you, just the same. Please help my Patera and her family. You are the only one I could think to ask.

Your loving Aunt Ellen

Tris had held the letter in his hand for so long. He read it at least five times. She asked him to do again what he had done for her daughter by an accident of instinct.

What *had* he done? Could he do so again without knowing?

That same night, he packed and quietly left the manor without telling anyone; he left only a note for his mother saying he would return soon. The journey took lonely days and nights, though it gave him some relief in solitude. He arrived in Ceskú in late afternoon, asking the shy and suspicious townsfolk where he could find the local candle shop. When he did find it, Patera had been expecting him.

She welcomed him kindly as the nephew of her former employer. But this was the first time he looked into eyes staring back in hope and fear. Some of that fear was for him—some of him.

He had no idea how to hunt a spirit.

The following night, he was awakened by screams somewhere in the town. When he rose, he hesitated, but no one in Patera's house came out of their rooms. The door of her and her husband's bedchamber remained closed in silence.

Tris barely left the house when another scream sounded in the dark night, drowning every other sound. He ran toward it and spotted dim red-orange light wavering out of the open bay doors of a dirt-floored smithy. Rushing to those doors, he first found a young, shirtless man twitching on the floor, a forge hammer either dropped or tossed aside nearby. Before he could crouch next to the man, he saw a disheveled girl backed into a far corner behind a scarred and burned wooden workbench.

Her quivering mouth gaped under eyes that never blinked and did not look at him. This time no scream came out of her, and he followed those wide eyes to the smithy's far side.

There, in the darkness lit only by the forge's dim glow, he saw a white, transparent form without a head.

It drifted straight toward the girl through the forge, coals and all.

Tris had no time to guess at what else had happened here, or why a girl was in this smithy at night, but he had no fear of the spirit. None at all. He lunged in two steps without thinking and shouted.

"Here! Look at me!"

The white form beyond the forge turned his way. Its headless body was shirtless and muscular, and the opaque shapes of chainless shackles were on its wrists. The smithy became so quiet that Tris went still where he stood.

What should he do now?

Everything that had happened in facing the boy ghost with Alaina had . . . just happened. It was not happening this time.

The headless spirit rushed at him straight through the forge.

The girl screamed.

Tris raised his hands, ready to hold off the headless man, if he could. Cold, white, thick hands as transparent as vapor went straight through his own and latched around his throat.

Determination turned to shock when he *felt* those grips crushing into his flesh and then bone. His breath was cut off. If the girl screamed again, he did not hear it. He tried to latch hold of the spirit's wrists.

Unlike with the boy ghost, his hands went straight through, as through icy mist.

This was not the way it had happened the last time, and he could not protect anyone if he could not protect himself.

Me . . . not you . . . I Tris . . . not you, Tris . . .

Everything became worse when he heard the whispers again.

Beyond the headless spirit, night within the smithy gathered and swallowed the forge's dim glow. It turned and turned in a darkening whirlpool hanging in the air.

. . . my Tris . . . me Tris . . . not you . . . Tris . . .

He stared into that swirling void beyond over the headless spirit's stump of a neck. It manifested just as it had before, on the night with Alaina. Had he called it up again somehow?

. . . my Tris . . . my life . . . not yours . . . Tris . . .

Unable to breathe, he tried again to grab the spirit's wrists. His fingers sank in like gripping winter-chilled water. It did not matter how that opening into death had formed again; it was his only hope. He planted both hands against the spirit's chest.

His fingers and palms sank again, but this time like in thawing mud. The void beyond the ghost spun in place, and Tris shoved with his whole body.

That murderer's ghost gave ground.

He struck outward with both arms against its grips upon his throat. Those grips faltered, and he slammed his palms against its chest—solid to his touch this time. Both grips broke, he gasped a needed breath, and then he heard running footsteps halt behind him.

"My gods . . ."

He did not dare turn at that low male voice speaking strangely ac-cented Belaskian. Instead he shoved even harder. The headless one lurched back but not enough and then came at him again.

A white wisp shot past him . . . and another . . . and another.

They swirled in the smithy's air, and he lost focus as one dove at his face. He ducked and then did feel a hint of fear. He had not seen those since that night at the manor when he was thirteen.

"I will deal with the pests," that strange voice barked to him, this time in Stravinan. "You get Silas into that . . . that portal!"

The headless one grabbed for Tris's head with both of its hands.

"*No fear!* That is what they need—*want*—and it can kill just as quickly."

Tris stalled at that shout, and the spirit gripped his head. Cold sank into his skull like none he had ever felt in any winter. He flattened both of his hands into its chest and thrust with his legs.

"Harder—*now!*"

Tris needed no urging. Inch by inch, he gained ground on the black void, driving the headless one toward it. He had no fear of this headless ghost.

But somewhere beyond that opening into death waited the other *him*.

The headless one began to tear apart. That murderer's spirit shredded like tatters of threadbare cloth. Pieces spun in a swirl, sucked into the pure black before Tris's eyes. This time, he did not back away.

He wanted to see what was in there—in that black void.

Someone grabbed the back of his vestments and yanked.

Tris spun, stumbled, tripped, and fell in a tumble across the smithy's dirt floor.

"Are you stupid, boy?"

At that sharp retort, he righted himself and looked back, but not to whoever had shouted at him. The last of the black void drained like swirling ink, sucked into a hole in the world, and vanished. Not one white wisp still raced about the smithy. Everything became so quiet—enough to hear boots shift on the dirt.

A sigh made Tris flinch and look up.

An elder man stood close by, smirking down at him. Dressed in well-groomed attire, from charcoal-colored felt vestment to chocolate-toned canvas pants and high black leather boots, he had a long face curtained by silver-gray hair glimmering by forge light. Fifty years old at a guess, he was poorly shaved.

Tris had seen men who did not care to shave; they sheared back facial hair whenever it grew long enough to do so. In the man's left hand, dangling at his side, he held a round and flat silvery disk more than a hand's length in diameter. Strange, engraved markings lined its outer edge. Again, Tris looked about for any remaining white wisps in the dim smithy.

All had vanished, and he glanced at the disk again.

"Who are you?" he asked in Old Stravinan.

The man slowly dropped to one knee and snorted with a half smile.

"Heilman Tavakovich," he answered in Tris's preferred language. "Most around these parts know me as Heil."

Tris again studied the strange silver-gray plate. "What is that?"

"An Ether shield," the man answered, "fashioned by four of the five elements—Earth, Water, Air, and Fire. The void of the fifth—Spirit—gives it the power to leach Spirit from whatever it touches. Thereby it can . . . *repel* ghosts."

Tris was still staring at the plate; though he had understood every word, little of it registered but for one thing in that moment.

"It is possible to make *weapons* to use against spirits?"

The man rolled his eyes. "Do you see any spirits left? However, you got rid of one with your . . . natural talent."

Tris had never heard the word "natural" applied to anything about him. This man seemed to know more about what had just happened—more than he or anyone he had ever met. That was disturbing, and none of what had happened appeared to startle this man.

"I am—"

"I know who you are, baron's boy. Even if not, there were those whispers as well."

Tris went suddenly chill. This man had heard the whispers? No one could have known he had come here, and no one but him knew of the black one. Even those who had been present when it entered the living world were all dead.

"You . . . *heard* . . . it?"

Perhaps the elder man chuckled, though it sounded more like he had cleared his throat. He flipped the silver-gray disk, catching it like a toy, and shrugged.

"Your aunt thought you'd need assistance," Heil said casually. "Or some guidance, though to date, I've yet to hear of someone who could *grip* a ghost."

Explanations aside, all of this was too much in the moment for Tris. Was this man the "herbalist" that his aunt had mentioned? Had she told this Heilman anything about what had happened with Alaina? What he had come here to do?

And this Heilman had heard the black one?

Tris glanced again at the disk in the man's hand.

Heilman—or Heil, if he preferred—arched his back, as if stretching out a kink.

"Don't just sit there," he grumbled. "Pick yourself up."

Hesitantly, Tris did so. After another long moment of staring at Heil, he looked around the smithy. The girl and the downed man were both gone.

"She dragged him off," Heil said, turning away for the door. "Likely that'll be the last she does for him—or to him—after his wife hears about this."

Again, Tris stalled at this stranger taking everything that had happened as if it were commonplace. When he finally hurried to follow outside, he rounded Heil wide, watching the man carefully. All the would-be apothecary did was flick his hand for Tris to lead onward. So he did, but not without too many glances back, until Heil caught up and walked beside him.

Neither spoke along the way to the candle shop, though Tris often watched his companion in side glances. When they reached that shop, Heil surprised him further.

"You've a rare gift but no idea what you're doing," the herbalist said. "Not from what I've seen. I suppose you'd best come to Strîbrov with me, young baron."

"Do not call me that," Tris warned without thinking.

He wanted no connection to a father who treated him like a curse in the flesh. And it did not matter this was how he saw himself as well.

Heil shrugged, a thin smile spreading across his stubbled face. "Very well . . . Tris."

And then Tris grew eager at this stranger's offer—anything to find a way out of the life he had been given—any way to elude its loss as well. Yet he could not simply leave his mother. Her desperate love smothered him in the absence of his father, and the loss of her only child might damage her even more.

"I cannot come, not now," he mumbled out.

Heil cocked his head, long and silver hair curtaining one eye.

"The offer stands," he said. "Whenever."

Heil turned away without another word, gone too quickly in that night that now seemed so long ago.

Crouching before that one hut in the sprawling village amid the woods, Tris knew what had to be done now. Delaying longer gained him little, though he could not strike too soon and betray his presence. Creeping forward, he peeked through the seam between the front window shutters. All inside was as black as the other *him* who would never stop coming.

Mari slipped in and out of the darkest night shadows along the way, but it wasn't long before it didn't matter. She paused, peered ahead wide-eyed, and even let her other half rise a bit more. The night brightened in her sight, but the scent was gone.

Tris was gone.

Panicked, she crouched, dropped to all fours, and sniffed the ground, over and over. She had to find him, see what he was up to, to figure out once and for all if he really was the one she'd been hunting for so long.

Mari smelled nothing that helped.

How could she have lost him?

She'd forced herself to join him, eat with him, and sleep idly nearby until certain she'd found the right prey. And now, just when she might've gained another scrap of truth about him, he was gone.

It wasn't possible. She could track anything—anyone.

Mari rose, sniffing the air in quick pants, and still nothing came of it. Clearing her thoughts, she quickly scanned the village shadows for any sign of where he'd gone.

After all three questionings during the day, he'd seemed to lose interest in everyone they'd sought out. But something slightly different had happened when they'd gone to Cecilia, and that stuck in Mari's head.

Touching items and putting his hand on a wall, he'd lost interest in questions—or answers—even quicker than before. And he hadn't had Mari herself ask Cecilia about the severed locks of a dead girl's hair. Right after leaving that hut, he'd stated his offer and price to the zupan, Alexandre.

Mari darted across the village path, slipping from shadow to shadow, trying to trace her way back to Cecilia's hut.

Tris remained as silent as the dead, as he had done so many times. He peered through the split in the shutters and waited until his sight adjusted to the deeper darkness within the hut. Slowly, he made out the barest orange-red glimmer.

That was from the dying, charred logs in the hearth.

Shifting his head slightly and steadily, he slowly studied the rest of the outer room. There Cecilia stood with her back toward him, halfway toward the hut's rear and the cupboards beyond the kitchen's table.

She backstepped once more toward the main room. When she turned, it was too dark in there to see her face. Her head was tilted down, as if she looked upon something gripped tightly in her upheld right hand.

That hand flattened to her chest, over her heart, against a floor-length garment like a heavy nightgown.

She moaned, *"Brianne*, stop . . ."

Though she went on, Tris did not understand the rest and did not care as he waited while watching.

Mari slipped in next to the hut's side and away from sight along the village's main path. All her senses widened again, and with one hand tracing along the wall, she crept toward the hut's front corner.

She stiffened and halted halfway at a moaning voice heard through that wall.

"*Brianne*, stop, please . . . Come only to me, no one else, not ever again."

At those words in Belaskian somewhere inside the hut, Mari's fingers curled like claws against the damp planks, and she flattened one ear against the old boards to listen.

"A hunter was called to kill you, my child, this time forever!"

Mari's breath caught as a strange panic set in upon that last word—*forever*. Was that how these peasants saw him—Tris? Someone who wouldn't just banish but "kill" the dead a second time?

Something in this horrified her. Did it mean nothing would be left, not even the spirit? Was that what *he* did—what he'd done to her mama, her papa, and all others that she'd loved? A fear-fed anger brought one more question.

Where was Tris now?

She pulled her head back from the wall, and her senses sharpened to a peak. If he'd thought as she had, he was somewhere close by. She looked again to the hut's forward corner, and as she drew one of her hands from the wall, she heard Cecilia's voice again.

"Oh my, my dear child."

Mari waited to hear more. A sudden chill ate through her palm and into her forearm.

She snatched her other hand from the wall in a backstep of shock.

Tris waited and watched, understanding no more than a fourth of what Cecilia whimpered. None of this mattered. The only thing that mattered was that the dead did not belong among the living.

For too long nothing happened, even for all of a mother's pleading.

He kept still outside, barely breathing as he watched. Then the night's cold wormed into him like iced needles, and still Tris did not move.

That was the first sign for which he had been waiting.

Darkness within the hut's front room appeared to swirl like char black smoke. The cold through the split in the shutters intensified on his left eye and cheek. The air before the hut's hearth shuddered.

A twisted glimmer of white formed.

Brianne appeared suddenly before her mother, still as white, pale, and translucent as on the night she had gone at Mari. Her visage matched that of her unearthed corpse: starved with her illusory skin stretched tightly over her bones. Only the darker circles around her eyes unsettled Tris, for he had seen such before.

Something at the barracks in Soladran had touched the girl, and her wasting death had been the result.

Cecilia moaned something out while taking a quick step toward her daughter's spirit.

About to act, Tris hesitated again. The mother was now too close to the daughter. Soon, his own presence and intention would open that swirling hole into death. But his intention was only half the cause for the portal's appearance. The "other" him was also somehow connected.

It was as if Tris's need to banish the dead was matched by the black one's desire to take him, to take his life and replace him in the world of the living. That tension of desires was what breached the barrier between the worlds of the living and the dead. Or at least this was Heil's theory.

And each time the portal opened, Tris heard the black one taunting him, and he felt its dark longings.

It was as if it waited for the next time it could manifest. As of yet, it had not attacked Tris, but at each appearance, it longed to come at him. Its manifestations had a schedule, which Heil had calculated based on past attempts. The next time was nearing, and worse, each time Tris banished a spirit, it felt as if that other *him* grew stronger.

He feared it would soon be stronger than him, and then it would act on its desire.

There was nothing to be done about this for now, and Tris shook off indecision. The dead did not belong among the living. Worse so, as tools to be used in finding him when that other *him* broke from the realm of dead yet again.

Inside the dwelling, Brianne stretched out both arms toward her mother, but her fists were clenched. Not the pleading gesture Mari had described from her own encounter. Brianne's gaunt face twisted in anger as her mouth gaped. Only more darkness showed between those shriveled lips, and she mouthed one silent word.

Cameron.

"No!" Cecilia shrieked.

Tris could not follow the rest of her hysterical rant. When Cecilia held up her hands, one clenched in a fist, he already knew what she held.

Dangling out of the bottom of her hand was the tail of a ribbon illuminated by Brianne's phosphorescence. That ribbon had to be what bound a lock of hair cut from the girl's corpse.

The girl had not come back for love of a man. Her mother had done this somehow. But now that Brianne's spirit *was* here, all she wanted was to return to the man she loved.

Tris pulled back, a chill in one eye and on his face from peeking through the shutters. He needed to catch daughter and mother unaware— and quickly—to banish one and save the other. This time, however, there might not be a need to risk that opening to the realm of the dead.

Rising, he sidestepped to the door and shoved sharply with both hands. The instant the door slammed open, he lunged one step into the

BARB & J. C. HENDEE

front room. Both mother and daughter turned his way as he locked focus on the second.

In Brianne's presence, the room began to brighten slightly in Tris's sight. By now, the color had likely drained from his irises, though it was an effect he had never seen for himself. Cecilia whipped the fist clenching the ribbon behind her back, but Tris remained fixed upon Brianne.

The daughter's spirit wavered as she attempted to vanish. Fear filled her gaunt features at failure, and she tried a second time. She remained there, locked in his sight . . . by his sight.

Tris glanced at Cecilia only once. "Release her or I will banish her my way."

The mother charged him with an anguished cry. "No!"

Tris did not flinch. Attempts on his life had been made before, though most people feared attacking him openly. Not so when they felt cornered or that he was trying to take away something—or someone— dear to them.

He thought nothing of slapping her groping hands aside. When she swung back again, he simply blocked her lead arm with one hand and grabbed the trailing ribbon with the other. He ripped it free of her grip, and there it was:

The lock of Brianne's hair bound in the ribbon's knot.

Fingernails raked Tris's right cheek.

He shoved Cecilia aside in a lunge for the hearth. A quick toss, and both ribbon and hair landed on a charred log still glowing faintly with embers. A scream behind him drowned out the sizzle of burning hair.

Tris felt the mother slam into his back.

She grabbed for the collar of his shirt and pullover. He twisted, throwing her off again, and looked for the daughter. Destroying a fetish should release a bound spirit, which was better for all than forcefully banishing it back into death. He barely righted himself when he saw the result.

Brianne still floated there, just within reach.

Her shriveled lips parted as if in a sigh of relief. He tried to grab for her. She turned and fled straight through the hut's front, through the shutters where he had first peeked in.

Cecilia slammed into him again. He shoved her off and bolted for the door.

Mari had just rounded the hut's front corner when a scream made her halt.

"No!"

There was no one outside the hut's front, so what was happening if Tris wasn't here?

Mari heard a struggle inside and then the peal of shrieks. As she made a lunge for the front door, something white came out of the front wall at her. She barely spun away into the open path—but not quickly enough.

Agony and numbness shot through her right shoulder.

It sped up into her neck and down into her hand and the whole night began to tilt in her sight. Panic followed the chill that ate into her, freezing damp night air in her lungs. She hit the ground but didn't feel it, and lay there gasping for air.

Panic became terror.

She tried to breathe or move and couldn't do either. Numbness spread through her, until she felt neither cold nor heat. Out in the path, she saw *him*—sideways—where he stood before something that glowed in the dark.

It was the ghost, the girl, the same one that Mari had faced last night in the common house's loft, before Tris had torn it apart in the air. And there he was, gripping the girl's spirit by her wrist.

Mari lost awareness of anything else.

A man holding a spirit? That was impossible.

No, not for *him*!

Night swirled inward behind Brianne, blotting out the shapes of huts across the way, which began to turn even darker in Mari's failing sight. The spirit thrashed but didn't break free, and then she began to shred in wispy tatters, sucked into that whirling black hole in the night.

Once the spirit vanished, along with that black hole, the last thing Mari saw was him—Tris—turning around and freezing at the sight of her. His eyes were glowing again, as they had last night. Then they were like pinpricks of white light just before everything went black in her sight.

That light sparked all of Mari's fury within the cold numbness spreading in her flesh.

Tris had held the spirit in place before the portal and shut out those whispers of the other *him*.

No! Brianne had mouthed, thrashing to get free, and then, *Cameron!*

He had not reacted to her pleading expression. He'd held her there before that black vortex until she began to come apart. Only then did he release her and watch her form tear from this world. It happened far easier this time than many times before. Perhaps upon death she had lacked as much strength in spirit as in body—thankfully. He was exhausted, as always, after a banishment, but the years had conditioned him against giving in to fatigue.

Tris turned away as the portal finally collapsed—and he stopped one step later.

Mari lay sprawled in the village path with her eyes slowly drooping shut.

"Mari?" he whispered in another step; she neither answered nor opened her eyes. "Mari!"

Where had she come from? What was she doing out here? How had she found him? She should be asleep up in the common house loft and not here for any of this.

He ran to her, dropped hard on his knees, grabbed her shoulders, and shook her slightly. Nothing changed. Even in the dark, he saw her face and hands were pale—too pale for anyone, especially the dusky complexion of a Móndyalítko.

An agitated spirit had touched her.

How? When?

Something screamed just before it rammed him, sending him sprawling. As he lay prone on his back, it was on him again, raising something high.

Tris saw the carving knife come down in Cecilia's grip where she crouched atop him. Back inside the hut, he had already tossed the mother aside into the table and chairs to go after the daughter. He barely caught her wrist, and the blade's tip stopped a hand's length from his throat.

Cecilia's mania pushed the blade downward.

"Murderer . . . my child!" she screamed.

Tris grew more exhausted with each pant. He was too spent by another banishment to face another enraged villager, even one smothered in grief. And not at the cost of his own life.

He jerked back his other hand holding her off and struck her with the heel of that hand.

Cecilia's head whipped back.

He hit her again, and she tumbled off to one side.

Tris rolled the other way. Struggling to his feet, he turned and saw her rush him again, knife still in hand. One foot seemed to catch on something.

Cecilia suddenly slammed to the ground, face-first, and Tris flinched in shock. Just beyond the woman's feet, Mari barely held her face up.

One of her hands was latched tightly about the anguished mother's left ankle.

Tris flinched again. Even in the dark, he thought he saw her eyes shift, change as they fixed on only him.

"My . . . my . . . ," she struggled to say, as if barely able to breathe. That vicious, broken hiss sounded like the lynx that had torn apart a man one night before the journey here.

Still pallid, Mari closed her eyes, and her head dropped facedown on the ground. Her grip remained latched tightly around the sobbing Cecilia's ankle.

"My . . . *prey* . . ."

Mari went limp upon the ground after that last hiss.

Tris stood panting in the dark and looked between Mari and Cecilia.

Mari had saved him again, but why would she call a grieving mother *prey?*

He took the knife out of Cecilia's hand, threw it off into the woods, and stood there, looking down at both women. Dealing with one of them was all he could manage, and all this noise would surely have roused others in the village to come.

Taking hold of Mari, he struggled to pick her up, and somehow managed to carry her back toward the common house. Perhaps he heard voices left well behind him whenever he paused to check if Mari still breathed.

———————

Mari awoke, sat up, and shivered with an inner chill, though she was covered with a wool blanket. She was still dressed from last night, but her clothes were stained with mud and dirt. Blankets hung around her as curtains. So she was back in the common house loft, but how had she gotten here?

The last thing she remembered was seeing *him* on the village's main path. After the girl's spirit ripped into shreds, she'd seen his eyes with their irises glowing.

Where was he now? Had he brought her back here?

She rose, slapped the blanket-curtain aside and the next across the center path, but his space was empty. The blanket there was folded up next to the bedroll and his gear, as if he hadn't been there all night. When she turned back, she started to shake . . . to vibrate all over.

It wouldn't stop, and her mouth was filled with an acrid, metallic taste that made her gag. She started spitting to clear the taste.

Her spit on the floor was colored a rusty green.

What was that?

She stuck a finger in her mouth. Under her tongue was a clump of something. She scraped it out, and her finger was coated in a paste colored like her spit.

With no other choice, she headed down the stairs and heard muted voices, which made her run down the passage to the front room. When she slammed through the end door, there he was.

Tris turned, suddenly startled where he stood on the near side of the farthest table. On the table's opposite side, nearer the front door, stood Erath, Zupan Alexandre, and others as well. Alexandre looked over, as did Erath and the others.

Tris stared at Mari as if shocked that she'd appeared. He looked bad to her, as if he hadn't slept in days or nights. By light sneaking under the door and through the splits of the shutters, it was well into morning. So what had he been doing since last night?

And what had happened last night?

Noisy peasants babbling all around made him cringe, though he didn't look away from her. Likely he hadn't understood most of what anyone said or asked of him. The way he kept looking at her, so concerned, kept her stalled in the hallway's door.

"It's done, then?" Alexandre demanded of her.

At first, she didn't know whether to answer, but she nodded. That much she did remember from last night.

Tris strode around the other two tables toward her. The worry in his narrow features made her wary.

"You left Cecilia lying in the street," Erath said quietly, almost accusingly.

Mari's gaze twitched to the elder woman. Yes, now she remembered that as well, and Tris neared, still watching her. The grieving mother had gone after him, though Mari couldn't quite remember what else.

"Sorry about that," she said to Erath.

Erath's expression softened a little, and Mari tried to remember more. Had there been a fight?

"But Brianne is gone?" Alexandre pressed.

Halfway to Mari, Tris stalled and looked back, likely catching only the name. Obviously he hadn't made anything clear to these people. He turned back.

"Are you . . . well enough?" he whispered.

He looked doubtful. She wasn't even sure what had happened to her—or how she'd gotten to bed.

"Yes," she answered.

He relaxed a little and whispered, "Please clarify for them."

Mari hesitated but looked to Erath and Alexandre. "Brianne is gone. I saw him . . . send her off."

Erath closed her eyes in relief or grief or both. Reactions differed among the others, whom Mari didn't know. She watched and listened as Alexandre explained to them, but Tris still studied her.

Under his exhausted gaze, Mari remembered something else she'd heard last night, something Cecilia had said.

A hunter was called to kill you, my child. This time forever!

Mari began to shake slightly. Though she was still chilled to the bone, fury began heating her within. She thought of her family and that black thing in the Wicker Woods—*him*—who had taken everyone who mattered to her.

"Your payment."

Mari twitched at a chink of coins.

Alexandre had dropped a small pouch upon the table closest to the front door. The others around him except Erath turned away for the door. Whispering among themselves, each stole a last glance at the Dead's Man—and at Mari.

"You'll be on your way, then?" Alexandre asked.

It wasn't really a question.

"Yes," Mari answered, as it was most likely true. Nobody wanted them—*him*—here anymore.

Now that the village's ghost was gone, these people were in a hurry to be rid of the one who'd done the deed.

With a curt nod, the zupan steered his wife toward the door.

"I left warm rolls for you," Erath called over one shoulder.

Then they were gone, and Mari was alone with Tris. She glanced toward the far end of the first table, and rolls weren't all that Erath had left on a wooden platter.

"Are you certain you are well enough to be up?"

All her muscles tightened at the concern in his voice, false as it had to be. He hadn't even looked at the pouch Alexandre had dropped.

Why?

She stepped wide around, still watching him until she gained some distance. That appeared to worry him again.

"Are you sure you—"

"Stop asking that," she cut him off.

Reaching the first long table, she didn't pick up the pouch. Instead, she looked to the table's far end. A bowl of broth for dipping sat with four rolls along with two steaming mugs. But she didn't feel hungry, though she should've, and she turned about.

"What did you do to that girl, her spirit?"

. . . this time forever!

"Banished her back to the dead. Why?"

He was lying, if Cecilia was right, and Mari remembered Brianne tearing apart into that darkness darker than the night.

"What does that mean?" she asked. "Gone for good? Dead forever?"

Her mouth began watering again with that foul metallic taste.

He quick-stepped toward her. "Do not swallow!"

Mari faced him in a half crouch. "What'd you do to me?" She spit on the floor.

"The only thing I could," he answered. "Do not swallow it, though it should not—"

"What did you put in my mouth?"

"Something to save you. Though it only worked once before."

"Save me from what? You? From what you did out there . . . to that dead girl?"

His exhausted eyes locked wide.

"No, from her," he answered, "from the spirit."

Mari shook her head in confusion.

"A spirit that agitated is deadly by a mere touch," he continued. "All the more after someone's own fear peaks in facing the dead. Especially a type—a form of death—that cannot be stopped by the living."

Something in his words did make sense. Something cold had struck her, something she hadn't seen, as she'd rushed for the hut's door.

"I did not know you followed me, again," he added slowly, as if speaking tired him more. "You should not have. That is why I left without you . . . one less person to watch over. Brianne must have collided with—through—you . . . when she fled through the hut's front wall."

Mari remembered that deep cold striking her, eating her away, until she fell in the dark.

"Rinse your mouth." He pointed at the mugs. "Do not swallow until the taste is gone."

He continued staring at her, as if amazed that she stood there alive at all.

Something more of last night came back.

Cecilia had gone after him with a knife.

At that, all of Mari's fury had doubled, cut through the cold in her flesh with its own heat. Some other predator had tried to take her prey. For that, both halves of her couldn't—wouldn't—die and let that happen.

Mari stalked along the table and grabbed one steaming mug of herb-steeped water. She rinsed her mouth and spit on the floor, over and over, until the water was clear. Looking at the rolls and the broth, she still couldn't find enough hunger to eat.

There had been no fear, no terror in her last night, for she'd never seen Brianne coming. There was only her fury—and long grief—and desperate need to establish enough certainty to kill *him*.

But a greater fear was rising. Now that he'd completed his task here, he would be going home. She was not ready to leave him yet. She hadn't yet learned the truth. But how could she possibly justify walking south with him? What reason could she give?

Picking up the pouch, she held it out.

He glanced at it as if momentarily confused. "Oh . . . Take out your share first."

After a slow breath, Mari removed four coins, the money she had earned, and handed him the rest.

"So, now you go back home to Strîbrov?" she asked.

"No. I'm going to Soladran, to the barracks there."

Her heart jumped. "Why?"

"To find out what it was that touched Brianne and caused her death." He paused and asked carefully, "Are you still traveling north?"

With a mix of relief and trepidation, she saw a chance to remain with him and learn more. "I am. I could walk with you. There is safety in numbers."

"That is true."

A short while later, they were both packed and ready to leave. She loaded the warm rolls into her own satchel and then slung it over her shoulder.

Tris walked to the door and went outside. As he turned to leave the village, she fell into step beside him.

CHAPTER SIX

Mari led the way back toward the main road, listening for his footsteps following behind her, making sure he was close enough.

He seemed tired today, and his pace was slow.

They stopped several times for him to rest. At one point, she made him eat a roll she'd stashed away. As they finally reached the main road and turned northward, doubts about the previous night still nagged her, and she half turned.

"When did you know Brianne's mother called her back with that hair? And how?"

He dropped his satchel and plopped down next to it without answering. In daylight, except for his pale face and light eyes, everything about him looked so dark.

"Did you hear me?" she said.

"Yes."

"So?"

He was silent a moment longer. "There are rituals. Most require something personal from the deceased to recall a loved one. Hair is the easiest, and the least gruesome to acquire. Sometimes a ritual is unnecessary, if desire is overwhelming."

Where had he learned this? And she hadn't missed his choice of two words: *loved one.*

"But why would Cecilia do that?" Mari asked. Even with her own long grief, she didn't understand. "What good was it to her?"

Tris tilted his head aside. He frowned slightly. "It does not matter."

"Everything matters, everything we do," she countered, and then, in a whisper: *"Everything."*

Tris struggled up, grabbed his pack, slung it over one shoulder, and walked on, away from her.

Mari stood shocked for a breath.

She rushed after him, grabbed his arm, and jerked him around. He wrenched free and turned on her. She backstepped once, ready to draw her dagger if necessary. Right now, she wanted answers.

"Brianne wasn't dangerous," she challenged. "She didn't seem the kind of spirit to hurt anyone, even for what happened to me. So what did *you* do to *her*?"

"As I told you, I sent her back into death, however you or anyone chooses to envision that. The dead do not belong among the living, for they only bring misery or . . ." He faltered, perhaps held back something, and then said, "Or more death."

She wasn't letting up. "And how'd you do that? How can you grip a ghost?"

"I do not know," he answered tiredly.

"How can you not know?"

His expression turned even darker as he lunged a step in on her.

"And what of you, *shifter*?"

"*Yai-morchi!*"

After a pause of locked glares, he continued.

"As you wish, but do you know why you were born that way? Have you reasoned this out? Has anyone among your people ever done so?"

Mari couldn't answer. Yes, her people had beliefs about this—only beliefs. In some ways, she'd been blessed.

Better to be born a "shifter"—*yai-morchi*, two-fleshed—than a "mocker"—*yai-dôytri*, two-minded—let alone a "tween"—*yai-urvai*, two-spirited. Mockers . . . *yai-dôytri* . . . were the cursed ones who changed only in mind. Little more than wild animals trapped in human form, they recognized only their most loved ones, and sometimes not even those.

Not like her.

In one flesh or the other, she was always . . . Mari.

"I thought not," he added, before she could gather an answer to his challenge. "But I do know the dead do not belong among the living! Not for any reason."

His tone had changed to match his spite. For him, hunting the dead seemed a feud he wouldn't let go until one or the other side was gone. The problem was that he saw all ghosts as the same.

Mari wasn't so sure.

Even more, it troubled her that he could take hold of them. What did that make him if not like them in some way? This unsettled her all the more, and the title of Dead's Man took on more meaning.

But if like her, he'd been born this way, without a choice . . .

Her thoughts went blank in a held breath. When had she started thinking of *him* as anything more than that black spirit, now somehow hiding in flesh?

Somewhat like she could in her other flesh.

They both fell silent again as they walked on. She couldn't stop dwelling on old pain, old furies. If he *was* the one who murdered her family . . .

Unwanted memories pushed up, though she struggled—and failed—to put them down.

As a child, she'd been passed off from one Móndyalítko family or clan to the next. None wanted her around after learning about the Wicker Woods. It didn't matter even after she'd learned to shut up and say nothing about it. Sooner or later, at some passing or gathering of families or clans, bits of the truth came out.

This went on so long that later she could barely remember the names of the first ones who'd taken her in. Even so, she'd always been listening for any mention of the one who'd done this to her and hers.

Blacky . . . Ebony Einan . . . Shade of the Night . . .

Death's Boy . . .

That thing ended up with so many names through all the rumors and tales that traveled quickly among her kind. There were worse ghost tales to frighten most children, but none were as bad for her.

And that was the way it was for years.

She could've increased her value among her people if she'd revealed herself as a *yai-morchi*. But she didn't. Her secret was one of the few things that belonged to her. Alone in the forests, she began shifting and hunting for herself, eating raw, wet, and hot in her other flesh or waiting to cook what she'd caught away from anyone else.

Mari never told anyone. Why should she hunt for them if they didn't want her?

One night, when she was fourteen, while camped with a family from the line of Džugi clan, she made a plan. She stole and hid a burlap sack, and then night by night stuffed it with a blanket, food, a flint, a small knife, and anything else needed that she could steal.

Then she was gone, and she never went back.

And the years passed.

She'd sought stories of spirits, ghosts, unnatural dead things that preyed on the living. Another cold night when she'd barely passed twenty years old, she was drinking tea and eating soup, this time in a remote tavern. Someone at another table whispered not so quietly about "the Dead's Man."

All in black—black as the dark—he called spirits to himself and commanded them. One of a kind, he was the only one in all of the Farlands—Stravina included—who possessed such power over spirits of the dead.

Mari sat still and silent, her spoon hovering above the wooden bowl. She didn't finish that meal. She began searching for more tales of the Dead's Man. And a few scant years later . . .

She might be walking beside him right now.

How could it not be this Tris, who commanded—gripped—spirits? Yet nothing he'd done or said had offered certain proof—if she killed him—that she had the right man.

She still needed certainty.

She needed to know that she could finally escape grief through revenge.

"What's wrong?"

Mari was startled to awareness.

He was watching her as they walked. Had her face given her dark thoughts away?

"Nothing," she answered.

He looked pale to the point of being white.

"Do you need another rest?" she asked.

"No."

They continued north. At first they passed only sparse travelers on the road, most on horseback or driving wagons. Tris always slipped off to one side until any horses passed, though she saw a few buck slightly, snort, and whip their heads until they got past him. For the most part, he ignored them and returned to the road once the horses were out of sight.

And the two of them kept walking in silence most of the time.

Mari knew Soladran was getting close when more and more people on foot or on horses or in wagons began to pass by. Tris moved as far as he could to one side of the road and stayed there. Not long after, the city's front gates appeared ahead.

"Do you know Soladran?" he asked.

Mari answered without thinking. "Yes. Some of the families that I'd . . ."

She'd almost let slip that some families she'd been with had performed regularly in Soladran. That was how most Móndyalítko earned coin for commerce with outsiders, versus barter and trade among their own kind. They put on shows with music, dance, storytelling, and sleight-of-hand magic, with a bit of fortune-telling thrown in, as locals expected of "those people."

Tris was still watching her, waiting for her to finish what she hadn't said.

"So?" he asked.

"A few times. I didn't pay much attention, though."

Then she realized that she was the one who'd be navigating again. He was asking if she knew what he didn't: how to get around in that place.

He couldn't speak any language but his own. His knowledge of anywhere beyond his own territory was likely questionable. How had he managed to hunt anything on his own, let alone ghosts wherever he'd been called?

But Mari didn't mind leading, so long as she kept him in sight, close enough to spot the last truth about him when it came. Up ahead, guards before the stone gate arch didn't stop or question anyone coming and going. That would change after nightfall, like in most cities.

Soladran was a vast, walled city, home to thousands. The soldiers who protected it commanded respect from all citizens within and from the entire nation. From what she knew, it had been the first settlement of the territory later to be called Stravina. That it was on the border of what was now called the Warlands came about by chance and events over the following centuries. The great wall had come later. And now, as well as guarding Soladran, its soldiers patrolled all along that northern border.

Stravina was bordered on the west by the sea, the Vudran Bay. To the east was the impassable Blade Range, beyond a deep forest. The friendly—or at least civil—nations of Belaski and Droevinka sat to the south. Only the northern border offered a threat from the chaotic rule of the warlords who lived in those ever-changing territories known as the Warlands.

Soladran soldiers were vigilant and disciplined, or so Mari had been told by some of her people. She'd tended to avoid soldiers of any kind in the past, but now there was little choice. Tris had come to learn how and why Brianne died for love of one of them, and to hunt whatever had killed her. The irony didn't escape Mari that she'd likely found—walked with—the one who'd murdered all those she'd loved.

Closer now, the front gate was daunting in its sheer size, with a stone arch overhead taller than the heights of three men.

And it'd grown so cold that Mari could see her own breath as she stepped under those high stones. Four guards in white tabards, padded armor, and fur-trimmed helmets shifted on their feet to both sides of the archway. With their expressions drawn, eyes wide and constantly shifting, they weren't even looking at the people passing into the city.

So what were they looking for?

"Do you know the location of the barracks?"

Though spoken just above a whisper, the question came too close to her ear.

Mari eyed Tris sidelong, and then realized she didn't know where she was going. The families she'd traveled with coming here in summer gained permission to park their wagons near large open-air markets—the best place for performances. They kept their distance from soldiers.

"Not exactly," she answered. "North side, near the border, I think. At least that makes most the sense."

Of course he wasn't satisfied with that.

"Ask one of the guards," he ordered.

They'd barely stepped into the city, and he was already making her bristle. It wasn't the first time he'd tried that master-to-servant tone with her.

"I'm not your dogsbody to order about," she said, not looking up at him.

The two of them standing there, blocking the way, forced others entering the city to veer around them. Tris shifted to avoid a passerby.

"Would you like me to find someone I might ask?" he returned, quieter this time. "I doubt the guards would understand me—or I them."

She sighed. All right, so that was true, but it irritated her even more. Arguing with him was like snatching at a shadow. Stepping around him, she headed toward the nearest soldier and then hesitated.

"Pardon. Where do I find the main barracks?"

The tall soldier with stubble on his face blinked in distraction. He looked her up and down.

"Why?"

She almost backstepped at his challenging tone. "I have business there."

"Not today, you don't." He shook his head. "No civilians near the barracks."

Her first instinct was to argue, but she thought better of it and turned back to Tris.

"Something's wrong," she said quietly. "He just said to stay away, no civilians allowed, at least not now. Something's happened."

Tris turned, heading into the city. "Of course it has. That is why we have come."

Mari followed him. What else could she do?

They cut left through the comers and goers at the first cross street and paralleled the outer wall. The barracks were on the northernmost side, but Soladran was huge. They'd need to pass through the city and do some exploring.

First, they reached an internal gateway she hadn't expected.

The guards there watched them but didn't challenge them.

Upon passing through, Mari saw elaborate two- and three-story houses of fine stone. Soladran boasted an unusual layout with the wealthier inhabitants living here on the south side—as far from the border as possible. These streets were wide and well maintained, though nearly as crowded as the central ways. Most people walked with quick purpose, heading elsewhere, perhaps to business or market districts.

Mari didn't like this. Even the side streets were wide, with little place to hide. She expected to continue on. Instead, the clink of coins pulled her attention.

Tris stopped and was fingering through the contents of a pouch. He looked up once, and she followed his glance to a wooden stable half a block up on the left. Out front of it, young men sat atop wagon benches with harnessed horses at the ready. What were they waiting for?

"Hire a driver to take us to the barracks," Tris said.

Mari looked back to find him holding out two copper groats. Hiring a local driver would solve several problems at once.

Taking the coins, she asked, "What about the horses?"

"I will sit in back, out of their sight."

With a doubtful nod, Mari stepped onward, approaching the nearest wagon at the back of the line. She held up the coins in plain sight.

"I need transport for two to the city barracks," she said.

"The barracks?" the young man echoed.

His expression darkened with worry, and he almost shook his head of brown hair, cropped as short as could be without being shaved off. Then his eyes fixed on the coins.

Two copper groats seemed quite a lot for a ride.

"All right," the driver agreed. "I'll get you within sight of it, but that's all."

He reached down, rather than step off the wagon, and took the coins. Then he offered his hand to pull her up. She had no intention of getting up there with him.

"We'll both sit in back." She tilted her head toward Tris, still standing ten or more paces behind the wagon.

The driver nodded and turned away to unlash the reins. Mari slipped around behind the wagon, and Tris came to her just as she hopped up and settled against the wagon's left side. He took the right side. With a snap of the reins, the wagon pulled out.

Tris hunched down a bit as they passed the other wagons and teams still waiting.

He still looked worn. Whatever he'd done in banishing Brianne had cost him.

Soon enough, the houses passing by became smaller, and most were constructed of wooden planks or with tile or slate roofs. Farther on, they passed between small shops, tall but narrow inns, and noisy little eateries. She spotted only one place that might be a tavern, though there were two men standing post outside it, maybe private guards. And then the wagon reached a large open-air market.

Mari could smell roasting sausages and freshly baked bread.

The driver slowed his horses to inch through thicker crowds along this way. On the market's far side, the shops became shabby. A tavern occupied nearly every block. And the wagon continued on.

Mari knew the city was large, but she hadn't realized quite how large. Thankfully, they didn't have to walk it. Soon they passed smaller dwellings with thatched roofs; this went on far longer than any other portion of the passage. Finally, the wagon slowed along the city's wall once more, and then it stopped. Mari craned her head to look about.

"There it is," their driver said, pointing beyond the horses, "but I won't go any closer."

Mari jumped off the back of the wagon and rounded its side to see a tall, timber barracks, at least the length of two city blocks. Its lower half was made of mortared dark stone. The back was almost right up against the wall to the far side of the huge northern gate.

And the gate was open.

Tris joined her, and she looked up at the driver.

"Thank you," she said, though he'd already begun turning his team and wagon back the way they'd come. Without waiting for Tris, Mari walked slowly toward the gate's near side and spotted soldiers just outside it, half of them with bows at the ready, though none with arrows drawn.

They were all looking into the distance, either by one or in sets of two and three.

Open and cleared land sloped to a wide, ice-fringed stream at least fifteen paces across and running east to west. On the water's far side, the ground rose to a field of browned wild grass, partially matted. And in the distance was a tree line of huge firs and pines marking the edge of the foothills farther on.

The reaches of the Warlands were still and silent below a dull gray sky.

Mari started slightly when she noticed Tris standing near behind on her left. She followed his attention back to the distant tree line with white-capped mountains far beyond it.

"The stream is the border," she said barely above a whisper.

When he didn't respond, she looked the other way to the barracks. A number of soldiers milled about outside it. One looked over, spotted her, and immediately came at a swift stride.

He was short and wide, about thirty years old, and wearing a worn cloak over his white tabard.

"No civilians allowed here," he said in Belaskian.

His voice had an edge. Dark shadows of sleeplessness showed beneath both of his hazel eyes.

"I need to speak with a guardsman named Bródy," she countered. "It's about his . . . mistress."

Tris remained silent at her side, looking toward the barracks.

"His mistress?" the guard echoed, and then snorted. "Which one?"

His pert tone got to her, and she fought down a counterretort. "Could you send for him, please? There has been a death."

The soldier frowned.

"Sergeant!" a sharp voice interrupted.

Pulled by that voice, Mari saw a very tall man striding toward them.

He was dressed as the other border guards in a crestless white tabard over padded armor. But he wore a fur-lined cape, steel-scaled gloves and vambraces, as well as plain polished armor on his shoulders and shins. A thin prong of gold sprouted a finger's length above the nose guard of his fur-trimmed helmet.

He looked about thirty years old with long, sandy blond hair that hung out his helmet and fell across the shoulders of his cloak. He turned on the other soldier, who backstepped and stiffened to attention.

"Orlov, what are these people doing here?" the officer demanded of the wide sergeant. "I told you to keep this area clear!"

"I just spotted them, Captain," Sergeant Orlov replied, not daring to look the captain in the eyes. "I was about to send them off."

The tall captain turned toward Mari. His gaze shifted right and left, likely on Tris, and he hesitated.

"Captain Stàsiuo," the man said as introduction, and spoke directly to Tris. "At present, civilians are not allowed in this vicinity, as we have . . . a situation. Please turn back into the city."

Polite as it was, it was not a request.

Tris stared at the captain for a moment, and without looking away, he said, "Tell him we have come from Jesenik, where a girl who recently visited these barracks was just buried by her family. I need to speak to whoever is in command."

About to translate, Mari hesitated at the slight shake of the captain's head.

"You don't need to have her tell me anything," the captain answered in Old Stravinan. "And currently, I'm in command. What does your presence have to do with this dead girl?"

He didn't speak Stravinan as well as Mari, but well enough, and she looked to Tris.

Both men assessed each other before Tris answered.

"If we remain out here," he replied quietly, "I will have my companion translate everything for the sake of absolute clarity. Unless you wish your men to know every detail, we should speak in private."

Not long after, Mari followed Tris and the captain into what seemed the barracks' common room. A huge stone hearth in the back wall was piled with burning logs, which filled the place with welcome warmth after a cold, long walk. Stools and tables were scattered haphazardly about, but only three other city guards sat at a table playing cards. All three looked over at the newcomers entering. Two of them eyed Mari the longest.

"Back to your posts!" Captain Stàsiuo ordered.

One man hesitated but then followed the other two in a rush out of the hall.

The captain turned to Tris. "What exactly do you seek here?"

"Truth," Tris answered, and then he lied. "We work for the family of the deceased."

The captain looked Tris up and down. Crossing his arms, he didn't appear impressed.

"Are you that rumored ghost-hunter, the one some called the Dead's Man?"

"Where did you hear that?" Mari interrupted.

He barely glanced at her. "It's a city. Any rumor ends up—spreads—quickly here."

"The girl's name was Brianne," Tris answered, ignoring all else. "She was involved with one of your men—Guardsman Bródy—and came to see him. While here, something 'horrible and white' touched her. She rushed home but died shortly after returning, appearing to have starved to death."

Mari watched the captain's reaction.

Stàsiuo glanced away. With a tired sigh, he sagged a little and ran a hand over his face.

"Brianne?" he asked. "With red-gold hair?"

Tris nodded once as Mari answered, "Yes."

Stàsiuo closed his eyes. "I'm sorry." And when his eyes opened, they'd hardened again. "But if she's dead, why have you come here?"

"I am after the *something white*," Tris said quietly.

The captain turned away and started for the door. "You can inform the girl's family that we're doing what's possible to resolve the situation, and please send my condolences. But we don't need a . . . ghost-hunter. You'll both leave immediately."

Mari looked back and up, surprised and confused. A pained expression crossed Tris's pale features. He didn't answer back for two breaths, as if struggling with something.

Captain Stàsiuo reached the door.

"Captain," Tris called out, "I am Tris of the house Vishal, son of Baron Gerold Vishal."

The captain froze in the doorway. He was slow in turning about.

Mari was stunned as well.

As little as she knew of nobles and politics, even she'd heard of the Vishals. They owned—ruled—a good portion of southern Stravina, including the Wicker Woods.

Those woods were within sight of the Vishal manor.

She stared at *him* as her insides heated up.

Stravina was a monarchy, somewhat more so than Belaski or

Droevinka. In theory, ruled by a king and a queen, but as in most mon-
archies, much of the power was in the hands of local nobles and their
local forces.

The captain's mouth was flat and tight as he repeated, "Son of Baron
Vishal?"

"Yes," Tris confirmed, just as cold and soft. "Now, what is happening
here?"

Mari still couldn't believe she'd slept so close to him without knowing. All those nights on the road, and he'd let her think he was just a
traveler, like her. Of course, he wouldn't have told her—so why let it slip
now, just to whip up this officer?

Much else now made sense—his aloof manner, his inability to speak
any language but Stravinan, and a too-formal form at that, and his
manner in often expecting to be served. He was what she expected from
one of them.

But again, if he'd been hiding his status, why let it slip now, when
she'd hear it?

Stàsiuo lingered in the doorway and then appeared to recognize
defeat. In a deep, silent breath, he stepped back into the common room,
paused for a semiformal nod to Tris, and gestured to the closest table.

"Baronet Vishal, would you have a seat?"

Mari waited.

At first, Tris hesitated, looking away from the captain with a brief
twitch in his left eye, as if uncomfortable. Then he sat down. Mari
rounded to the table's far side. She settled slow and silent, still watching him.

The captain sat last in a position between them. "I assumed—was
promoted to—command four days ago. But this . . . mess started half

a moon back. We've lost three guardsmen and another lieutenant since then."

Only at this did Mari look away from Tris to the captain. "Lost?"

"They're dead," he corrected, "like Brianne, seemingly starved. We found the first, a guardsman, in his bunk one morning with no clue to what happened. We found another one three days later, the same way. Both looked . . . worse than any Warlands peasants fleeing for the border stream before a warlord's militia ran them down. And in both cases, they'd died in a single night."

"And then?" Tris prompted.

"My colonel worried it was a plague, though it didn't look like any sickness I'd ever seen. He quarantined the whole barracks, but the physicians couldn't figure it out. Lieutenant Curran went next . . . but that time was different."

"How?" Tris prompted.

Stàsiuo glanced at him briefly. "I heard Curran screaming in the stable and ran for him. He was already down when I found him, unmarked, no wounds."

Tris sat waiting, and Mari fixed solely on the captain.

"I tried to lift him," the captain continued. "He babbled about something passing *through* him. He was in too much pain to say much, and he was already . . . withering. We tried to feed him, but whatever he could get down didn't help. By morning he was gone, with his eyes still open."

"And the deaths continued?" Tris asked.

"I've seen too many deaths, but nothing like these. There was another guard, and then the colonel, only his death was the worst because he lasted almost three days." The captain closed his eyes. "I didn't know about Brianne. Bródy has a number of lady friends."

"You spoke with your colonel before he passed?" Tris pressed. "What of the other man? Did they both relate the same story as your Lieutenant Curran of something white appearing and passing through them?"

"Something like that," Stàsiuo half whispered. "Or maybe in pain and fear they just repeated what they'd heard. Reason often fails before the last of life."

When the captain fell silent, Mari's attention once again fixed on Tris.

"Is this barracks still under quarantine?" Tris asked.

"To a point. I've tried to keep most people away, but without a sickness verified by physicians, it is difficult. Some of the men have families, sweethearts, and so on. The women sometimes visit in the evenings, and I cannot deny them any longer. The men are already on edge in having to live here full-time."

"That may be the problem," Tris said. "You are dealing with a malevolent spirit, not a disease."

Stàsiuo scowled as if he might lose his temper. "You keep that talk to yourself! I don't care about your rank when it comes to maintaining order here, and I don't believe in any of that nonsense."

Mari couldn't stop herself. "Then how do you explain it?"

"It's a ruse!" the captain answered. "Someone is trying to hurt us from within, to frighten the men and destroy morale. I don't know who or why, but I'll find him . . . or them!"

Tris studied the captain.

"I am here to stop this," he said. "We require private quarters in the barracks, and I expect full cooperation, or the king will hear of it."

For an instant, Mari thought the captain had had enough. Breathing too hard, he rose off his stool and then just stood there a moment.

"I'll have my sergeant find you accommodations . . . my lord."

Mari saw Tris flinch. How strange—confusing—that he so disliked wielding influence and power over the living, considering what he could do to the dead.

Shortly after this, Tris found himself following Sergeant Orlov and Mari out of the common room. Orlov led them through a door at the room's back and into a much longer space with rows of double-stacked bunks to both sides of the center aisle. Only two city guards were present, both sitting on top bunks as they talked in low voices.

Both turned and looked. Both focused on Mari.

Tris barely held in his anger, which was mostly for himself. It revolted him that he had seen no recourse but to play upon his family name in remaining here until the cause of the deaths was uncovered.

He had no intention of ever taking his father's title. That world was no longer his and never would be again. There were no ties between him and the house of Vishal. At least he had succeeded in this—or so he told himself, over and over.

Though somewhat troubled at the prospect of staying here at the barracks among all these soldiers, he held fast to his request for quarters. Finding lodging elsewhere would hamper his investigation and cut him off from events taking place here at night. This was when most spirits appeared of their own volition. The unimaginative captain might not believe in spirits, but some of the men here would think otherwise by now. That was also an advantage, for likely the captain would not be among the men at all times.

They might speak more freely without him present.

Tris had three things to learn: who the spirit had been in life, what it wanted, and why. All three were necessary before he could find the right place and time to catch and deal with it.

Sergeant Orlov led the way through the long room and through a door to another long room exactly like the first. Then out another farther door into a passage that turned left.

"We have a few private chambers for visiting officers," Orlov explained, stopping before a door and glancing at Mari. "Do you need one room or two?"

This was obviously a polite way to inquire about the guests' relationship.

Mari's eyes narrowed.

"One," Tris said.

She turned on him with a half-vicious, half-surprised expression, but she said nothing.

He added in Old Stravinan, "I'll sleep on the floor if there is one bed, but we should not be separated. I cannot protect you if we are the next targets."

She appeared to settle after that and nodded once, but with some reluctance. Though what he told her had been true, the fuller truth was that he did not like the way some men were looking at her. From those among his father's men, he knew the ways of some soldiers—married, attached, or not. A pretty, exotic Móndyalítko might be more enticing than other women.

Tris flipped a hand toward the door.

"As you wish, my lord," Orlov said, pushing open the door and then stepping aside.

Mari glanced at him with hard eyes as she stepped forward and slipped into the room.

Tris was well aware she could take care of herself. And for what these men here might not know about shifters—*yai-morchi*, as she would say—anyone bothering her would face much worse than a slap or a punch. Still . . . he would rather she not be bothered in the first place. If the men here believed she was *with* him, it might stave off unwanted advances.

He followed her inside. As he was about to turn and close the door, the sergeant did so from the outside. The sound of boots clomped away in the passage outside. And Tris was again alone with this woman.

Glancing around, he felt some relief; the room held two beds, one against each sidewall. A small window with actual glass, frosted outside at its edges, was centered in the far wall opposite the door. Before it stood a tiny table and two stools plus a pitcher with a basin and a single-candle lantern. At the foot of each bed, toward the door, were good-sized chests.

Mari stood off next to the one on the left, watching him. Her gaze was still hard, and her arms were crossed.

"It is wiser to share one room," he said.

"No, it's not. Not with *you*."

He tried not to wince, thinking she must be angry about his recent revelation. "And who am I, a noble? No!"

She blinked twice, as if his explanation caused confusion.

"I left that world, that life, far behind," he continued, "and regret returning even briefly."

Turning to the left-side bed, he dropped his pack on the chest at its foot.

"It's not that."

At those words, he glanced back and found her still watching him. For an instant, those eyes were too much those of the lynx in her other "flesh."

"You can't change . . . what you are," she added, breathy and low.

Was this a reference to him not being able to change his noble status?

A part of Tris regretted Mari's company. They had saved each other twice—or one and a half times each, for at one time for both of them, they had not truly needed to be saved. He did not regret her help but rather that now of all times she was too close.

Others had been close when that other *him* came again into the living world. That was before he had met Heil, who had later calculated the black one's future reappearances. The schedule was not precise to the day but close enough.

Tris did not want anyone near when this happened again. Too many had already died for this—though not him, not yet. Exhausted and numb, with midafternoon light slanting through the window, he wanted the closest thing to privacy possible now.

"I will wait to question anyone until evening," he said. "We should rest, for we may be up late."

She nodded, dropped her pack on the other chest, and rounded to sit on the other bed's edge. Scooting back, she lay down on her side, facing him, then reached back and ripped free the inside edges of the bedcover and blanket, pulling both loosely over herself, boots, cloak, and all.

He took off his boots and cloak and lay down, feeling some relief at the chance to rest. He needed to regain his strength. Whatever he'd be facing here, he had a feeling it would fight much harder than Brianne.

To his annoyance, it bothered him that Mari now knew the truth about his birth. He hadn't wanted her to know. It would change the way she looked at him, and it shouldn't. He was exactly as he'd represented himself to her: a traveler with a single purpose.

As he tried to rest, unwanted memories began to rise again, but this time, he didn't fight them. He let them wash over and through him.

Closing his eyes, he was nineteen again, feeling trapped and smothered at home in the family's manor. His father was away—as always—and his mother needed his company. In her early forties, she was still lovely without a single gray hair or line in her face.

The only sign of her mania and desperation was in her soft brown eyes.

She expected him every night at the dinner table, where she would grasp his hand and say again, "My darling boy."

He was no longer a boy. He fell asleep every night thinking of the strange, silver-haired man he had met in Ceskú, who could make weapons to use against spirits. And Heil's last words repeated over and over in Tris's desperate thoughts.

You've a rare gift but no idea what you're doing, not from what I've seen. I suppose you'd best come to Stríbrov with me, young baron.

Tris felt like a hangman's noose, stretched tight and ready to snap by the weight of a condemned man's corpse left dangling too long. He couldn't leave his mother, with his father essentially having abandoned both of them. So, he stayed, night and day after night and day.

Then one evening when they dined once more together with only servants near at the ready, he noticed beads of sweat trickling down one of the faces of those servingwomen. What was her name? Matiya?

Normally, he would not notice such a thing, but the room was cool, and the woman appeared to waver slightly on her feet. His mother's gaze followed his, and her brow wrinkled.

"Matiya?" she said with concern. "Are you unwell?"

The servingwoman crumpled to the floor stones; she was the first.

Other servants soon followed, and then some of the guards grew ill. Agnes, the family's elder head of staff, called it "sweating sickness." Nearly half who fell to it died.

Tris did not contract the illness, though he watched many others pass. Only then in the spread of death did he realize something else. He had never been sick even once that he remembered.

Another odd blessing of his cursed existence.

He watched his mother work night and day to care for those suffering. She sent a rider with a message to tell Tris's father what was happening, but the baron did not answer. A week after Matiya had dropped, Tris noticed beads of sweat on his mother's face.

His breathing slowed.

He dragged her to her room, insisting that she rest, and she was too weak to argue. By that night, she was so hot he had to sponge her face, and she barely recognized him. He was unskilled in caring for the sick, but he tried. Near the mid of that night, she grasped his hand. Her grip was weak.

"My darling boy," she whispered again.

Those three words were the last she ever said to him. He was still sitting beside her the following morning, though she was long gone, and his guilt came from knowing he would not follow her.

The final tie with anyone who cared for him was broken.

It left him hollow, and yet it left him free.

He was still there beside his mother when Agnes patted his back.

"Your father will be home soon, my young lord. He must be home soon."

Tris did not care. If anything, his spite only grew. His mother had been left in loneliness; but she was now beyond that and all else for which his father had abandoned her.

At the first light of the next day, Tris left. He took no money, no heirlooms, nothing that might belong to his family.

But he headed for Stříbrov.

Mari didn't sleep. She lay listening to his quiet breaths.

He didn't sleep either. She could tell.

Why had he been embarrassed by his noble status? Maybe she read him wrong in that, but not likely. So why? And if he'd hidden that much of himself, then he could certainly be hiding more.

And one day, no matter what he claimed now, he would take his father's place—if she let him live.

He was more devious than she'd even suspected. Worse, she couldn't shake off her reaction when he'd announced they'd stay in the same room. She'd been . . . relieved.

Some of that was having a private place to finish all of this without anyone watching, but there were other things. Certainly he needed her protection more than she needed his in this place. She still possessed her people's instinctive need for safety in numbers, traveling in numbers and living in close quarters. But that wasn't it, or at least not all of it.

She'd learned to be alone, and yet for some reason, he wanted her company. In some moments, he'd looked at her as if concerned—as if wanting to protect her? She'd seen it on his face when he'd ordered that sergeant to place them together in one room.

Why?

No one had behaved like that toward her since her papa.

Mari heard footsteps down the hallway outside and opened her eyes. The room was fully dark, though her eyes adjusted quickly. Tris still lay on his back with his eyes closed. She counted the footsteps coming.

Seventeen long strides later, a knock on the door followed.

Tris opened his eyes. He didn't look at her, just at the ceiling beams. "Yes?" he called.

"Supper's in the common room, m'lord. Captain says if you want to eat, come feed yourselves."

After a moment, Tris answered flatly, "Thank you."

Mari sat up and swung her feet over the bedside, still in her boots. She sat there watching him until he finally rolled his head toward her.

And he looked at her, as if he could see her in the dark.

"If the guards gather to eat," he said, "we will be able to talk to several of them, to piece together different versions of what happened. I need you to translate the full details that I cannot catch in their language."

She said nothing, for there wasn't anything to say. Her task was no different here from in the village.

Without warning, he swung his legs over the bed's edge and sat up.

"I do not know if we will be compensated this time," he said. "Rewards sometimes come of situations like this one, sometimes not. If nothing comes of this, I will pay you more out of the funds gained at Jesenik."

Mari cared little about that. If she finally finished him, she'd take it all anyway, and she was more fixed on uncovering more secrets, now that he'd revealed one because he had to. Then again, if she didn't act concerned about the money, he might get suspicious.

"Works for me," she said. "Tell me what you want from them, and I'll get them to talk, if they know something."

Tris stood up, hesitated, and went to his pack upon the trunk at the end of his bed. Whatever he was looking for, he either didn't find it or thought differently about retrieving it. In a slow, deep breath, he turned for the door.

Mari took a step to follow.

He turned to look at her, and she froze.

"This spirit will not be like Brianne," he said. "When I tell you to run, do so immediately, away from me. Do you understand?"

She had no intention of doing so. She had no intention of letting any spirit—let alone anyone—get him before she did, if it came to that. But she needed to see what else he could do, of what else he was capable.

"Just as you say," she answered. "I've had enough of your ghosts anyway."

He dropped his gaze, stood there a little longer, and nodded—maybe to her or not. And with more waiting and watching to come, Mari realized it had been too long since she'd last eaten.

Dinner waited.

CHAPTER
SEVEN

U pon entering the common room, Mari paused, surprised to see three women present.

Then she remembered Captain Stàsiuo had mentioned letting his men decide if their wives or sweethearts could visit. It appeared a few of them weren't worried about the safety of their women. Or perhaps they believed only soldiers were being targeted.

Stàsiuo also hadn't known what happened to Brianne, so maybe no one else did. Hadn't Guardsman Bródy said anything? Maybe he didn't know she was dead. From what Mari had gained from Tris, Bródy must've been nearby and seen what attacked her.

Again, all of this was second- and thirdhand.

She braced for more questioning as Tris's mouthpiece, but tantalizing scents in the air filled her nose. A table to the left was laden with food and bowls, and a portly man in a soiled apron set down a heavy cast-iron pan on a wooden plank table's far end. At the near end were large pitchers and mugs and plates of sliced oat bread. In between were piled tin and wooden plates.

A number of people stopped eating, drinking, or chattering to stare at her and *him*.

None of the men wore their helmets, and somehow that made them look different—less like soldiers, more like people. Several picked up bowls and scooped spoonfuls of something out of the pan. And the closer Mari got to the table, the more saliva welled up in her mouth.

"Fish pie," she said to Tris.

"Hmm?" he replied absently. As usual, he probably didn't care what he ate.

"Made from trout caught in the stream this morning," came a voice from beside her.

She looked over—and up—into the dark brown eyes of a young man. He was beardless and slender, not much taller than she, and wore an expression as drawn and worn as all of the others'. When he smiled, it didn't last, though he seemed open and friendly.

She didn't smile back but answered, "I like trout."

"Better get some while it's warm," he said, and led the way.

Mari first looked to Tris, nodded to the table, and headed over. If she didn't remind him to eat, he might forget. Handing him a bowl, she pointed to the pans of fish pie.

The young man waved her ahead, stepping aside. "I'm Guardsman Farrell. Sergeant Orlov said the captain gave you quarters here. Who are you?"

As he was blunt enough to catch her off guard, she stalled in dishing up her bowl.

"Mari," she said. "This is Tris. He doesn't speak your tongue, so you'll need to talk through me instead. We're here to help find out what's been . . . has happened, and why."

She expected his eyes to widen, narrow, or something. Instead he looked at Tris.

"Is he the one some call the hunter, the Dead's Man?"

She hadn't anticipated answering questions instead of asking them. Chatter around the food table died off and others were now watching and waiting.

Mari didn't like so many eyes on her. "Yes," she answered.

Farrell nodded and turned to filling his bowl. "Good. We've been waiting for the captain to get some real help."

He wasn't smiling in the slightest anymore.

The captain hadn't sought out her or Tris, but Mari wasn't going to correct this soldier. She studied the other men as she again waved in Tris to fill his own bowl. How much of this talk had he followed so far?

Farrell ducked behind her to the table's other end and grabbed several mugs by their handles with his free hand.

"You and ma'lord can sit with me, Rafferty, and the sergeant," he said, tilting his head toward a nearby table.

She half turned her head toward Tris, lowered her voice, and switched to Stravinan.

"We've been invited to sit. What's your first question?"

He stepped around her, handing her another bowl he'd filled. "Get their separate accounts of what happened to those who died. We need information to uncover who the spirit was in life."

"In life? Does that matter?"

"Yes."

He did not elaborate. When she looked back, Farrell waved her over as he settled at a table with two others.

She recognized Sergeant Orlov and nodded to him. The third man was about Farrell's age but with paler, freckled skin and carrot red hair. She went to join them and pulled out a stool for herself.

"This is Rafferty," Farrell supplied, motioning to the redhead, and then turned to Orlov. "It's what you thought. Captain's sent for the Dead's Man, though he mustn't have realized who these two were when they arrived. Mari there"—he nodded to her—"says the hunter can't speak much of our tongue, so talks through her."

Orlov raised an eyebrow at Mari. "So, that's what you do for him? I wondered."

She tensed, almost went for her dagger; then a hand closed on her forearm.

Mari turned her eyes on Tris at his touch. He showed no reaction and barely shook his head once. She realized she'd almost lost control— of herself and the conversation—before even asking the first question.

Orlov was going to be trouble. Questioning these men wasn't going to be the same as with the villagers. Peasants looked at Tris with a different kind of fear, as someone to be obeyed, and for reasons not connected to him being noble.

These were soldiers on the edge and kept isolated too long. Farrell looked slightly embarrassed by Orlov's insinuation and had better manners, but no one at the table looked impressed by Tris, let alone afraid of him.

Mari's puzzlement over their lack of reaction to sitting with a noble quickly passed; after all, his title didn't put her off. Quite the opposite. And now she had to take back control of the discussion.

"When did all this start?" she asked.

"Start?" Orlov poked at his food. "Fourteen—maybe fifteen—days ago. That's when we found Jamison dead in his bunk."

"No one saw what happened to him before then?"

"No," Rafferty answered, this time through clenched and crooked front teeth. "Nor the next, when we found Dixon."

"The lieutenant was different," Farrell cut in. "When Curran died . . . it was different. He was screaming before the end about something *white* coming at him, through him, and he couldn't stop it."

All three men fell silent, though Orlov still pushed loosened fish bits about his bowl.

"Henrik went the same way, said the same thing," Farrell went on. "And then the colonel, may the gods rot him!"

"Lower your voice," Orlov warned.

"Why?" Farrell asked. "The captain's in charge now, and the sooner he makes colonel, the better. I'm not answering to anyone but him, not in this or anything else."

Mari felt she was losing control again. But at least they were talking freely, and there might be something to learn from that. Shifting only her eyes, she noticed Tris hadn't eaten a bite.

"What was that last comment about the captain?" he whispered.

Mari whispered back Farrell's exact words, and Tris looked around all three at the table.

"So the colonel will not be replaced by someone of current rank from the outside? The captain will be promoted and given permanent command?"

The three men fixed on him and clearly hadn't understood him. Farrell was the first to look to Mari, and she repeated both questions in Belaskian.

"Yes," Orlov answered in strange relief.

"That leaves other ranks here unfilled in the change of command," Tris continued. "Will someone else be promoted to lieutenant in the meantime or later?"

When Mari translated, Farrell nodded. "Most likely. The council of nobles and upper officers usually promotes from within." He straightened up with visible pride. "We're all chosen for a reason, the best riders, trackers, and bowmen. Only the best patrol the border of the Warlands."

Mari stalled for too long, and Tris tapped her leg under the table with one finger. She translated the answer and felt his tension before looking at him. He said nothing more.

Something troubled him—something she'd missed—and she couldn't ask with the other three present. Tris dropped his head, picked up his fork, and began separating pieces of fish from the crust.

It seemed he had no more questions, which made Mari wonder what he'd learned that she hadn't from his questions and the answers.

Looking about, she saw others were dishing up, heading for stools, or sitting and talking in low voices, but she fixed on one man by instinct. Tall, solidly built, with thick, red-brown hair that hung to his collar, he had handsome features and dark green eyes. Right beside him sat one of the three women, by far the youngest and the most beautiful.

She had a mass of wavy black hair down well past her shoulders and the pale coloring of one who'd never worked much outside. Her red gown was cinched tightly. She never looked at anyone but the man beside her, and Mari had seen that kind of hunger before. The woman smiled playfully at him, picked up a spoon in the bowl with a scoop of food, and slipped it into his waiting mouth.

Mari dropped her own spoon, and her gaze, slightly sickened by the display. She looked up after a hard breath through her nose.

"Do you know him?" she asked Farrell, cocking her head.

Farrell straightened, looked over, dropped his spoon, sat back, and crossed his arms.

"Not you too?" he said, frowning at her as if she were the one fawning over that lout. "Orlov said you'd asked about Bródy. You look smarter than that."

Mari began to heat up. What was he suggesting? Before she could shoot something vicious back at Farrell, many heads within view began to turn elsewhere. She couldn't help but follow all that attention.

Another young woman with silver-blond hair and a sky blue dress stood near the common room's outer doorway.

Guardsman Rafferty snorted with a brief smile. "This should be interesting," he half whispered.

"Why?" Mari asked.

Rafferty barely glanced at her. "That one never comes midweek, and he's usually better at keeping any of them away from Sabine. Bródy's in for it now and not for the first time."

Mari looked back to see the young woman in blue scan the common room. Her gaze halted on the handsome guardsman and the dark-haired woman in red.

So that was Bródy, and what had Rafferty called the dark-haired one? Sabine.

Sabine had already spotted her opponent.

Her vapid, lovely face turned cold in a way that put Mari on guard. The hate in Sabine's eyes went beyond anger.

This woman was capable of violence without regret.

Mari realized she held her breath. She let it go and waited for an ugly scene to explode—but it didn't. Bródy finally noticed Sabine's glare and followed it. Instead of remorse or even fright, he smiled at the newcomer, instantly got up, and strode across the room.

"Elora," he said as if nothing was amiss.

The rest of their talk was too quiet for Mari to catch beneath the murmurs and whispers of all others in the room. The girl, Elora, acted agitated at first, and whatever she said came fast and sharp.

Mari let a little of her other form rise and listened in as the room's other sounds grew louder as well. And caught only a few phrases from Bródy over the other noise.

". . . finishing some business . . . friend of my mother . . . can't talk now . . . on leave tomorrow . . . the Gray Dove for wine . . . can't wait to see you . . ."

And all the while, Elora's anger appeared to drain, until she smiled at him, glanced at Sabine with a puzzled wrinkle of her brow, and turned to leave.

Mari just stared. How could any woman be that gullible?

"Oh, blind gods!" Farrell breathed in disgust. "They believe anything he says."

"That one won't be as easy." Orlov jutted his chin toward Sabine.

Mari continued looking over as others around the room looked away, as if eager not to be noticed staring while Bródy strode back to his table, still smiling. Sabine watched him coming, and her simpering smile was gone. He sat and grasped her hand, speaking to her too low to hear, but he was still smiling.

Mari couldn't hear what they whispered.

"Those two deserve each other," Farrell said quietly. "One no better than the other, but I pity any other girl who gets near him."

"Why?" Mari asked, though she felt she already knew.

Farrell shifted uncomfortably. "Just the way she acts, as if owning him. But no matter his hunts elsewhere, he always goes back to Sabine, though he had one other recently who was a bit different from the others. I felt sorry for that one—kindhearted and not so much a fool."

"Brianne?" Mari blurted out without thinking.

Farrell's eyes widened a little.

Tris nudged her. "What are they saying?"

She ignored him and remained fixed on Farrell.

Farrell shrugged. "Yes, Brianne. She seems to know what he truly is and cares for him anyway. I've had the feeling Bródy might throw off Sabine for her, but if Sabine ever got wind of that . . ."

He shook his head.

Tris nudged Mari harder this time, and she quickly translated. She was about to press Farrell about the last time he'd seen Brianne when Tris spoke again.

"I need something to drink. Come with me."

Mari looked at his bowl, and from what she saw, he still hadn't eaten a bite. So he wouldn't need something to drink. Still, he got up and walked off toward the food table. Frustrated by the interruption, she stood and followed.

He stopped beside the long table's near end, looking toward the room's entrance without touching a mug or pitcher. Mari ducked around to face him.

"What?" she whispered.

It was two breaths before he answered. "We may have been wrong. These deaths may not have been caused by a spirit . . . by someone already dead."

He sounded almost angry, and his comment took her off guard. But as she thought about it and all that she'd heard, it made some strange sense. But how, if not why? And even if, why would that upset him? Catching a living killer would be less trouble than catching a dead one.

But the victims—or those who'd lived long enough—said something "white" attacked them . . . passed *through* them.

"How?" she whispered, though no one else could understand them speaking Stravinan.

"I have seen it once before," he answered just as quietly. "Heil and I were called to a noble manor in Droevinka. Four sons, three had died, leaving only the youngest. All three died of a wasting sickness, and before their deaths, they claimed to have been attacked by a spirit."

Mari said nothing to this, though she leaned a little to catch sight of Sabine with one eye. She glanced back toward the entrance as well. Still, none of this made sense, for why kill off others who'd had nothing to do with Bródy's rutting ways?

"All three described the same grotesque image of a bloated ghost with red eyes," Tris went on.

He stopped, as if reliving this event.

"And?" Mari asked.

"The youngest son had studied herb lore and created a toxin to induce hallucinations. And with that, it took only suggestions to make his victims believe in what they saw. At the same time, he was slowly poisoning them."

Mari shivered. Tris lived in an ugly world. Her own was no paradise, but most of her struggles involved her own survival. It wasn't hard for her to see what the youngest brother was after.

"Youngest" really meant "last" in succession.

She didn't even have to say it.

Tris nodded once to her. "He wanted his father's title, eventually, and would not likely have risked applying the same method to his own sire. Though Heil and I discovered the truth, there was nothing for me to hunt."

At this last, he sounded bitter, but she kept thinking on his story—and the events happening at this barracks.

"Yes, but what kind of poison could make someone look as if they'd starved to death so quickly?" she asked. "Where would it come from or how would it be made?"

"Heil would know that, not I."

Mari pondered this further. She tilted her head to one side. "Such an act would take someone very clever, with great knowledge."

"Does anyone here strike you as that clever?" he asked.

Mari hesitated. "No, not that I've met."

"People can be deceiving."

Mari stared up at Tris. *Yes, they can—or they think so.*

His brow wrinkled. His lips parted and—

The outer door slammed open, startling both of them.

Mari spun about as all soldiers in the room stood suddenly with a racket of scooting stools.

Captain Stàsiuo stood in the entranceway. Without looking back, he came through the door, calling out, "At ease."

The captain headed to the table nearest the door, still empty and with one chair instead of stools. He dropped there, and a young guardsman hurried toward the table.

"I'll get your dinner, Captain," that one called.

Tris lowered his gaze to Mari. "Come and sit. I need to speak more with him."

Mari didn't move. "He speaks Old Stravinan, so you don't need me."

Tris frowned. "What? Why?"

The story about the deadly ruse of the nobleman's son still lingered for her.

"I need to track something else," she said. "I want to hear more from Farrell and Orlov."

His frown deepened. He glanced over toward the table they'd left and back down at her.

What now? Was he feeling protective again?

"Stop it," she whispered. "Talk with the captain on your own. We can learn more this way than with me following you around."

She turned away, heading back to where they'd started.

"If we get separated," he called, "meet me in our quarters."

Mari didn't answer, didn't look back, and grew even more unsettled by the notion of her own prey watching over her.

Tris still waited and watched as Mari left to rejoin the three soldiers. He knew he could not stop her and that she could look after herself. And still he watched, even as she settled on a stool again.

Then he walked to the captain.

"My lord?" Stàsiuo rumbled.

With a slow breath, Tris pulled up a stool to sit where he could face the captain and still see Mari.

Stàsiuo was young for a captain, let alone commander of a border garrison. He was a guarded person from what Tris could guess, yet his men appeared loyal to him, even to expressing preference over the deceased colonel.

Had someone orchestrated this change of leadership? Or was some other purpose the goal of these recent deadly events?

"Stàsiuo," Tris began slowly. "An unusual family name."

"My friends call me Stasi. You can call me Captain."

So this man did not care for nobles . . . or perhaps just the Dead's Man himself.

Tris ignored the slight, turned the other way, and nodded toward where Mari sat with Farrell, Orlov, and Rafferty.

"Those men said you would be promoted to colonel and put in permanent command here."

When he looked back, the captain was fixed entirely on him.

"Did they?" Stàsiuo asked slowly.

"Is it true?"

With a sigh, the captain leaned back.

"Yes, I've had a letter from the council," he said. "The king wants someone familiar with the border patrol, the men here, and the . . . limits under which we labor, unable to cross the stream to defend anyone fleeing the Warlands until they cross to our side."

Every word sounded more strained than the last. It could not be easy to defend the city sitting on the border of another realm from which so many wanted to escape. Everyone knew of the Warlands and why they had been so named. Even the number of the provinces beyond those distant trees often changed as one self-proclaimed "king" or just tyrant over there sought to annex a competitor's territory.

"I've been second-in-command for several years," the captain went on. "I do not know if—when—my promotion will come. Soon, most likely."

"That will make your past position vacant," Tris countered, "as well as that of the dead lieutenant's. Both positions will need to be filled. Who will make those promotions?"

Stàsiuo's jaw muscles tightened and then released. "I will."

This was no surprise. "Earlier today, you said you did not believe in malevolent spirits. And that the deaths may have been committed by someone within the ranks?"

"A guess, a possibility only."

"And with your elevation comes the power to elevate others, because of your own promotion."

"Watch yourself, young baron!" the captain said as he leaned in. "Rank only protects one so far. And I'd never harm one of my own, 'elevation' or not!"

A few heads turned their direction.

Tris did not react.

"I do not think you would," he said calmly. "Or we would not be having this discussion. But others might be more ambitious. Has the motive occurred to you?"

Stàsiuo settled slowly back in his chair. "Yes. Of course it has."

"And who would you promote?" Tris asked. "Someone now in this room?"

When Stàsiuo remained silent, it was Tris who leaned forward this time.

"Help me," he whispered, "or I cannot help you. Who is most likely to succeed you as captain?"

Stàsiuo glanced to the left. Tris barely turned his head, looking farther with only his eyes. Beyond the food table were two smaller tables. Only one was occupied.

A dark-haired soldier the same age as the captain or slightly older sat speaking quietly with a plain-looking woman of like age.

"Tragos," Stàsiuo said quietly, and Tris turned back. "The other lieutenant . . . the only one in this division who could replace my post, the only remaining officer."

As he was about to ask more, Tris was stopped by a shake of the captain's head.

"But he's steady and solid," Stàsiuo continued. "And he wasn't here when all of this started. He'd been on border patrol for almost a moon."

"Who would fill his position if he were promoted to yours?"

Stàsiuo shook his head. "I'm only replacing Curran, if I'm promoted. I can get by with one lieutenant and a captain. Simpler that way." Then his gaze shifted toward a table. "Only two guardsmen—other sergeants— could step into the lieutenant's post." He paused before adding, "That's Cotillard with the shaved head. Kreenan's sitting to his left."

Looking over, Tris saw two young men drinking ale with a number of comrades. One had a shaved head with strangely near-white eyebrows. The other had light brown hair pulled back at the nape of his neck in a long tail down his back.

"Are they the only sergeants?" Tris asked.

"No."

"Then why those two?"

"Because their families have money."

Tris turned back at the venom in Stàsiuo's voice, and the captain was glaring at him. Tris felt no embarrassment over the insinuation in the captain's eyes. Yes, his family had wealth, as did most nobles, but not him. But he was also well aware that an officer's commission had a high price.

He quickly turned attention from himself. "Does either one of that pair strike you as ambitious?"

"Both," Stàsiuo answered. "Both are second sons who'll gain no title or lands of their own, except by the pity of an elder brother." He paused. "Kreenan's strong-willed but fair-minded and gets on well with the men. Cotillard's an exceptional tracker, but he's easily slighted, even when no slight is made."

Tris had noted Stàsiuo seemed fair-minded as well—and also easily slighted, though he kept his temper, until his honor or reputation was impugned, even by innuendo. Both attributes could be useful and used for or against him.

Two voices grew louder, and Tris turned again as Guardsman Bródy and Sabine's argument peaked. Bródy's slick smile was gone.

Tris turned back, and found the captain watching the pair in open disapproval, but he didn't appear ready to interfere.

"If your advancement is approved, how soon will it come?" Tris asked.

The answer did not come for a moment.

"Days," Stàsiuo murmured. "A few . . . no more."

Tris pondered the captain.

There were always those who sought to climb whatever status ladder they could, and by any means when not born to such affluence. More than once had Tris seen or heard of those willing to do nearly anything to scale such heights. Yet this man appeared reluctant—even forlorn— by the manner in which it was happening for him.

Tris looked about the room again; someone here or near was not so reluctant.

Mari couldn't help feeling more comfortable sitting in the company of the soldiers than with Tris or the captain. Guardsman Farrell was friendly without being overly friendly and his dislike of Bródy showed some good sense. Rafferty was quiet, and Orlov, though bitter, was well suited to a sergeant's role: blunt and to the point.

The argument between Bródy and Sabine grew more visibly heated.

"The captain's going to have to do something, sooner or later," Orlov growled, eyeing those less-than-loving lovers. "She's gotten braver again since the colonel died."

Mari's full attention fixed on the sergeant. "The colonel didn't like her?"

Farrell snorted, chuckling under his breath. "Gods no! She's trouble, and not just for Bródy. The colonel didn't like dealing with such things, so he made Lieutenant Curran handle it, told Curran to either run her off or make Bródy do it. But now . . ."

He looked over at the low-voiced squabble, and the humor left his face.

"She's been looking very comfy," he whispered, "now that the colonel and lieutenant are both gone."

Mari's eyes followed Farrell's back to Sabine.

By the woman's expression, she'd clearly just whispered something venomous at her lover. Bródy smiled just a little as he shrugged, and Sabine struck out, slapping him hard enough to whip his face aside. She was on her feet before he righted himself, and she stormed away a few steps, but then stopped.

Mari tensed as Sabine stepped back in a lunge.

Grasping the back of Bródy's head, she pulled it back and kissed him passionately. Jerking her mouth from his, she whirled and headed for the door, not stopping this time. She was gone in an instant.

In following Sabine's path, Mari caught sight of Captain Stàsiuo, who'd watched the woman leave. He didn't look pleased.

Bródy flashed a smile at the two men watching him from the nearest table.

"It seems my evening plans have changed," he said lightly. "Anyone for cards?"

The two men laughed and shifted tables to join him. Chatter in the room resumed.

Mari looked to the common room's entrance again and stood up. "I have some things to attend. Excuse me."

Farrell stood up as well. "Do you need an escort? May I, Miss Mari?"

Not many days past, she'd been no one, shunned by everyone else, and digging in the dirt to steal carrots. Now she was "Miss Mari," and a soldier of the Soladran barracks was asking permission to guard her.

"No," she replied quickly, and then swallowed, trying to find some manners. "Thank you, but I'll go on my own."

She started for the door again, and as she passed Tris, he looked over.

Mari shook her head once as he started to rise. She waved him off as well and continued. While everyone else finished supper or set to something else, she slipped out to track Sabine.

CHAPTER
EIGHT

S till sitting with Captain Stàsiuo, Tris started to rise as he watched
Mari walk past. She waved him off, and then she was gone. Somehow, he kept his seat.

Stàsiuo sat watching his face.

"Pretty girl," the captain said carefully, as if waiting for a reaction.

Tris forgot whatever he was going to ask next.

"Maybe a little exotic," the captain added. "So, what is she to you?
And don't tell me she's just your servant."

Tris did not respond—did not know what to say.

He worried she might be following some lead of her own, though he
had no idea what. She was clever and resourceful, but she was not *him*.
If she had begun considering herself a hunter akin to himself, that was
worse. She had no idea what she might encounter from the living or the
dead. She had been stunned by his story of a youngest noble brother
killing his elder siblings.

Such things and worse did not shock Tris; they were or had been a part of his world.

Mari might know her own world's darker side, but she did not know the same of his. She did not comprehend the darkest depths of the living, let alone the dead.

"She is a recent companion," he finally answered the captain. "I needed assistance with translation, and she was willing."

Whatever Mari was up to, Tris had to leave her to it. He had his own lead to follow and could not abandon it until he reached its end. The two sergeants in line for promotion—Cotillard and Kreenan—interested him the most. Though both had motivation to clear their paths to advancement, he did not see why either would have targeted Brianne.

Across the room, Sergeant Kreenan rose from among others now at his table, and his long tail of brown hair swung around one shoulder.

"Sorry, no cards tonight," he said to the others. "I've got duty on the wall."

"Pity," Cotillard answered, light from the wall sconces glinting off his head. "I wanted to win back some of that coin you took off me last night."

As Kreenan walked away, he called, "Soon enough, but not for the next few nights." Then he was out the door.

Cotillard chatted a few moments longer with the others at the table. Then he rose and stretched. "I'm too tired for cards anyway," he said with an exaggerated yawn and stretch. "I'll find my bunk early."

Tris could not help noting the expressions of relief on the faces of the other men, and he remembered what Stàsiuo had said about Cotillard having a temper and taking things too personally. Perhaps he was not a graceful loser when it came to cards.

"This early?" one of the guards said. "Bunks are a dangerous place these days. I hope you wake up tomorrow."

A few of the other guards winced and glanced away.

Cotillard glared at the speaker. "Don't worry about me. I'll be fine." He sauntered out of the common room.

One of the other guards at the table looked at the man who'd spoken. "That was stupid. He may be our next lieutenant."

The card game resumed, but the mood of that moment seemed to spread throughout the room.

"I too am weary," Tris said to the captain. "Travel was more difficult than expected. Please excuse me."

Stàsiuo nodded without a word, and Tris left the common room behind Cotillard.

Mari didn't need to track Sabine.

There she was, still in sight down a main street into the city, though now a cloak hid most of her red gown. Her black mass of hair was easy enough to spot, along with her gait—she was graceful but still rolling her hips.

Mari hurried out of the courtyard and followed at a steady distance from her quarry. Sparse streetlamps offered just enough light for her eyes. Along the way, she started thinking again about Tris's story of the young nobleman who'd poisoned his elder brothers in a way that looked like they'd been slain by a spirit.

That took a dark heart, which was something she knew about. Was Sabine that dark?

Back in the common room, Farrell had said that both the colonel and Lieutenant Curran had been against Sabine's presence at the barracks. She clearly thought she had a grip on Bródy and might not stop at anything to keep that hold.

Would she think to remove anything—anyone—who tried to get between her and him? And what of Bródy and his predatory ways, hunting other women's hearts? Would Sabine put an end to that as well? After murdering men at the barracks, it would be a short step to removing rivals like Brianne.

As of yet, Mari didn't see *how* aside from the *why*. So she followed Sabine into the city. Shadows deepened between the taller buildings, offering Mari cover for whenever Sabine absently glanced back along her path. Soon, Sabine turned down a side street.

Mari followed.

The structures to both sides grew more dingy, filthy, and decayed with each cross street Mari passed. Her senses told her she might be headed toward the city's northeast side. Fewer lanterns lit the way. The string of shabby dwellings and tenements to either side was broken by half-decayed shops and faded taverns.

Then Mari stalled in frustration as Sabine turned abruptly into one sloppy, slat-roofed, single-floor building on the right. When she jerked the door open, raucous laughter rolled out for an instant.

Though there was no sign out front, Mari knew it was a tavern by its stench. After approaching the front door, she hesitated. She couldn't simply walk in. Sabine had seen her at the barracks and would spot her in an instant.

What to do? Was there a back way in? Perhaps she could slip in that way and take a look without being seen. If a proprietor or a maid challenged her, she could pay either of them off. She had money now. This thought caused her to waver. Her real goal should be watching Tris.

What had she been thinking in letting him out of her sight?

But a part of her still wanted to learn what had happened to Brianne, perhaps even avenge the dead girl if Mari couldn't yet avenge herself.

Mari spun from the door and crept along the front wall, looking for a way around to the back. She found one between the tavern and a rickety cobbler's shop, and she was just about to head for the tavern's rear door when it suddenly opened.

Yellow-orange light spilled out along with a voice, which made her flatten against the tavern's rear wall.

"Not inside; out here," said a woman.

Mari crouched down into a ball in the darkness.

"I had a good hand going," a low, male voice argued. "What do you want that can't wait?"

Two figures emerged.

Sabine's cloak was brushed over the backs of her shoulders, exposing her fitted red gown. Following her came a half-shaved, wiry man in his mid-thirties. Even by moonlight, Mari still saw his filthy clothes. Not tattered, just soiled, as if he didn't care to wash them, let alone bathe himself, by his stink, which overrode the alley's stench.

Reaching past the man, Sabine pulled the rear door shut.

"I have a job for you," she said.

"Tonight?"

"Or tomorrow if need be. But finish it by tomorrow night. I mean it, Raylan."

"You can skip your tired tricks," he grumbled, stepping in on her. "Make a promise to me and this time you'd better keep it!" His eyes moved to the tops of her breasts, pushed up by the laced bodice of her dress.

She reached slowly into her low bodice, hooked a finger into the loop of a string of leather, and pulled out a small pouch.

"I don't need to make promises this time," she whispered back. "I have money."

Her hand rose up in the dark. A *clink-clink-clink* sounded as she poured coins into her other hand. By the angle of Raylan's head in the dark, he still wasn't looking at the coins at first. And then he did.

"Where'd you get those?" he asked.

"Does it matter? They're yours if you can do it."

"I'm not killing anyone, not for you."

"Not kill. Just make sure anyone who looks at her face will look away just as quickly . . . for the rest of her life."

"Ruin her face? Cut it up with my blade?"

"Did I suggest that? What a clever idea," she returned, followed by a soft laugh. "Half now, and that's all, until it's done."

A pause followed. Then Raylan asked, "Is it that Brianne?"

"No, she hasn't been back, and he hasn't gone to see her. I may have to deal with her later, but this is someone else."

"Who?"

"I'm sure you've seen her with him at the Gray Dove. That's where he goes to meet her. A skinny little harlot named Elora Tanner. She's so pale she has almost no color at all. I don't know how she's trapped him. There's nothing to her."

His short laugh sounded as filthy as he smelled. "If there's nothing to her, why come to me?"

Sabine didn't answer that, though her voice hardened. "Will you do it or not?"

He was a little long in answering. "Give me all the money now, and I'll get it done—you know that. I've got a debt to pay that can't wait."

Reluctantly, Sabine handed him the coins. "Not just a slash or two. I want her face ruined."

"I know what to do."

He seemed ready to leave, and Mari was about to back away before she was spotted.

But Raylan headed toward the building's far side instead. Appearing satisfied, Sabine pushed in the back door and disappeared into the tavern.

Mari crouched in the dark in thinking on all she'd just heard—and what to do about it. All of this had more than answered her own suspicions.

Sabine wasn't clever or skilled enough for a scheme using herbs, suggestion, and poison. She was nothing but a street wench hiring some thug to cut up Elora's face. And she didn't seem to know anything about what had become of Brianne.

If the barracks killer in Soladran was someone still living, as opposed to a spirit, it wasn't Sabine.

Mari found this disappointing in more than one way. She'd found someone with a motive, and it had all come to nothing. For both learning more about Tris and finding the barracks killer, she'd have to go back and start searching for a new lead. But Sabine's malicious prod stuck in her head.

Not just a slash or two. I want her face ruined.

Elora had done nothing except be taken in by Bródy's charm. If anything, he was the one who deserved a bit of slashing. And yet this girl would suffer just the same—maybe for the rest of her life.

It wasn't Mari's problem. But as she slipped from the alley toward the street, intent on heading back to the barracks, her frustration began to seep to guilt—which grew into anger—until she turned the other way and began tracking Raylan.

Tris shadowed Cotillard through the barracks passages, trying not to be heard or noticed. He was somewhat gratified that one of his suspects had gone off alone, and it was fortunate the man had not left the barracks.

Following someone in the dark of a city he did not know would have been far more difficult.

Tris hoped the sergeant would do exactly as he'd claimed and head for his bunk. In this, he might learn of any nearby personal storage to later search. It had almost pained him to learn there might be no spirit to vanquish at the end of this hunt.

His one purpose was to rid the living realm of spirits of the dead—which in turn might lead him to something more for his own need: to finish or banish forever that other half of himself.

A foolish hope, for he did not know what that might cost him, maybe his own life.

Up ahead, Cotillard turned a corner, still heading toward the first bunk room. Upon reaching the corner, Tris stopped out of sight, for the next passage was short.

He might be seen.

A moment later, he heard a door open and close.

He remembered from his earlier walk through the barracks that there were two doors at the end of this short passage. One led straight ahead to the first bunk room; a second door on the left wall led out back of the barracks. He leaned out just enough to peek around with one eye.

The short passage was empty, and both doors were closed.

As this was the same path that led to his given quarters, he stepped out, walked openly and slowly to the bunk room door, and opened it. Inside were a few men getting undressed, lounging in bunks, or chatting. A few glanced his way, some puzzled or surprised.

Cotillard was not in the bunk room.

Tris asked, "Has Guardsman Cotillard come through here?"

The closest man on a top bunk leaned on an elbow. "Haven't seen him, m'lord."

Tris suppressed a flinch at the title. With a curt nod, he backstepped and pulled the door closed. Quickly and quietly, he stepped to the other door and opened it. At a squeal from weather-beaten hinges, he clenched his jaw, pushed the door wide, and stepped out, having lost any semblance of stealth.

The high city wall was no more than two arms' lengths away. He looked left and then right. Halfway down toward the northern gate he saw the bulge of a rounded barbican with an open stairwell.

Footfalls echoed out of the opening in the night. Someone had entered to climb to the top of the great wall.

Tris followed, pausing once to listen before entering the barbican.

Mari had no trouble at all tracking Raylan; his strong scent made it easy. He was also careless—maybe too self-certain—and never once looked back. Not that he'd have seen her.

Under the streetlamps, his clothing looked even dirtier. About five streets up, he stopped.

Mari sidestepped in under a shop's awning and flattened against the shop's front. The number of other people walking up and down the street helped to mask any noise of her movements.

Raylan turned his head toward a building on the left.

Mari shifted just enough to sharpen her hearing even more. She heard voices, laughter, a clink of glass and then tin, and then the slop of liquids being poured. This must be another tavern, and there were four men out front, three of them crouched while tossing dice.

"Brace!" Raylan barked.

He walked a few paces closer to the four. Only the one still standing turned, startled, and then folded his arms and spit.

"Never thought you'd show your face here again."

One of the others spun while still crouched. Spotting Raylan, he rose and gripped the hilt of a large dagger sheathed in his belt.

Raylan shook his head and spoke to the first man. "I've got your money, so leash your dogs."

"Never thought I'd see that either," Brace drawled.

Raylan held up the pouch Sabine had given him. "Take it." He tossed the pouch.

Brace caught the pouch, emptied it into a hand, and counted the coins. "Betting you didn't earn this, so you must have gotten lucky for once." He gestured toward the dice on the ground. "Still feeling lucky?"

Raylan was already backing away. "Keep your crooked dice, and keep your dogs off sniffing after me . . . if you want to play those dice on any other fool."

Brace chuckled at the veiled threat. Raylan kept backing away, not turning to speed off until he'd nearly reached the street's far side—Mari's side.

She was stuck in place, until Brace turned back to watching over his game. By the time she soft-stepped through the shop-front shadows and caught up to Raylan, he'd crossed three side streets and veered toward a bulky shingle-walled place with a rain-bleached wooden sign hanging out over the street's edge.

Mari lost her fix on Raylan for an instant.

The wooden sign for the Gray Dove was gray all over. This was the place where Bródy and Elora had planned to meet tomorrow. Was she a regular in there, or was it just somewhere little-known that he met up with her?

Raylan had come straight here after paying off his debt, so he seemed to know right where to go. Perhaps Elora was a serving girl who worked in the Gray Dove, since Bródy would not be visiting tonight.

It seemed Raylan planned on earning his coin right away. That said something more about Sabine, if he hadn't thought to cross her. Glancing around, he slipped into the nearer cutway toward the place's rear.

Mari had no idea how he planned to catch Elora alone. But she couldn't wait any longer and ducked back the way she'd come, heading for the alley. When she neared it, she slowed and peeked around the back of another building. A stack of crates along with an old barrel up the dark alley was close enough to the Gray Dove's rear.

And there he was.

Raylan crept in upon the tavern's rear door.

Skulking along silently, Mari crouched to strip off her clothes. She'd already felt the shift coming as she pulled her tunic over her head. And the pain came.

The first time, she'd been barely past her sixth year. She'd been hungry, for making camp had come late that night after the family's wagon had broken a wheel. It took an afternoon for Papa to replace the wheel from the nearest town with help from Uncle Tavio and Cousin Brita. As Mari wandered in the nearby woods feeling hungry, a tufted squirrel ran right across her path.

It was both painful and shocking when she fell and writhed in the dirt.

With some of her pretty clothes having been torn in the change, she lay gasping, whimpering, unable to move. Every sight seemed too bright, every sound too loud, every smell too strong, until she was overwhelmed and couldn't even scream.

She just huddled on the ground.

And it was so long before Mama came searching and found her in the dark. That was all she ever remembered of that night.

"It's hard the first time," Mama whispered the next morning. "Horrible, from what I know. But you're all right now, safe, my *mahkai-tah* . . . my little kitten."

Mari began shaking, even wrapped up in Gran-mama's musty quilt of faded maroons, teals, and ambers. Mama pulled her close in the bigger bed in the back of their warm, wagon home.

"And it won't get better," Mama said. "But you'll get better at getting through it, knowing it for what it means, like your great-uncle Shy'nann."

The two of them lay there most of that day, with Papa peeking inside several times to check on them. And no, the pain never got better, though she learned it meant something better.

It meant power, freedom, and survival in a life she'd never imagined as a child.

Yai-morchi.

Mari once might've wept in remembering that first night and the next morning, but not anymore. In the alley, the instant her dropped pullover hit the alley's soiled cobble, her other flesh took her in less than two breaths.

Bones warped and shifted. Fingers shrank as her nails changed into claws. Skin became downy fur. She crouched on all fours as flesh and muscle bulked and rippled. Her face elongated, her mouth reshaping around her teeth. Though the act still hurt, now the pain was nothing but joy.

Night brightened and sharpened in her sight. Sounds grew and mounted on others not heard until now—like her prey's shallow breaths in the dark.

Mari was on all fours when she charged. He never heard her until the last instant.

Raylan stopped and looked back over a shoulder . . .

Mari slammed into him, flattening him.

They both slid on the cobble. Even before they skidded into a pile of empty crates, his stench filled her muzzle, nose and mouth, clogging her head. She flexed her fore claws into his chest, cutting off his first scream in a suck of breath with pain. A hissing snarl through widened jaws and fangs silenced him the second time.

Mari slammed a paw down on his right cheekbone, wrenching his head to the side and pinning it. She cocked her rear legs in to shred out his guts. His panicked pants came fast, and the one eye of his that she could see locked wide on hers in terror.

She froze there with him pinned down.

Dead or maimed prey meant some constable or even the city guard would investigate. Evidence of a wild animal in the city would make it harder to get about. But she had to stop him from hurting the girl, Elora—stop him marking her, cutting up her face.

Mari flexed her paw upon the side of his head.

Claws distended, pressing into skin.

If only she could speak like this . . . *I'll shred* your *face instead!*

She remained for a while, panting into his face through bared teeth. The scent of urine filled her nose when he wet himself, and she hopped off him in disgust.

Raylan scrambled away, tripping, falling, and breaking the crates, making a good deal of noise. Then he ran down that alley without looking back.

Mari wheeled around the barrel for her clothes; she wasn't done with him yet. As she changed flesh again, the pain stalled her for a moment as she heard the tavern's back door swing open. Still naked, she ducked low behind the barrel and peeked around it with one eye.

One step out the open back door stood a young woman with bright blond hair backlit by yellow-orange light spilling out of the tavern. Over her sky blue dress she wore a soiled and stained canvas apron.

Elora looked both ways along the alley, frowned, shook her head, and went back in. The instant Mari heard the door close, she hurried to pull on her clothes, pants and then boots. Then she went running up the alley while struggling to get the jerkin over her head.

It wasn't that hard to track a terror-stricken man fleeing through the night streets. He didn't even hear her coming as she drew her narrow dagger and simply dropped her cloak.

Mari kicked in the back of Raylan's right knee at a run. He crumpled and tumbled across the cobble, and she was on him as he rolled over on his back. When she slapped the blade flat against his throat, she thought he might piss himself again.

His mouth gaped more than his eyes, but his breath caught before he could scream.

"Shut it!" she hissed in his face, pressing the blade until his skin bulged over its edges.

Raylan's mouth snapped shut.

She leaned in, snatching him by his hair with her other hand. "That cat is mine, and it does whatever I say . . . to whoever I don't like."

His breathing quickened.

"Touch the girl, or go near her again," she whispered, "and you'll never even see my little kitty as it comes at you for the last time. Understand?"

Still breathing hard, he finally nodded once.

She eased back, about to hop up, but all her fury and heat just wouldn't go.

Mari dropped down on him again, catching his jaw with her free hand and sliding the flattened blade up across his cheek.

"And when Kitty's done, I'll take your face off!" she rasped. "And nobody will know you when they find your carcass."

She slammed his head aside to stun him. Lunging backward off him, she spun and grabbed up her cloak as she ran off. After weaving through the streets, she made a final turn and spun in against a building to peek back the way she'd come.

She didn't see him, which meant he'd run off some other way.

Mari turned onward, sheathed her dagger, and whirled the cloak over her shoulders. Still, she couldn't help regretting that the barracks murderer was not Sabine. Mari had solved nothing tonight, and too many pieces of this puzzle were missing. This thought brought her back to what had really happened to Brianne here in Soladran.

It was time to speak to Cameron Bródy.

Tris climbed the barbican's stairwell as quietly as possible. Near the top step, he paused upon seeing a pair of boots left there, exposed by a little flickering from a distant brazier. Someone who had come up here did not wish to be heard or spotted.

Tris remained in the barbican long enough to remove his own boots.

He emerged atop the north wall, its stone still chill, even through his socks. Braziers burning along the wall's top did little to illuminate much of anything, even the walkway itself. On such a dark night, he wondered how far out there lay the forest's edge of the Warlands. The border stream was barely visible, though he heard it if he held his breath. And then he looked both left and right.

To the right, a man walked away, though his footfalls on stone made no sound. Moonlight glinted off his shaved head. Farther beyond him, and nearing the north gate, someone else in a helmet walked away.

Tris fixed on Cotillard again, who had left his boots behind to follow the other figure. What was happening here? He followed Cotillard but maintained a distance.

Whenever the far figure slowed or paused, so did Cotillard, who moved on only when the other man did so.

Tris's intuition and reason both told him to stop whatever was about to happen. But if the sergeant was here to do something illicit or deadly, he needed to be caught in trying to do so. Suspicion would not help if Tris was mistaken in . . . whatever Cotillard had come here for, boots or not.

The other guardsman never looked back in his casual stride along the way. He had likely walked this path so many times that he knew each step, even in the dark, and had little need to look down at his steps or back along this way.

Tris waited for Cotillard to act—to do something. The man only continued his silent stalking, now and then shifting in between the wall's top crenels. Tris decided to close the gap as quickly as he could without being spotted, and then one more detail caught his attention. Out the bottom of the farther guardsman's helmet, a long tail of brown hair hung down his back.

The man Cotillard stalked was the other sergeant—Kreenan.

Cotillard raised both hands, palms out for a final charge.

Tris almost cursed aloud for his stupidity.

Cotillard might be clever to a point, but not with herbs and poisons and the ruse of spirits. He was about to push his rival off the wall's end over the north gate. Why here, with other guardsmen below on duty? Perhaps because it was easier than wrestling an opponent over the wall's outer crenellations, somewhere unseen, or knocking him off to the wall's city side.

A scream or shout at night during the fall would still attract attention. A death in a remote location would draw three times the suspicion. But a fall over the gate within the sight of others—scream or not—would more quickly be ruled an accident.

Tris charged along the wall's top. "Kreenan!"

At that shout, the other sergeant turned. Both he and Cotillard froze in surprise, the first in seeing the second, and the second in suddenly being revealed by Tris.

Kreenan backstepped, reaching for his sword. His left foot faltered as its heel crossed the wall walkway's end. Cotillard rushed in, dropped low, and kicked Kreenan's other leg.

Kreenan's feet slid off the wall's end. His chest and head hit the walkway, and his sword clattered out of his hold. Even though he'd been caught by surprise, for a trained soldier, his actions appeared clumsy. Though both men had been drinking earlier, perhaps Kreenan had consumed too much. As he fell, he barely caught hold of the walkway's edge.

Someone below started shouting.

Cotillard spun, reaching for his own sword.

Tris stopped and froze before he could close. Cotillard was larger than him, a trained soldier, and now armed.

"Dead's Man!" Cotillard spit. "You'll be dead enough now, noble or not."

Kreenan still held on, but from the scrabbling of his boots on the wall, he could not find purchase and would not last long. Even by the sounds of other guards below, they would never find a ladder or anything else to save him in time.

Tris was unarmed; he sank his weight into his feet and readied himself. Time with his father's guards had taught him a few things.

When facing larger and/or more skilled opponents, he had learned to make the other person take the first move. The element of surprise was his first defense.

Cotillard charged, and Tris shifted his weight to his left foot, toward the inner and open edge of the wall. Cotillard stepped a little wide, toward the wall's crenellated side, likely to get an angle of charge for driving his target toward the wall's open edge.

Tris used his weight-loaded left foot to lunge to the walkway's other side, dodging the sword's thrust and striking his opponent's jaw as he rushed by. Then he kicked down into Cotillard's nearer ankle.

It almost worked.

Cotillard stumbled, shifted weight to his outer foot, and teetered for an instant near the walkway's inner open edge. Somehow he still slashed with the blade.

Tris lurched away against the wall's crenellated side. As he righted himself, Cotillard's booted foot slammed into his left calf, and his leg buckled. Crumpling, Tris spun along and down one crenel and slammed on the stone walkway. As he was barely rolling over, a boot's heel came at his face.

It never connected.

A large helmet struck and careened off Cotillard's right cheek. As the helmet clattered and tumbled off the wall's top, the sergeant wobbled, wide-eyed and stunned, and the flat of a broadsword's blade smashed in his nose. His head snapped backward as he toppled, hit the walkway on his side, and began to slide over the wall's inner edge.

Still caught in shock, Tris rolled over too late in an attempt to grab for Cotillard's arm.

Someone kicked his arm aside and stepped in his way. Lost in confusion, he reared back as two more men rushed past toward the wall's end at the gate. Two more came in from the other side but halted short and stood poised with swords in hand, ignoring him.

When Tris looked, he saw Cotillard's face just visible where the man clung to the walkway's edge. His mouth and chin looked blackened by blood running out of his smashed nose. Above him stood Captain Stà-siuo, with his back turned to Tris and looking down.

Tris could not see Stàsiuo's face, only the back of his head, helmet missing; the broadsword was still in his hand. For a moment, Tris wondered if the recent captain would kill one of his own men, here and now.

"Get him up," Stàsiuo growled softly, and then louder, "And lock him up!"

The two nearby guardsmen rushed in as the captain backstepped out of their way. Tris remembered someone else left in danger, and looked down the wall. The first pair of guards had pulled Kreenan back up. How he'd managed to hang on was unknown. Then something suddenly blocked all the brazier light, and Tris looked up.

The captain stood over him. His face was not clear to see, but he could not be in a good mood, even as he reached down with his empty hand. Tris reached up and barely gripped that hand before he was heaved to his feet. He began to explain.

"One of your sergeants decided to—"

"I know what happened," the captain interrupted. "Or did you think I wasn't watching these two?"

Tris stalled, at a loss. The last two of the four who had come with the captain hauled away Cotillard just as the other pair walked a wobbling Kreenan nearer. Before Tris could speak again, the captain spun on his other sergeant and grabbed the front of Kreenan's vestment.

"Listen up!" Stàsiuo barked. "I know everything, and Cotillard will be dealt with. As to you, I've been lenient, considering all that's happened to us in the last moon. It ends now—no more drink on duty!"

Kreenan, leaning on a comrade, dropped his gaze in whispering, "Yes, sir."

"Go to bed and sleep it off," Stàsiuo ordered, and then to the other guardsman: "Desún, take his watch."

The second guardsman nodded and headed off toward the gate's end of the wall, while the first led Kreenan down the walk the other way.

Tris still hesitated; apparently the captain was aware of far more than he had first thought.

Stàsiuo turned on him again. "And I don't want a dead noble to explain to my superiors! You keep out of anything to do with the garrison until you clear it with me . . . *my lord*!"

It appeared a title and nobility did not hold much sway with the captain.

"So . . ." Stàsiuo took a deep, slow breath. "Is Cotillard linked to any of the other deaths, by your estimate?"

Tris shook his head. "No. Whoever killed the others is either a spirit of the dead or someone possessed of skill and knowledge to fake such. If Cotillard were such a man, he would not have resorted to killing a rival at this stage. It was too reckless, too opportunistic."

"Agreed," Stàsiuo growled. "That leaves nothing for the rest, no?"

"No."

As Tris stood, facing toward the city amid failure and unnecessary complications, something more nagged at him. Where was Mari? He decided to check their quarters. That was where he had told her to meet him.

"Captain, we should return inside," he said.

"Yes, for your . . . attendant?"

Tris did not like the reference, but it served for now, and he nodded.

Upon reaching the barracks, Mari headed straight for its common room but paused in its doorway. The room was still half-full, and the men present chatted in low voices or played cards. She didn't see Farrell, Orlov, or Rafferty, and all the women were gone. No one looked her way, and so much the better, as she was still heated from the night's hunt.

Bródy was still at the same table with a handful of cards, and she went straight at him.

"We need to talk—alone."

He leaned back, looked over and up at her. So did the rest of those at the table, who were suddenly all quiet.

"I don't think we've been introduced," he said with a lazy smirk.

Up close, he was alarmingly handsome, his red-brown hair both thick and silky-looking, and his green eyes were flecked with brown.

Mari wanted to rake his face off. And it wasn't just the heat of the hunt that made it so.

"Get up," she said.

He raised an eyebrow and smiled. "I've a decent hand for once to-night. Come and find me tomorrow."

One of the other men scoffed and threw his cards on the table.

"All right, let's do this here," she countered. "Brianne's dead."

That wiped the smile off his face. The other men exchanged glances; one whispered something to another, but she kept her eyes on him.

Mari jutted her chin. "Out in the passage, now."

Still lingering, Bródy tossed down his cards and rose. He towered over her, but she didn't back up, and he no longer looked lazy or comfortable. After three breaths, she turned without waiting, as if it meant nothing to turn her back on him. She heard him follow soon enough as she headed for the door to the back passage.

Once beyond the door, she turned and blocked the way to cut him off. He stared at her with no expression, leaned his back against the wall, and crossed his arms.

"Well?"

The door was still open. Mari took one step and kicked it closed.

"You don't seem surprised about Brianne," she said. "Why is that?"

"How do you know she's dead?"

"Because I saw her body. She looked starved to death."

At this, his cold expression wavered. "What do you want?"

"She came here to see you. She said something 'horrible and white' touched her, or so we heard. You abandoned her, and she ran for home."

"Abandoned her?" he repeated. "Who told you that?"

"Her betrothed, Leif."

He straightened up. "That pockmarked cripple? And you believed him?"

"I don't have a reason not to." She looked him up and down. "Still don't."

She could see that he counted on his looks to deal with women, and she was getting tired of this.

"The man I came with is hunting that *something horrible*, and you're going to help him stop it."

Mari couldn't stop the slight rise of her other form amid her heat. Everything in the passage grew brighter. Every sound from his breathing—her breathing—to the chatter in the common was loud in her ears. His heartbeats were quicker, and she could smell his fear.

"What did you see that night?" she asked. "If you stuck around."

He hesitated again, but she heard his breath catch.

"I didn't invite her. She showed up," he said, quieter this time. "Hadn't planned for it, being seen together that night, so I took her out and around the stable."

"Why? Who would've seen you?"

He didn't answer that, and instead said, "She asked what I would do if she broke off her engagement to Leif."

This didn't matter much, and it wasn't any surprise. Someone like him too easily turned innocent but foolish young women—girls—away from better men.

"What did you say?" she asked.

"I didn't know, still don't." His gaze sharpened. "I cared for Brianne, probably more than she knew, but I don't make promises I might not keep."

"I'm so impressed. Then what?"

He stared at her for a long moment.

"That *thing* appeared," he finally said. "A ghost . . . spirit . . . whatever you call it. It came at me first, one hand outstretched."

Him first? Why?

"What did it look like? Man? Woman?"

"Man," he bit off.

"Did you recognize him?"

Bródy broke eye contact, looking away. "No . . . or I don't think so. He was white, somewhat see-through, and like he'd nearly starved before he died. Maybe a beggar, since his clothes were tattered, and he had a head wound."

Mari pondered this—starved but wounded? So which had killed the man in the end?

"What kind of wound? What did it look like?"

He frowned and appeared to grow even more uncomfortable. "I don't know. Something blunt, not edged."

All she could think of after that was forcing better answers out of him. Just one good slash across his handsome face.

"Which side of his head?"

Bródy blinked, maybe confused. "The left . . . or on my left, meaning his right side."

If she'd given in and ripped into him now, she would've started with her right hand—paw—into his left cheek. Maybe it didn't matter, but that meant whoever had attacked the man had been left-handed, if he'd been facing his attacker.

"Did you recognize him?"

Bródy exhaled, shaking his head. "Maybe. I don't know. Every other moon or so, people . . . refugees try to cross the field, reach the border stream, and escape. We're not allowed to help until they're into that stream."

"Not allowed? Why not?"

"It's not as if those petty lords over there could start a real war with us, but the nobility here doesn't want to face the first slaughter should someone in the Warlands think otherwise. We're not allowed to interfere or help until someone's *in* the stream. They try to cross here at the gate because they know we'll be waiting to protect them."

Absorbing this, Mari tilted her head and didn't interrupt. She didn't see him as any kind of hero either.

"The ghost might have been someone who tried to cross," he said. "But I don't know. He just looked . . . somehow familiar. As if maybe someone I saw once running toward us. Most don't make it before they are run down by a Warlands soldier or his horse."

Struck down from behind? That suddenly made it worse.

If the spirit had been struck from the front, this would mark the killer as left-handed. From the back, that would be right-handed and far too common to help identify a killer. Not that this would matter if the ghost was one of the refugees who'd been running toward the stream and the only hope of freedom.

"You stood and just watched?" she asked coldly.

For the first time, he showed open anger and straightened up. "We can't interfere until they reach the stream! The colonel's orders, and he is—was—right. Doing otherwise puts our people—our city—on the front line of a possible war. We would lose far more than we'd save."

Mari almost sympathized—almost. "So you think this ghost . . . man was a refugee who didn't make it across?"

Bródy stood there too long and looked away. "I don't know. They have all started to look the same, too much alike."

She tried not to wince.

"That night with Brianne," he went on without any prodding, "that spirit came after me, at least first. But it stopped when it noticed her. I swear its eyes narrowed and it looked back at me and again to her. I couldn't move, and she backed away, shouting at it, calling to it, trying to get it away from me."

Mari's stomach tightened.

His voiced turned shaky. "It rushed her . . . and its hand went for—through—her throat. She couldn't even scream. And then I tried to reach her. The ghost turned on me. It smiled and vanished." He stopped talking briefly. "I've never seen anything like that smile before—cold, vicious, spiteful. When I got my wits back, I tried to go after Brianne, but she was gone. I couldn't find her."

Mari wondered about the last part, and maybe he saw this in her face.

"I didn't abandon her!" he insisted. "She ran."

"Was she still trying to draw it off?"

Bródy stalled, brow wrinkling as if he was trying to think. "I don't know. Maybe."

But he'd never gone far enough to find out what became of her.

Mari wanted to demand answers for that, but her thoughts turned to something else. She might have details she'd missed or didn't understand. Tris might know better, if she'd even asked the right questions.

"Come with me," she said. "Tris—my lord—is likely retired by now, and he's the hunter. I'll translate, and you will tell him all of this and answer any question from him."

"There's nothing more I haven't told you."

"I'm not *asking*." She backstepped to the passage's far wall, waiting.

Bródy watched her for a moment. With a resigned huff, he headed down the passage.

She didn't have to lead him. By now, everyone in the barracks would know where the Dead's Man, noble or not, was lodged. A few guards looked up and watched as they passed through the first bunk room. Then they passed through the second and down the shorter way to the room she shared with Tris.

Dim as the passage was at night, Mari looked up at a soft but sudden glow ahead beyond Bródy. He stopped, and she heard him suck a breath.

Only her instinct made her grab his arm and wrench him out of her way.

Mari stared at the white, transparent form as it sharpened in her sight.

Tattered clothing covered a bone-thin man, white skin stretched tight over his skull and jaw. The right side of his head near the temple was dark, like it'd been smashed open and bled down his face.

His mouth opened wide—and then wider.

His sunken eyes shifted from her to Bródy, and his mouth widened even more.

Mari could only guess what would come next. She couldn't protect Bródy any more than she could protect herself. Grabbing Bródy's tabard, she wrenched him back down the passage.

Tris had said she was lucky or something like in surviving Brianne's contact. She thought it was something else. Either way, she hoped one or both of them were right.

Everything in the passage lit up as fear called to her other flesh.

Only one cry escaped her as fury welled up.

"Tris!"

Tris paced between the beds in the room assigned to himself and Mari. Upon returning here earlier, and not finding her, he had walked the entire length of the barracks and then gone back out to the city's edge, looking for her. Peering out into the city streets, he knew he would not find her by leaving the barracks grounds. Soladran was too immense.

Instead, he returned to this room.

Ceasing his pacing, he sat and pulled off his boots. But he could not rest. He should have sent Mari away—for her own sake—before coming to this place. He should not have brought her here.

"Tris!"

His breath caught at that angry cry, making him think of the lynx he had once chased through a forest. Rushing to the door, he ripped it open.

"Tris!"

He lunged into the dark passage, and strangely it was not as dark as when he had returned. Turning left, then right, he did not spot her. Instead he was transfixed by the back of a spirit lighting up the passageway.

Beyond the grotesque spirit, Mari was backing away while shoving someone else behind her.

Tris lunged forward, both hands ready to rake and tear the spirit to ethereal shreds. His hands clawed nothing but air, and the passage dimmed sharply as the spirit shot straight through its left wall.

"No!" Tris whispered.

He slapped both hands against that wall. On its other side were his quarters. In a quick glance, he saw Mari still on her feet and wide-eyed. Her shock wore off before his, and she charged toward him.

He reached their quarters first, and just inside, he slid to a stop in his stockings.

The room was empty and dark.

Some distant light outside slipped between the worn shutters of the room's one window. He turned to run back out, in case the spirit had reversed in flight, but Mari stood in the doorway, her hands gripping both sides of its frame.

She looked directly at him and stiffened as she took a step back, as if she saw something strange.

His eyes. He knew she saw the white glow when he was about to dispatch or banish a spirit.

But was there no spirit here to banish now. She would have known—seen—if it had reversed into the outer passage. The ghost had fled. Tris breathed a curse. He'd been so close, and yet he'd been too slow.

For his failure, more deaths might come before that spirit was found again. Someone else then appeared behind Mari in the outer passage.

What was Bródy doing here with her?

Tris quick-stepped to the door but halted short. He thought he heard something scraping harshly on the wood. That sound pulled his eyes to Mari's curled fingers, her nails gouging the doorframe's wood.

"We're not dealing with a ruse anymore," she said tightly.

She was correct.

In a final hope, Tris turned for the window, unlatched and pushed the shutters open.

Of course, there was nothing to see, so he closed and latched the shutters, leaning his head against them.

CHAPTER
NINE

Mari didn't sleep much, but as she and Tris hadn't gone to bed until nearly dawn, they skipped breakfast and rested through most of the morning. Finally, giving up on the hope of real sleep, she rolled over and up on one elbow and saw Tris wasn't asleep either. He lay on the other bed gazing blankly at the ceiling's rafters.

Last night, his frustration at losing that ghost made him almost manic, worse than she'd seen before. He'd questioned her and Bródy so long that she'd finally cut him off. She'd had enough for that one night and wouldn't talk to him again.

By the tense set of his face where he now lay on the bed, his mood hadn't changed.

Well, neither had hers.

"Lunch should be set by now in the common room," she said.

He didn't answer or look at her.

Mari fought against her temper. His notion of someone playing a game to hide murder had been wrong, so what was his problem now? Wasn't a ghost what he dealt with best?

"Get up," she said. "Now that you know it's a spirit for certain, we can ask different questions and some of the men might be able to tell us more. We should go in while they are gathering to eat."

Not that she should care—so why did she care? Still, she couldn't stop thinking about last night. She'd saved one girl from suffering, but other people would mostly likely die if *he* didn't do something now.

Tris finally rolled his head to look at her. Swinging his legs over the bed, he sat up.

"This spirit chooses specific targets," he half whispered at first. "It is not killing at random or by happenstance. If it is . . . he was . . . a refugee now seeking revenge, we need to know why and against whom. First, we must learn when he died, specifically who was on duty at the border stream when he was killed."

Mari felt relieved. At least he was making sense now, thinking of things she hadn't.

"Bródy was there," she said, "whether he remembers or not. He said the men have orders not to act until someone reaches the stream on their own."

He didn't respond, and Mari's frustration left her feeling edgy.

Was this the man, the one she'd hunted for so long, with power over spirits? It unsettled her that such a murderer, if he was the one, was so necessary now. Sitting up, she reached down for her boots.

They both readied themselves for the day in silence and left the room, heading down the passage. Upon entering the common room, they found it already crowded.

The room smelled stale in the heat from the hearth, no matter the scents of food. She studied everyone present as Tris passed her, heading for the food table, and she followed. Guardsmen Farrell and Rafferty were sitting with Sergeant Orlov, but Captain Stàsiuo was missing and so was Bródy.

The food table was again filled with plates, mugs, and spoons along with a simple meal of tea, bread, and cheese.

Farrell came over to dish up a plate.

Mari elbowed Tris, who was just standing beside the food, and cocked her head toward Farrell.

"At dinner," she whispered, "he almost spoke out against the dead colonel. If we tell him what Bródy saw when Brianne was attacked, and what happened last night, he might—"

A loud horn outside cut her off, so loud that she instinctively covered her ears.

Everyone around them dropped spoons and mugs and rushed for the outer door.

Mari grabbed Farrell's arm before he was out of reach.

"What is it?" she asked.

Farrell pulled out of her grip. "Refugees, out of the far forest. Stay here!"

He ran on for the outer door. In less than three breaths, the common room emptied, and she was alone again with Tris.

Mari looked up at him. His face was tired and his eyes dour. She was about to say something when he stepped off after the others, so she followed.

Outside in the courtyard, men rushed into a nearby armory shed and back out, bearing long spears in addition to their swords. Maybe half wore helmets; the other half were as bareheaded as at lunch, likely not scheduled for duty. That didn't appear to matter now. A number of bowmen were already at the gate as the others ran out.

Mari tried to bolt after them and was jerked to a halt by her collar.

"Do not get in their way," Tris warned, and released her and they followed more slowly.

Mari tried to stay out of the way but had to see what was happening. She slowed to a stop just outside the gate. Soladran soldiers were fanned out along the upslope between the stream's near side and the outside of the city's wall.

"Some are coming from the trees," a man shouted from atop the wall.

Mari didn't look up, for she'd spotted Bródy a dozen paces to the right in padded armor and helmet. Captain Stàsiuo stood out at the stream's edge in his helmet, vambraces, and chain mail while holding a long spear in one hand. He didn't look back or shout orders and kept his gaze focused out across the stream.

All the men along the near bank stood waiting in silence. It was so quiet that Mari heard the captain's boot toes crackle against the stream's ice fringe when he shifted weight. She followed his gaze beyond the stream's far-side slope and across the grassy plain beyond.

There was nothing to see all the way to the distant trees except tall brown grass barely shifting in the still morning air. She started to shiver. It was frigid out here, and she hadn't had time to get her cloak.

She felt Tris hovering to her right. Then the captain half turned and spotted her.

"Get back inside the gate!" he shouted.

She ignored him, didn't budge, but Farrell was coming out of the armory shed and hurried over.

"Miss Mari," he said. "You shouldn't be here."

His gaze shifted briefly, probably to Tris, but Farrell didn't say anything to the "noble lord."

"Why was the alarm sounded?" she asked. "I don't see anything."

"You can't—not from down here, not yet."

He glanced up, higher this time. She remembered that shout from atop the wall, but before she looked up—

"It won't be long," Farrell added. "Now, please, get inside the wall."

Before she could say anything, someone shouted again from atop the wall.

"Three in the grass!"

Mari looked out across the plain.

Something moved out there. Stalks of brown in the distance spread in one path. Someone's head bobbed above those, then shoulders, and Mari saw hair whipping in flight.

It was a woman in drab clothing from what she could see.

Two more paths in the tall grass veered to either side of the woman's and paralleled her own flight in racing across the plain. Whoever they were, they were so small that they couldn't be seen in the grass.

"Children!" Mari said. "Those are children!"

Farrell's head whipped toward her. "Get inside—now!"

Someone grabbed her arm.

"Come," Tris ordered, pulling her.

She wrenched the other way. Though he didn't let go, she held her ground as she looked outward again.

Small heads appeared in those other two paths. Then more paths broke the stillness of the field behind the three. A taller boy and girl together, the latter marked with something red tied about her head. They rushed on faster than the first three. More groups of people emerged, all of them running.

A small band of men came last. Two appeared to stop halfway across the broad plain, as perhaps even more were still coming from somewhere beyond sight.

Then something much taller broke from the distant forest—a rider on a horse. The two stalled men turned and ran after the others. Mari's anger rose up, pulling on her other flesh as five more riders cleared the trees, charging after their fleeing quarry.

Mari's hearing suddenly sharpened, and she heard the hammer of hooves and the tearing grass.

The first rider swung something up, back, and down.

Mari clenched at the sound of the distant impact.

No scream came as the farthest fleeing man fell from sight. And that rider quickly gained ground on a trailing peasant woman. His mace arced down.

Mari heard the distant crack as its iron head broke the back of the peasant's skull. The woman pitched forward out of sight in the grass, and again, no scream, even as Mari could see the spatter of blood when the mace arced upward again.

She ripped out of Tris's hold and went straight to Farrell. "Do something!"

"We can't," he answered. "Not until someone reaches the water."

Those fleeing were now close enough to see their faces. The tall boy stumbled; the girl with him slowed, almost turning back for him. The next crack of a mace came from somewhere else as the boy righted and the girl grabbed his hand as they ran on.

Mari ran downslope.

"No!" Farrell shouted after her. "Get back."

Her boots cracked ice and splashed in the frigid water as she charged at the captain.

"Do something! Loose some arrows or . . . anything . . . before they're slaughtered!"

He never glanced at her. He only stared flatly at the stream's far slope and its crest. She thought she heard his grip grinding on the long spear's haft. He wore no gloves, and his knuckles were white.

"Get back through that gate," he said without looking at her.

Mari's attention shifted as she saw Bródy coming toward them, openly angry and panicked.

Someone grabbed her from behind, and she thrashed while reaching for her dagger. When she twisted about, it was Tris behind her.

He didn't have his cloak either, but he wasn't shivering. She couldn't see his breath when he exhaled.

"What are we doing out here," she demanded of him, "if we're doing *nothing?*"

Tris neither spoke nor moved in looking down into Mari's amber eyes. She shook from cold, rage, or both, and he glanced toward the far slope's crest. In the distance beyond there, he heard muted horses' hooves pounding earth, and then a yell that cut short.

Fear grew toward terror as he turned back.

Bródy closed on both of them but spoke sharply and directly to Mari. Tris understood only a few words.

. . . captain . . . doing duty . . . you leave!

Mari tried to wrench from Tris's hold to go at Bródy; she could have done so, but Bródy backstepped out of reach. Having her cut loose on a guardsman was not Tris's worst fear, though if she turned lethal here and now, it would add to the risk of what might come. Not because of her but because of what was happening here—and what it could summon in the aftermath.

No one but he knew what so many deaths in one place at a time might call.

So far, Tris had watched, absorbing every detail. At a guess, the So-ladran guardsmen fanned out above the stream might be a third—maybe half—of the barracks' complement. There was no way for Stàsiuo to know ahead of time how many of the Warlands soldiers might pursue the refugees. Aside from saving the latter, the captain's other challenge was to keep his own men from crossing the stream.

The noise of hooves and screams and shouts beyond the stream's slope was growing nearer.

This time Mari tore out of Tris's hold in his distraction. He had never seen her like this, shouting at the guardsmen to act, but her reaction gave him insight into the conflict displayed on other faces. Some stood cold and devoid of emotion, while others grew hardened, and others appeared desperate to take action.

Even this would make everything worse, after the end.

Mari whirled away from Bródy—who was useless—and almost went at the captain again in an effort to make him listen. She heard another distant crack, but couldn't see enough from where she was. She wanted to charge through the stream to crest the far slope, but instead she turned the other way, ran past Tris, and back up the near slope for a clearer view.

Out on the plain, some of those fleeing had scattered, making it harder for the six riders to run down all of them at once. Four riders held a charging line while the two outer ones swung wide in trying to drive scattered prey back together.

The riders were hunting like a pack of wild dogs and then there *he* was again. Mari locked eyes on Tris. He'd rushed after her when she wasn't looking, and now shook his head.

The captain was now ankle-deep in broken ice at the edge of the stream, his expression anguished.

"Archers!" he shouted suddenly. "Fire between the riders and refugees. Aim for the ground!"

Bródy strode toward the captain.

"Sir, no! We can't risk a war, even with those Warland sell-swords!" Stàsiuo ignored him.

After so many bow thrums, a swarm of arrows arced over the stream into the field. Most disappeared into the grass between the riders and those in flight. Horses veered, staggered, or reared. One rider lost his seat and tumbled off into the grass. Others fought to rein in their mounts as their mouths and eyes gaped toward the forces before the city wall.

People in tattered clothing kept running for the stream, but the two outside riders bore down on them from the left and right. Then three of the other four charged onward from behind. The one who'd fallen tried to regain his mount.

Tris cast his gaze wildly around, almost lost in fear of what could happen, though in his imaginings, he saw the worst outcome.

Mari lunged two steps as the first refugee rushed down the far slope. A woman with a dirt-streaked face, looking too young for the child she carried, stumbled toward the stream's far edge.

Two guardsmen rushed to the stream's near side.

"Hold!" Stàsiuo barked at them. "Not until her feet hit water!"

"Captain," one shouted back. "We have to cross now!"

The young woman stumbled again and stopped to keep from dropping the child.

Mari looked to the two guards hovering at the stream's near side. One of them was Farrell. She didn't know the other, but Orlov was three paces behind that pair. Two archers ran down to flank and cover them for a charge. Other men along the near slope inched forward, regardless of Stàsiuo's order.

One leather-armored and full-bearded rider crested the far slope. He held a raised spear in his free hand. His horse skidded as its hooves struck sloped ground.

The young woman was still trying to regain a hold on the child.

Mari couldn't stand there any longer.

"No!" Tris shouted from behind her.

She ran down the slope, jerking her long dagger from its sheath, and her lead foot cleared the ice fringe to splash down in the stream.

Tris panicked as Mari plowed into the stream.

Before she reached the midpoint, the water was up to her thighs and climbing. Her hips and waist sank and forced her to slow even more. He heard the crunch of breaking ice and saw the woman refugee with the child stagger into the stream's far edge.

Tris ran straight between two guards and into the stream after Mari.

Not far in, cold water filled his boots and sucked away his breath for an instant. He barely gained midstream by the time Mari reached out for the woman and child. An enraged Warlands soldier on the far side charged his horse straight downslope at them, and the rider launched his spear.

"Mari, down!" Tris shouted.

Everything else stunned him into stillness.

Someone shouted one word.

Six arrows sprouted from the rider's chest.

The man toppled sideways in the saddle, unbalancing his mount.

The horse twisted, losing its footing under the sudden shift of the rider's weight. The spear arced for the woman's back. The mount fell, tumbling straight downslope over the top of its rider. Mari thrashed toward the edge of the stream and reached for the woman and child right in the horse's path.

Tris barely lunged another step through cold water as the spear thrust into the woman's back. She fell straight into Mari. Both went down and sank beneath the stream's surface as the horse rolled toward the water, kicking, thrashing, and squealing.

Woman, child, and Mari did not resurface.

Tris could think of only one thing to do—for horses did not like him. He surged toward the animal at the stream's far side, and still Mari did not resurface. The horse smashed ice and splashed water.

As it struggled up, he shouted, waving his arms, and it saw him.

The animal's eyes widened with insane fear. It screamed but stumbled back, kicking and twisting to get away from him. A sudden splash blew up over Tris, startling him.

Mari rose with a loud gasp, soaked through but with the child in her arms. Before he could reach her, she spun in the water, looking every direction. He knew what she sought.

There was no sign of the woman, not even by a spear's haft sticking up above the stream.

Tris heard Stàsiuo shout something he could not understand. He did not care and struggled to reach Mari. Guardsman Farrell crashed past him, through the stream, and to the slope. The downed rider was not moving, but Farrell still rammed a spear into the man's chest. He jerked the spear out as he charged up the far slope and into the grass field beyond sight. And the captain was still shouting.

Tris grabbed Mari's arm, the dagger still in her same hand.

She whirled on him, as if to slash at him, but then turned farther, looking all about again.

"She is gone," Tris half shouted at her. "The mother is gone!"

Other refugees now scrambled, tripped, and tumbled down the far slope toward the stream, trying to cross as more Warlands riders bore down on them from above. Shouts everywhere made it hard to hear any one voice. Nearly half the Soladran guards were in the water, and more noise came with them. Still, the riders surged over the far crest, no matter how outnumbered.

Tris yanked Mari's arm to drag her out of the mayhem. He noticed one noise was missing. Not a sound came from the soggy, bundled infant in Mari's other arm.

Could it mean another death—and again, he was in the middle of all of it?

"Get the child out of here!" he shouted at her.

Cold and shivering, Mari appeared too numbed to react. Tris dragged her on toward the Soladran side of the stream. Whether the child still lived or not, at least this would get her—and himself—away from the slaughter.

So much death at once in Tris's presence could bring something far worse by nightfall.

Mari sat shivering by the common room's hearth, even though wrapped in a wool blanket. Once Tris had shoved her through the front door, he'd run off into the barracks and come back with two wool blankets scavenged somewhere. She was now wrapped in one and the other was for the little boy in her arms.

Three years old at most, at least he lived; his mother had not, though Mari didn't really know if the woman lost in the stream had any connection to the boy. He lay sleeping in her arms with shallow breaths, another child orphaned like her. She looked up.

Tris paced the room, stopping only to peer—stare—at her, again and again.

She had no idea why, but this went on so long that she began to ignore him, growing tired as the warmth from the hearth finally sank in. Her eyelids and head began to drop, and she lost all sense of time.

The outer door burst open, startling her awake.

Outside, daylight was beginning to wane. Winter days were short here, and the remainder of the afternoon was nearly gone.

The chaos of shouts made her flinch and rise as soldiers hauled in the wounded: their own or refugees. Some who'd escaped across the stream were still on their feet but soaked through.

She hefted the boy and tried to get clear of the hearth. Others now needed heat more than she. Tris stopped pacing as the bleeding, broken, and weeping flooded the common room. He just stood there at the food table's inner end staring blankly, as if every face he saw held a threat.

In his expression she saw fear on the edge of panic.

He'd faced—no, commanded—the dead, and likely seen more death than she had, at a guess. He was the Dead's Man, so why did all of this frighten *him* now?

Captain Stàsiuo came striding in among another cluster of wounded and refugees. He was drenched and one side of his face was badly bruised. Sergeant Orlov was right behind him, carrying a middle-aged woman.

"More blankets!" Stàsiuo barked. "Anyone on your feet, move, now!"

Mari ducked aside as two more guards ran by toward the bunk rooms, and almost stumbled into the captain's back. Both men were bloodied and wet, but neither acted as if badly injured. The sounds of crying, prayers to whatever gods, and pleas for the missing filled the place and her ears.

Mari felt her own panic rise as she clung to the boy.

"Orlov," the captain half shouted, and then lowered his voice. "Gather an able team."

She looked back to find Stàsiuo gripping the sergeant's arm in close talk.

"Gather the six bodies of those Warlands riders and get rid of them," the captain said. "Have another team get their horses out of sight and in the stable for now. Move!"

"Yes, sir," Orlov answered with a curt nod.

Mari absorbed this. So, all six of the riders were dead, and now the captain was trying to hide what had happened.

"And, Sergeant," Stàsiuo said through clenched teeth.

Orlov looked back.

"When you're done," Stàsiuo finished, "find Bródy and arrest that coward for questioning orders."

Orlov nodded with satisfaction. "Yes, Captain," he answered, and headed for the door.

"Tichen?"

Mari spun at that panicked plea. A young woman with one arm in a crude sling turned about in the crowded room looking everywhere.

"Where's Tichen?"

One old man in soaked, tattered, and soiled clothes pushed through others but stopped short upon facing her. His wrinkled lips parted as if he was about to say something, but he only shook his head.

Tears began to fall down her stricken face. She looked vacantly about the room and finally fixed on the captain.

"You!" she cried at him. "Why didn't you do something sooner? You had archers . . . could've saved us all!"

Stàsiuo didn't answer. He dropped his eyes, the muscles of his jaw tightened, and he turned away.

"Get the rest of the rescued in here *now*," he snarled at his own men.

The woman started after the captain, fingers hooked like claws.

Mari thrust the bundled boy into the arms of someone else and lunged in to grab the woman's wrist.

"Don't," she whispered.

The woman turned on her.

For an instant, Mari thought this one might come at her, at anyone, in anguish. She knew fury seeded in agony, but the woman only sagged and crumpled. Mari had to catch her, though they both dropped to the floor.

"Tichen," the woman whimpered.

She had lost someone. No one had been there for Mari on the night she'd lost everyone who mattered, so she held on as the woman choked in silent sobs. How long they remained like that she didn't know or care. Then someone's wet, ankle-high boots slapped the floorboards next to her. She looked up into the vacant eyes of the same old man.

He didn't say a word amid the noise in the common room and crouched down with pained effort. Reaching out, he gripped the young woman's shoulders with his worn, gnarled hands.

At first, Mari didn't want to let go, not until the old man whispered, "I 'ave her, miz. It's a'right. See ta' the others."

It wasn't all right; nothing was. Just the same, Mari let go, rose up, and looked about the room. At first, all the misery and loss crowded into this place hid one change from her. Then she realized.

Tris was gone.

Tris met no one as he strode through the barracks; everyone, including Mari, was too busy with the battle's aftermath. When he reached the room he shared with her, he entered and quickly shut the door. He fixed on that one shuttered window in the far wall between the beds.

He had to get out of the barracks—and the city—before full darkness set in, without being followed. What was coming would not care who got in its way. His satchel and other belongings still lay on the chest at the foot of his bed, though he did not touch any of those. If someone noticed him gone from the common room and came looking, they would eventually come here. Better to leave all possessions behind and let others think he was here somewhere. In the end, he would not need anything—except perhaps the cloak.

Tris grabbed his cloak, about to hurry to the window, but then paused and turned back. There was one more thing he needed.

Digging into his satchel, he pulled out the small knife he used when making camp during a journey and tucked it into his belt. Then he hurried to the window, shoved the shutters open, and climbed out.

Quietly, he closed the shutters before slipping away in the night.

Mari hurried through the barracks, pausing here and there only to see if Tris had gone into one of the bunk rooms. All she saw were guardsmen scavenging blankets or settling their wounded into bunks. Ducking aside as two of the guards jogged out into the passage, she ran on for the room she shared with Tris and burst in.

He wasn't there.

All of her and his belongings still lay on the chests. At this sight, she ran back out and down through the rest of the barracks, even opening doors to other rooms, but she never spotted him—never smelled him.

He couldn't have doubled back without running into her, unless he'd gone out some side door, but why? He shouldn't be overwhelmed by anything that had happened beyond the city wall—and which was now spilling into the common room.

He'd seen more death than anyone here, even her, given what he was.

Mari's thoughts drifted to second-guessing.

What he'd seen would've always been after death. Not while it happened, not like she had, one night in the Wicker Woods. Or had he? Had he been there as well in those woods, just as she'd once thought?

Yes—he must have been there. Who else could it be?

She doubled back to the room, its door left wide-open. Entering, she stood between the beds and drew air deep and long through her nostrils. He wasn't here, but his scent was strong, though that might be from the bedding.

She looked about the room one more time.

Something was wrong. Even with a risen tinge of her other flesh, it didn't take heightened smell or sight to catch one more detail in the dark. Something was amiss here. Then she saw it.

The window shutters were closed, but the hook latch dangled open. She hadn't done that.

He hadn't done it earlier in the day before they left, and she'd never opened those shutters even once since they'd first arrived. Even if so, he wouldn't have left them unlatched.

Someone had gone out through that window, unable to close the latch from the outside.

Mari kicked the shutters open, climbed out, and sniffed the air.

"I must leave—now," Tris ordered. "Open the gates!"

All four guardsmen fidgeted before the closed northern gate. He did not recognize any one of them, though this did not matter. None were officers that he could see, not even a corporal or a sergeant. They exchanged panicked glances at a lord's order, and one man shook his head at the others.

"Sorry, m'lord, but . . . ," that one began. "We can't, m'lord. The gate stays closed tonight. Captain's orders, m'lord. It won't be open again until daylight, when the guards on the wall can see out into the field."

Following just enough to understand their meaning, Tris stared at four bewildered, suspicious, cowed, or panicked faces that might soon pale in death. That was all that would be left of anyone within his sight if he did not leave this place.

It would be pointless to run for another city gate. He would not have time to reach one, and it seemed the northern gate was locked tight in fear of reprisal from some petty tyrant across the border stream in the Warlands.

Neither this wall nor the gate could protect anyone near Tris this night.

He glanced up to the city wall's top, turned without a word, and ran toward the back of the barracks, leaving the four confused guardsmen at their post.

Mari lingered behind the barracks' back corner, peeking around with one eye to watch. Her ears caught everything said, every harsh breath, especially strained words from one guard denying the command of a noble "lord."

Why did Tris want out? There was only the stream, its banks, and the field beyond, all recently cleared of corpses.

Could that be why?

A fresh lot of dead; fresh spirits perhaps easily called by the Dead's Man. Another host for another slaughter in the night, like what had happened to her family. But why? What would it gain him?

Mari didn't care. It wasn't going to happen, not to those refugees in the barracks suffering for ones they'd just lost.

Tris turned from the gate and ran into the darkness between the barracks and the wall.

Mari backed around the corner, tracking his footfalls by sound. From what she'd seen and heard, she couldn't get out of the city either. If she killed him now, she'd need somewhere to hide the body where it wouldn't be found for days. Then again, she'd be gone by the time anyone found his corpse.

He'd shown his intentions this time, no matter the strange things about him that'd given her doubts, over and over. She'd watch him die in agony for everyone he'd taken from her.

Tris bolted by, never looking her way; Mari readied to sprint, spring, and take him down.

He swerved toward and into the barracks' stable out back.

Mari's breath caught. He was making this too easy, which was suspicious for someone—something—like *him*. She ran quiet as a cat to hide to one side of the bay doors and peeked in.

Tris ran from one stall to the next, even around two horse carcasses piled off in one corner. Horses in the stalls began rearing, kicking, squealing in trying to get farther away from him. They didn't like him, and maybe he didn't like them. Maybe he was even afraid of them as well, but he didn't show it.

The stench of fear in the stable became thick.

Mari looked back toward the barracks and the corner where she'd hidden. All this noise would soon attract attention. If he was doing all this in secret, then why a racket and rush?

When she peeked back in, Tris held coils of gathered ropes, and she knew what he was going to do. There was only one other way out of Soladran: over the wall. Did he need to be out there, where death had come for so many? Good enough. What better place for him to die? And better for her before a horse's screech called someone else.

As he ran out the other end, Mari sped through the stable. Again, horses reared, bucked, and snorted, this time stomping at the scent of a predator come too close.

She followed the sound of his flight, lost track of him for a moment, and in that pause heard the echo of steps on stone. That sound came out of the open arc of a half tower in the city's wall, and she followed it.

Mari lingered inside the tower stairwell's base, listening to every sound carrying downward over spiraled stone steps. She'd heard his hurried footfalls pause somewhere above and didn't dare take him until sure he was alone up there. Maybe he'd stopped to check that the way was clear. Or he'd second-guessed trying to get over the wall and out.

Waiting ate at her, until she heard him take another step . . . and two more. The sound changed. It no longer carried down the stairs. He was out atop the wall.

Mari rushed upward but stalled at the top, keeping back out of sight.

She could see one far-off guard walking away to the east, and she risked a careful peek the other way toward the gate—no guard that way, and so she stepped out. There was no sign of Tris, but it took her no time to spot a rope looped over one of those raised parts of the outer wall. She hopped up between those stone protrusions and looked downward.

The rope still wavered slightly against the outer wall, but she didn't see him below. Her hearing sharpened on instinct, and she caught footfalls, strangely staggered, two steps separated by longer pauses.

Had he injured one foot or leg in a final drop? Then came the sound of splashing.

Mari spotted his dim shape wading through the stream, though it maddened her that he'd gotten so far out of reach. She grabbed the dangling rope, swung out, and scrambled downward.

The rope ended more than a man's height above the ground, but the drop into a crouch was nothing to her. Splashing sounds from the stream ended.

He was already across and out.

Mari ran for the stream toward the last sounds that she'd heard. She slowed before stepping into the frigid water to avoid splashing about and attracting his attention. Drenched again to the waist, she waded out on the stream's far side. She needed to catch him unaware, not the other way around.

Shivering, she crested the far slope. Her feet were already numb, and it was getting even colder. She'd have to do this differently than she'd planned over the years.

Mari began stripping off her clothes. She piled everything out of sight in the tall grass beyond the slope's crest and dropped on all fours. She even left the long, narrow dagger as well, her one and only visible weapon.

A quick, silent kill might've been safer. For all his deceptions, confusing her over and over, she wanted more than that now. But she'd make sure he didn't—couldn't—scream.

Mari shuddered on all fours and not from cold this time. Bones shifted, but that pain brought a welcomed freedom. Fingers thickened and then shortened as claws extended, piercing the ground. Her eyes rolled up as her jaws clenched with other teeth, and when those eyes rolled down . . .

Night brightened, even under a quarter moon.

Her sight took in thickened forepaws fully furred.

She wanted to run, charge, hunt, but she didn't.

Mari skulked through the grass, silently tracking her prey.

Tris huddled down in the grass, positioned where the battle site was directly between him and Soladran's northern gate. This was as close as he dared stop within sight of the city but close enough for what would come. Though he pulled his dark cloak tighter about himself, this did little to stop his shivers.

Not that sickness had ever been or was a concern.

Heil's calculations had not accounted for two past appearances of Tris's other self. Because of these anomalies, it had taken the elder alchemist almost three moons to roughly calculate when the black one would next reappear. It was through this that Tris finally learned the true terror of the danger he posed to others.

Those of the Vishal manor were not the only victims of the plague that had taken his mother. Large numbers of people in Stravina had died of this sweating sickness. He had been naive about the world, let alone his own nature, at that time, though being spared had not surprised him. It had made him feel only even more alone.

Tris had never been ill, not even with sniffles as an infant.

This should have been one warning, among others to come, when he finally left his family's lands for the last time.

Along that journey, he neared a village called Yan'vul, well after sunset. On that quiet night he heard weeping somewhere ahead. He should have turned back, turned away. A torch's flicker was at first no more than a distant light ahead. As he neared, its flutter revealed much more. It was mounted atop a pole planted in the middle of the road. Dangling from a lashed crossbar was a torn, plain white cloth as a banner.

It was a warning that the plague had come to Yan'vul.

Tris walked on until spotting the settlement's outskirts. He paused where the road breached the sparse trees surrounding the village. At first he saw nothing but scant torch poles and lanterns along the main path. Then the weeping returned but not from any cottage in sight.

The sound carried from the dark trees to the west.

Tris rounded the nearest mud-bricked cottage, all of its windows shuttered and dark, until he spotted a glow far out among the trees. He followed that beacon slowly, so as not to startle whoever was out there, and lost sight of the lantern now and then but never that sound.

Sorrow guided Tris in among fresh mounds of turned earth—graves hastily dug and more hastily marked with bits of board. Names he could not read in the dark were scratched into the wood with a knife or some farmer's hand tool. They were everywhere he turned, until he again spotted that one light.

Between the trees upon a rise ahead, a woman in a drab head shawl knelt hunched over upon the slope. By her weeping, she was the one he had heard before, though her sorrow broke in long silences.

He stepped carefully off and around, trying not to disturb her. He did not know why, but he had to see why she was here alone. He already knew, though he did not know how small a reason she had. Once he was far enough to the right, he saw another mound.

It was small—tiny—compared with all the others.

Tris backed away quietly, retreating to the village. Along the way, he noticed other dim lights among the trees. Small flickers of white light seemed to appear one after another. There were so many mourners burying dead in so many places that he stopped, unable to find any path that would not disturb someone's grief.

One white flickering light appeared to move. Someone was done with mourning or at least with burying the lost.

A scream made Tris fix on that one light—and another one moved— and another.

The next scream cut short suddenly. White lights once shifting began to race about, flickering as they passed behind tree trunks and then reappeared. And their shapes began to grow larger and change as they neared.

Tris did not wait. So many spirits at once heralded something worse, and he did not know how to face so many at the same time. He ran toward the village as he heard the weeping woman scream a name.

"Mi-Michelle, my baby . . . no!"

When he reached the village's main path, others awakened by screams appeared in open cottage doors. For an instant, he thought to shout at them to run. Then he saw it.

A darkness like a young man took form while walking inward from the village path's far end. It never halted, never faltered. The shape of its black head, like Tris's own, never looked aside. It kept on straight toward him, even as the first white wisp burst through the chest of an old man in an opened doorway.

Tris stumbled in a backstep and then turned and ran.

Mari crept through the tall grass along the matted path left by his passage. She was close now; she could smell him more and more with each step. When she heard him breathing quickly in the night, she veered away into the grass, rounding that sound in an inward spiral, until she spotted him.

He just sat there with his back to her, huddled in his cloak within a space of crushed-down grass. His breaths came harsh and quick. She watched and listened, savoring her coming release, now at hand. This was going to be so easy. She'd finally be free of the pain, the sorrow, the grief and rage and guilt.

Mari poised to take her prey, coiled for a charge. But she hesitated.

Why was he panting? Why wasn't he doing something? And then she thought she saw a glint in his hand for an instant.

Why would he bring that little food knife with him?

It vanished as he shifted positions, perhaps tucking the blade away.

She saw him shaking. No, that was just a shiver from cold; even she felt it through her fur. Still, there was not a sign of a ghost or any shimmer in the darkness nearby. If he'd come out to raise another host of spirits for slaughter, where were they?

He just sat there, shuddering.

Careful and silent, she ducked back before padding softly around to the right and his far side. She stopped where she knew she'd glimpse the side of his face. Soft and slow, one paw so careful at a time, she stalked in until she saw him clearly through a thinner barrier of grass stalks.

Mari froze again, watching him.

Were those smeared tears on his face, or just a glistening left from wiped-off water splashed from the stream?

Tris now knew what he had done that night in Yan'vul. It had been his own presence—and his connection to that other him—that breached the barrier to the realm of the dead. Heil had reasoned this as the only possibility for how the black one had appeared outside of the calculated schedule. Once this was known, Tris had understood much more.

That other half of him formed during his stillbirth needed to take his life directly.

This was the only way it could remain among the living in replacing him, and that gave him one way to avoid unleashing his own horror into this world. It was a choice he had pushed out of his thoughts until now, for he had always shied from any place of too many deaths at once.

Tris separated his cloak enough to look down as he slipped the knife out of his belt.

If he died before being taken, it might end all of this forever. No one else need ever face another night like in Yan'vul—face that other *him*. No one here would suffer loss. He pressed the knife flat against his tunic's abdomen, not wanting to look at it anymore but still needing it ready, as the night's cold sank deeper into his flesh.

Black Tris was coming.

Mari was exhausted. It had been years since she'd last stayed in her other flesh this long, though not that long since she'd stayed awake all night. She felt half-frozen and couldn't stop shuddering, no matter being covered in fur. And Tris hadn't moved once all night.

What was he waiting for? It wasn't spirits, or he would've called, conjured, or whatever some of them by now. And why had he been crying, alone out here in the night? She shouldn't have cared, didn't want to. She was tired of doubts stalling her concerning him.

Tris raised and turned his head, looking to the east. Mari stiffened.

Long moments later, the sky began to lighten. She'd known it was coming, but how had he? But he still sat staring, as if surprised the sun had come up at all. When he began to rise, she backed deeper in the grass. Again, he stood there looking eastward, as if another sunrise meant something. She heard his first limping step, so he had hurt an ankle or a foot in the drop from the wall.

She waited until he almost slipped from sight before following.

Before Tris had even reached the stream, she realized she might now have trouble getting back inside. In all likelihood, he'd pull up the rope after he climbed the wall. Where would that leave her?

A loud grinding sounded. Turning her head, she saw the north gate opening. Daybreak had come, and the men were reopening the gate. With a soft sigh, she decided she might have to wait for the guards to change out, and then she could bluff her way back in.

Tris stood alone in the barracks' common room before the hearth, trying to get warm again. He had hauled up the rope after climbing the wall, careful to first watch above for a passing guard, and then returned the rope to the stables.

Once inside the barracks, he checked his room first and found Mari not there. He had lingered a moment and decided not to stow his knife away. Then he came straight to the common room.

Along the way, he noted that the rescued refugees had been lodged in other bunk rooms. A long night's vigil alone left him more anxious than exhausted, though he knew this would soon reverse for lack of sleep. At least the night had passed without anyone or anything coming for him.

It troubled him that Mari was not here either. Where was she? Could the scene at the stream yesterday have been too much for her? Had she left this place? No, back in the room, he had noted all her belongings were still in there, so she would have to return for those.

Yes, she would—had to—return, much as he should have sent her off long before now.

He needed tea, and hoped that breakfast would be laid soon.

Then he heard the barracks front door open and turned. Mari stepped in and stopped at the sight of him.

"Where were you?" he asked without thinking.

There was something in her face, something he could not read, though perhaps not the tinge of ire always just below the surface. She appeared troubled.

"What is wrong?" he asked.

He waited another two breaths. And why was she wet to the waist?

"Nothing," she answered.

Dropping her gaze, she came in and rounded him widely as she approached the hearth's far side. What had he done now to offend her?

"Where were you?" he asked.

She sat before the hearth to pull off her waterlogged boots.

"Out," she answered, gazing into the flames. "Searching . . . Didn't find anything."

Searching for what, and why was she wet? Hopefully, she had not been foolish enough to go hunting that one spirit on her own, not that she could have found it. As he was about to ask, he heard boot-falls coming from the rear passage.

Guardsman Farrell entered, carrying two mugs of steaming tea. In a half pause, he scowled at Mari, though she did not look to him. He set one mug down next to her and held out the other to Tris.

Crouching beside Mari, he said something somewhat lengthy that involved several pauses. His accent was so thick that Tris caught little of his Belaskian speech . . . *gate* . . . *order* . . . *stupid*.

As expected, Mari twisted on him, and there was the Mari that Tris knew, ready to assault first. Tris intervened.

"What did he say?"

Mari let out a sigh. "He said what happened out there yesterday was my fault."

Perhaps true, but that crisis had been building far before her or Tris's arrival. And he suspected that Farrell's lengthy comment had involved more than what she'd related. Tris glanced at her boots, beginning to steam by the fire.

"Ask him how long this has been building up," he said. "These refugees trying to cross over, and why the leaders in the Warlands are so determined to stop them. Why risk losing trained soldiers over a few escaping peasants?"

Mari's eyes narrowed as if he had said something insulting, though he had no idea what. She finally spoke, not looking at Farrell, and her tone was a bit sharp.

Tris was lost in following their exchanges, which came too quickly to catch even a word or two. This went on longer than he had expected. Farrell was suddenly silent, and Tris turned full attention to Mari.

"He says if any commoners are allowed to leave, more would do so. The warlords wouldn't have enough left for farming and harvesting to feed what little troops they'd gained for striking at each other. Most commoners who try are caught before reaching the field. If not, they're cut down . . . always."

"So soldiers sent after them have orders to kill them all?"

She nodded. "Only soldiers with families are sent. Their families are kept as hostages to make sure they'd do as told . . . or else. It's been going on for years, decades. The border guards here always watch but can't do anything until any runners reach the stream."

Mari looked up at Tris, and the remaining anger in her face faded.

"It's hard on them too," she said, "watching people die under the old colonel's order not to cross the stream. Some of the guards here hope it might change, now that Stàsiuo's in charge, though others still agree with the colonel about not starting anything open with the warlords. Farrell's heard Bródy and some of the others call refugees things like 'Warland whelps . . . dogs.' They don't even want these people to make it across the stream."

Tris pondered this.

"Oh, yeah," Mari added. "And Bródy's been arrested for cowardice."

That did not surprise Tris.

"Of the other men with Bródy's viewpoint," he began, "was Lieutenant Curran one of them?"

Mari glanced up sidelong, then looked to Farrell and translated the question.

Farrell nodded tightly and offered a reply to Mari.

"So were all the men who've died," Mari translated.

Tris glanced toward the back passage out of the common room.

Vestiges of the mystery here were being stripped away. In the wake of last night and escaping the need to kill himself, the prospect of dealing with the vengeful spirit of a Warlands refugee was almost welcome.

"What now?" she asked.

"We lure out the ghost, so I can banish it."

"How?"

"With bait."

CHAPTER
TEN

S oon, the common room began to fill with guardsmen and refugees. Captain Stàsiuo was not among them. The portly cook laid out breakfast, and after giving Mari a few moments to wolf down some bread, Tris decided they needed to search out the captain. Hopefully, the man could set aside what Mari had done yesterday. For what Tris had planned, it would be best to gain the captain's permission first.

Tris motioned to Mari, and led the way out into the courtyard. She followed. As they emerged, Sergeant Orlov strode toward them, perhaps heading inside.

"Captain Stàsiuo?" Tris asked, knowing at least the second word would be understood.

Orlov pointed toward the rear stables without reply, though he nodded to Mari before passing by to some other duty. Clearly he did not share Farrell's harsher view of Mari's actions yesterday, but she had again fallen into silence.

Tris walked toward the stables.

He noticed now that daylight had arrived, the north gate was open again, and there were probably men posted once again at the stream. Mari glanced over at the gate.

As Tris continued leading, she paced him on the right. The muddy earth was still half-frozen and precarious. Mari said nothing in that slow and careful walk, but he glanced sidelong at her more than once. Something had altered in her. Though still harsh-eyed, still showing a shadow of frown, she was strangely withdrawn.

Upon entering the stables, Tris saw only a few guards. Fortunately, none had horses at the ready, and Tris kept to the center and away from stalls to either side. Some horses snorted; some whipped their heads, blew air, and danced aside or backed their rumps into their stall's rear wall.

The captain was alone near the stable's rear doors, stripping a saddle from his horse.

Tris halted at a distance, though Mari continued onward.

Stàsiuo frowned at the sight of her coming, and Tris could not blame him. She had been the first to ignore his command and started chaos at the stream earlier than the captain had wanted.

"Why did you wait so long out there?" she demanded in Stravinan. "You wanted to do something—I could see it—when the first of those people broke from the far trees."

Tris scowled this time, clenching his jaw. The last thing he needed was the captain pushed further into a foul mood.

Stàsiuo took a step at Mari, and Tris tensed.

"I had to wait," the captain growled. "And you should've obeyed and stayed out of the way!"

Tris understood—and agreed—but this had little to do with his task. He interrupted before Mari could retort.

"Mari," he said sharply, "tell the captain what Bródy told you about the night Brianne died."

He could have done so himself, but a firsthand account from her would be more accurate. When she cocked her head aside, glancing at him, he pressed her.

"Tell him."

Reluctantly, she related the tale Bródy had told her of the white spirit of a starved man in tattered clothing with a bashed-in skull, whom Bródy had identified as an earlier refugee who had tried to cross the border stream.

Stàsiuo grew only more visibly impatient, eyes shifting from her to Tris often.

"Bródy said the ghost started for him," Mari finished, "then saw Brianne and went for her . . . almost like it wanted to hurt someone he cared about, wanted to make him suffer."

Stàsiuo offered a soft huffing sound. "Bródy's just telling tales, cribbed from what he'd heard in Curran's ramblings before death. Don't believe anything that coward says, especially to save his own hide. That's all he's any good at."

"Then explain away what I saw last night," Mari asked. "Right outside our quarters, that ghost came at him again. I *saw* it, just how he'd described!"

"You saw a shadow!" the captain shot back. "Moonlight through a window, in the dark, and the rest was him playing your imagination."

Tris saw this was not going to work, but before he could act, Mari lunged toward the captain.

"I saw what I saw, clear as you! White, half-starved, tattered clothes and all, with a head wound."

Stàsiuo clearly did not believe her.

Tris had faced this before, too many times.

"And what did the spirit do?" the captain asked tiredly. "It didn't kill you or Bródy, for one."

"No . . . ," she answered and faltered, as if uncertain. "He—Tris came when I called out for him, and that ghost shot off through a wall. But we all saw it."

Stàsiuo shook his head in weary disgust, turning back to his horse. "You're both either mad or corrupt. Now I suppose you expect to be paid for ridding us of the ghost?"

"If you do not believe the murderer is unnatural, how do you account for the manner of the deaths?" Tris asked. "Healthy men starved to death in the space of one night."

Mari's temper broke free again. "And all of them, like Bródy, were ones who would not help refugees, didn't want them coming here!"

The captain ignored her and remained focused on Tris.

"I can't explain it away," Stàsiuo countered. "There *is* an explanation, and I will find it, but it isn't yours. I'm not a fool who thinks the barracks is haunted."

"What you believe or not is irrelevant," Tris said. "If you wish to save your men, assisting me will not interfere with your own investigation."

Stàsiuo still fixed on him but stood silent for too long. Tris hoped that using noble status would not be necessary again.

"What do you want?" the captain asked.

"To set a trap," Tris answered, "with something to lure the spirit again. It has appeared in or near the stables at least three times, and come twice now for Guardsman Bródy. I need your permission to use him as bait."

Tris knew that since Stàsiuo did not believe a spirit was responsible, he would do little to assist. Yet, the captain's answer still surprised him.

"Oh, you can have that coward," Stàsiuo said, "but not for another moon."

"A moon? Why?"

"Because he's been locked up. And you can wait until I'm done with him . . . my lord."

Mari barely controlled her fury. Maybe it was failure and more doubt after a night in the grass watching Tris. Or maybe she didn't like being called a liar—or mad—by this captain. Or that he'd used some foolish excuse not to help. When someone touched her shoulder, she twisted around.

Tris pulled his hand back and shook his head slightly at her.

Mari backstepped and looked away. For once, she didn't think of figuring him out or think on the death of her family. An image flashed through her mind of him sitting alone in the dark last night with a worthless little knife in his hand.

Pushing past him, she headed out of the stables the way they'd come in. When she'd reached the stable's bay doors, his touch came again.

Mari spun, snarling out words before he could ask something she didn't want to answer.

"How can he not believe me? Curran told the same story as Bródy, and I *saw* that ghost. I've nothing to gain by lying about it!"

Tris studied her.

"What?" she asked.

"From Stàsiuo's perspective, you might lie," he answered calmly. "I have been accused of creating visages in order to vanquish them for profit."

Mari blinked several times. He nodded, maybe thinking she doubted him.

"And worse," he added. "Some will never believe what they have not seen with their own eyes. To do so is to admit that there is too much in the world they cannot understand. The captain is such a person. He may not be able to dismiss me, but we will gain no further help from him."

Mari was lost for what to say to that. He was fully focused on banishing this ghost plaguing the barracks.

This was his hunt.

Like any predator, he wouldn't give up until the scent was lost. For one more time, every half certainty she'd gained about *him* started to come apart. That left her frightened, as all her pain welled up in the place of lost anger.

Again, doubts nagged her. Even worse, if she was wrong about him, she couldn't face the thought of years having been lost in hunting the wrong prey.

Tris stepped past her, not knowing the threat so close to him. Then he paused, glanced back without turning, and—

"Mari?"

She flinched to awareness and caught up as she answered, "Yes, I'm coming."

He didn't step onward.

Mari followed the tilt of his head and eyes toward the top of the city wall. One guard walked the wall top, slow and steady in his circuit. She didn't know his name, but her sharp eyes recognized him.

"Wasn't he one of those playing cards with Bródy the other night?" she asked.

"I think so."

Mari eyed the guard again. "He's the one who laughed after Sabine slapped Bródy and then kissed him."

"And not many here—and now—laugh."

"No, they don't," Mari whispered.

Earlier in the common room, Farrell said Bródy's comrades felt like him about refugees out of the Warlands. There was no way of knowing if the man on the wall was one of Bródy's friends, but it seemed likely. Would the ghost come for him as well?

Tris was already turning. "This way."

They walked slowly over half-frozen ground toward the front of the barracks. Soon, she spotted the half tower in the wall with the stairs she used last night in following Tris.

He went straight for those stairs, and on instinct, she grabbed his arm.

"Wait. I don't think we're allowed up there," she said quietly.

Did those rules apply to him? She wasn't sure. Both of them had been up there last night, but no one had seen them.

He frowned at her and went on up the stairs. Hesitating for an instant, she followed him up the curved stairs to the top exit archway. He slipped out, but he still stood on the walkway as she emerged. She couldn't help stepping to the outer wall to look between two protrusions and out beyond.

The first thing she looked for was that place where she'd watched him all night. The small, matted circle of grass was there. In the distance, beyond the far forest, the mountains appeared harsh and white, maybe beautiful in their own way.

Tris was already walking along the top of the wall.

Quick-stepping to catch up, Mari spotted the man they were after coming their way. Tris didn't stop until the guard was right in front of him.

"You cannot be up here, sir," the man said. "Please return below."

Mari looked at him more closely than she had the other night. In his mid- to late twenties, he might be considered handsome, but in a different way than Bródy. He was slender and had fine features, and a few strands of white-blond hair showed below his helmet's edge.

"Go down," he repeated more forcefully.

Mari didn't miss the arrogant hitch in his voice.

Tris didn't move.

"Tell him exactly who I am," he instructed her. "Then ask his name."

Though most of the men seemed to know Tris was a noble, perhaps they didn't know his full identity. For some reason, it didn't bother her a bit this time to use his title to bully a guard, especially one of Bródy's kind—though it did bother her that she still played the lackey.

"You're speaking to Baronet Vishal," she said. "His father is a member of the national council of nobles. And you are?"

To both her shame and satisfaction, the man blanched.

"Guardsman Lavich," he answered with better care, and nodded to Tris, though his voice was still laced with arrogance and assumed privilege. "Please forgive my manner, my lord, but please, you must return below. Civilians are not allowed on the battlements without an accompanying officer."

Mari wondered if this guard was one of those with family money. If so, why wasn't he an officer by now? Maybe they'd lost it all, and his only choice had been to join the local military.

Tris remained fixed on Lavich as he spoke to her. "Tell him what we need, why, and anything else necessary, including anything about Guardsman Bródy. Hold nothing back."

"We're not going anywhere," Mari said to Lavich. "Has Bródy told you what happened that night he was attacked behind the stable? Did he tell you what he saw?"

The handsome guardsman hesitated. "Yes," he answered, though he sounded uncertain.

"Do you believe him?"

"Does it matter?"

"This ghost only goes after certain guards. Ones not so willing to help the refugees bolting for freedom."

She watched his eyes, caught the twitch of the right one, followed by a quick ripple of resentment in his brow. Then came the rising scent of fear.

Maybe he remembered he was talking to the Dead's Man. Was he stupid—or just arrogant—that he hadn't made that connection until now?

"We need help to stop it," she added, and cocked her head toward Tris. "If the baronet can get close enough to touch it, he can banish it. And you—everyone—will sleep better. But we need to draw it out." She couldn't help a short pause before saying, "Care to be the bait?"

Lavich didn't speak for a moment. "And what makes you think I am such a person," he asked, "one of the men this spirit might go after?"

"Aren't you?"

She heard one of his boots shift back.

"If we are indeed plagued by a spirit," he said, "you've still no proof of why it's here. And I have my duties."

He turned, about to walk away.

"You're right," she agreed. "We don't have any proof, but you knew every man who died. I wonder what you have—what you *had*—in common."

Perhaps that hadn't occurred to him until now. His head swiveled back toward her.

"It'll find you eventually," she added, and again cocked her head toward Tris. "When it does, who do you want there—one of your friends or him?"

The rest of Mari's day slipped away. After she'd gotten Lavich's unwilling help as bait, there was little else to do. After a while, Tris suggested they both rest, and for that, she wasn't going to argue. Neither of them had slept last night, and he needed to be ready for whatever he'd do that she couldn't. Still, too many thoughts about him tangled in her head.

The quiet of the room, the bed, and the warm, wool blanket were still welcome. The next thing she was aware of was a banging sound.

Mari awoke, thrashed, and grappled for her blade in the dark.

What had happened? Was the rest of the day gone? Then a sharp scratch-'n'-hiss as a small flame lit the room.

Tris touched the ignited sulfur head of a stick to a candle, rolled out of his bed, and sat on its edge.

"You snore," he said. "Terribly."

Mari was certain that she did not snore, but before she could call him a liar, the banging on the door came again.

"M'lord? Dinner is served, if you'd like."

That was Orlov at the door, and Mari looked about the dark room, still surprised that the whole afternoon had slipped into night again.

"Bring your cloak," Tris said, rising up. "We will go out directly after dinner."

He went to the door and opened it, and Orlov stood waiting, lantern in hand.

"What about your cloak?" she asked.

Tris looked over. "It will hamper me."

She remembered he hadn't been wearing it when he'd dealt with Brianne. Somehow, she'd wager this next ghost wouldn't go as easily.

Mari pulled on her boots, grabbed her cloak, and checked her dagger before joining him. He blocked her way before she could step out.

Tris looked at Orlov, back to her, and tilted his head toward the sergeant. That he'd stopped here meant there was something more not for the sergeant's ears. Mari looked to Orlov.

"Thanks. We'll be along."

With a curt nod, Orlov went on his way.

Tris turned to her, speaking barely above a whisper. "Once this begins, your task will be to get Lavich away. When I tell you, you run. Do you understand?"

She didn't really, and she didn't care to be ordered about.

"I cannot deal with this spirit," he added, "and tend to your safety."

Now he sounded concerned about her again, and this twisted up everything inside of her. While he had risked himself for her before, she never knew whether to believe him as sincere or not.

"Mari!" he pressed. "Swear to me. Please."

His last word caused her to flinch.

"I swear," she said, though she had no intention of running off anywhere.

She needed to see what he did when dealing with something more dangerous than Brianne. Would he call upon something more . . . otherworldly? Would he give himself away this time for what he really was?

Shoving his arm aside, she headed off down the passage. It took him a moment to catch up, likely from snuffing the candle he'd lit. She reached the common room just before him.

Guards mixed with surviving refugees, all crowded into the place with too much noise. The young woman with her arm in the sling was feeding the little boy Mari had saved. With so many in the room, it took more than one sniff to catch the scent that waited at the crowded food table.

A savory stew, rabbit for certain, though with perhaps too much basil in the mix. For once, a decent meal didn't appeal to her, and she almost wished she hadn't come.

Tris whispered behind her, "Captain Stàsiuo must not learn of anything we will do tonight. Eat, whether you wish to or not. All must appear normal to anyone watching."

The prospect of finishing off this spirit seemed to have wiped away whatever had driven him out of the city last night. He'd been calmer since coercing Lavich into playing the bait.

Scanning the room, she saw Lavich again sitting with other guards, but she didn't remember if they were the same ones as last time. He glanced at her—or maybe Tris—and quickly looked away. As she stepped in, Farrell saw her at the same time she saw him, and he hurried over.

"Did you get some rest?" he asked.

It wasn't difficult to like him, even after his lecture this morning. He was honest enough to be unsettling, and everything he felt showed in his face, sooner or later.

"Yes, some," she answered, but her gaze wandered the room.

Though warm and fed, the refugees still appeared haunted by what happened the day before. She could see it in their eyes. Freedom hadn't freed them from fear and sorrow. The young woman feeding the boy looked stricken. And who had been her "Tichen" in life?

Husband? Brother? Whoever, he was gone forever.

"What'll happen to them now?" she asked.

Farrell shook his head. "I don't know. The colonel used to let them sleep here for a night or two, and then he'd make them leave. They have no place to go except into the city to look for work."

"Do they find it?"

He seemed uncertain and didn't answer her question. "I suppose they're still better off than in the Warlands."

Mari wasn't so sure now, though of course she'd never think to send them back.

"The captain will let them stay as long as possible," Farrell added. "Hopefully until they find work or somewhere to stay out of the cold."

That was something, at least, and maybe more than she'd have expected. Captain Stàsiuo was nowhere in sight. Tris pointed to the long food table, filled with a heavy, steaming pot, bowls, and wooden spoons.

"We should eat," he said.

Following him, she dished up a small bowl of stew, only half-full, reached for a piece of bread, and then decided to leave it for someone else. One pitcher held clean water. She poured herself half a mug and followed Farrell to a table with Sergeant Orlov.

Sniffing the stew, Mari felt hungrier than she'd realized. Of course, she hadn't eaten anything since early that morning. But she had barely licked a spoonful of the stew when the barracks front door opened and numerous heads turned. People shuffled aside as if letting someone enter.

Mari drew a sharp breath at the sight of Sabine. She looked as beautiful as the last time she'd left Bródy with a slap and a kiss. Tightly laced up in that red gown, her black curls of glossy hair hung around her face.

Of course, Bródy wasn't here.

Her dark eyes drifted toward Lavich, but he stayed focused on fiddling with the spoon in his bowl.

Entering the room, Sabine closed on Lavich.

Mari stiffened at the sudden scrape of chair legs the other way. By the time she looked, Sergeant Orlov was quickly headed to cut off Sabine.

"Bródy's not here, miss," Orlov said, polite and cold. "He's been arrested."

"Bródy? Arrested?" she asked, and then louder, "For what?"

"I cannot say."

Noise in the common room dwindled, but Sabine didn't appear to care about the attention.

"He's in the barracks jail?" she asked the sergeant. "I want to see him, now!"

"No visitors," Orlov returned, almost sharply. "Captain's orders."

The open anger in Sabine's face turned to something colder.

"We'll see about that," she said, turning away.

"The captain's given orders." Orlov took three steps to cut her off. "If you're found near the cells, he'll have the right to ban you from the barracks."

Mari caught only a little of Sabine's profile, but she knew the calm glare. Orlov had just made an enemy for life. She'd seen men hunger for strong drink, women, cards, and worse, even to the point of life's end. Mari saw that in Sabine—her need for Bródy—though linked with a predator's desperation.

Sabine's anger vanished as she stepped close to Orlov. "Let me speak to the captain, please."

When her breasts brushed his vestment, Mari dropped her spoon, letting it clatter on the table.

"Was that necessary?" Tris whispered.

Sabine didn't turn to look, but Orlov glanced past her toward the table.

"Come tomorrow," Orlov told Sabine. "I'll not bother the captain tonight. You can leave on your own . . . or with assistance, if you need it."

In a flash, Sabine swept around the sergeant for the door. Once it closed, loudly, Sergeant Orlov returned to plop in his chair.

"Like talking to a serpent," he said with a shudder.

Mari couldn't disagree, but she wondered. "Where is the barracks' jail?" Throughout this place, she hadn't seen anything resembling a prison.

"City side of the stable," Farrell answered instead. "Just one large cell with a stout door, and seldom used . . . seldom needed among our men. Bródy got off lucky, if you ask me, questioning the captain out there in front of everyone. He could have been run out or worse."

"He's not alone this time," Orlov put in. "Cotillard's in with him, and he *will* be run out and charged as well."

"Cotillard?" Farrell repeated.

Tris straightened quickly at that name, and Mari's attention fixed on the sergeant.

Orlov nodded. "I heard he tried to murder Kreenan on watch."

Mari stared at the sergeant, as did Farrell; when she glanced at Tris, he didn't look surprised, though of course he couldn't understand much being said.

"Doesn't surprise me, I guess," Farrell added. "He's been wanting that promotion so much since Curran . . ." He trailed off and looked to Mari. "Have you and the Dead's Man found anything yet?"

That caught her off guard, and she answered carefully. "Maybe. Not certain yet."

"Well, having him here might be helping," Orlov cut in. "We haven't had a death since you two arrived."

After that, they all ate with less talk and were close to finishing when the front door opened again.

Stàsiuo walked in and the guardsmen all stood up. He didn't look at anyone and headed for his small table. As he sat down, so did the men around the room. The same guard as the first night hurried to get the captain's supper.

Mari wondered a little about this. Certainly a captain didn't have to eat in here with the rest. This one did so with his men every night, or at least for as long as she'd been here.

When she looked back to Tris, he'd locked eyes with Lavich and nodded once.

Lavich lowered his gaze and dropped his spoon in his bowl. He didn't look happy when he stood up and headed for the door.

"Excuse us," Mari said, nodding to Farrell and then Orlov. "We've some things to do."

Both men nodded with short well-wishes in parting. With that, she and Tris left the common room. It was time to begin.

Mari was vibrating all over in tension.

Not long after, Tris hid behind the stable's rear end with Mari. She watched around the corner toward the courtyard, for she had the better eyesight at night.

Guardsman Lavich was out in the open, pacing back and forth. At each passage toward the stable's front end, he neared the place where Bródy had reported first sighting the spirit.

Tris was guessing on two counts: first about the location for this trap, and second about his choice of bait.

For the former, it was logical, if Bródy's word could be trusted. Spirits were often drawn to where they'd died or where they could find those blamed for their demise. Lieutenant Curran, Guardsman Henrik, and Brianne had all been attacked in or around the stables.

Tris leaned out to peek over the top of Mari's head. He could see the closed northern gate by the braziers at its sides. The darker stretch between there and where he stood was more difficult for his eyes.

For the latter part, Guardsman Lavich was tenuous at best for bait. This spirit was likely a dead refugee seeking revenge for being left undefended in the flight to freedom, likely but not certainly. But it was still unclear whether this spirit targeted men who had visibly refused to assist refugees. A large guess for as little as Tris knew of those who had died, let alone Lavich.

Lavich was a close companion of Bródy, who had been attacked, and saved only by the distracting presence of Brianne. Yet Lavich had been frightened when Mari had informed him of the possible link between the spirit's victims, frightened enough to be coerced into assisting tonight.

Tris now found this whole arrangement somewhat desperate. He had not faced a spirit this potentially malicious in some time. He closed both hands and did not realize they were clenched until they began to ache.

"Anything?" he whispered.

"Quiet," Mari whispered back.

Lavich reappeared, closing on the gate's braziers one more time. Other guards there looked over at him again. Hopefully none would leave their post to engage him.

The night was growing colder, and Tris second-guessed leaving his cloak behind in the room. He could have flipped it off when necessary, but now it was too late.

His hands still ached when Lavich returned to the front of the stable and then turned around to walk back in the direction of the gate again—twentieth—fortieth—

How late was it now? Sometime near the mid of night?

Lavich continued. The men here were trained for night duty in a chill climate, and he had probably walked the wall all night more times than he would remember.

"What if it doesn't come?" Mari whispered.

Tris did not want that question—his own question—spoken aloud.

Before he could shush her, a shout rang out in the night, causing his every muscle to clench. Two more distinct voices rang out, one from somewhere nearby, the last a deep baritone.

A woman screamed.

Startled, Tris failed to grab Mari before she bolted off in the dark.

CHAPTER
ELEVEN

Mari raced around the stable to its inward wall. There, between the stable and the barracks' nearest corner, was a door. Grabbing its latch, she found it wasn't locked and jerked it open, rushing in. The last scream had come from inside, though it was too muffled to have come from someone in one of the stalls.

Down a leftward passage in pure darkness, she skidded into an open area. The space smelled of old hay, dust, maybe dried mold, and worse. A sudden light, along with cries of fright or shock, caused her to turn around.

Sabine stood off to the right before a mottled iron door, and she was gripping the bars of its small, face-high window.

"No!" she screamed. "No . . . no!"

"Do something!" a deep voice called from inside the door. "Get the keys!"

Mari bolted straight at the door as Sabine broke into sobbing hysterics.

"Shut up!" she barked, slamming a shoulder into Sabine.

As Sabine sprawled across the floor, Mari gripped the door's window bars, standing up on her toes to peer inside. Her eyes met with those of a frightened guardsman just inside. She'd seen him before but couldn't remember where. His head was shaved smooth, and when she shifted left, he cowered rightward, away from a glow inside the cell.

Bródy knelt crumpled on the straw-strewn, stone floor, choking and gagging. Before him floated the white, half-starved ghost in tattered clothing.

There was so much hate in its grotesque face, and the ghost rammed a bone-thin hand through Bródy's forehead. Bródy screamed and straightened up on his knees, as if pulled by the ghost's hand embedded in his skull.

Mari wrenched on the door's bars and then the handle; neither gave nor opened. Sabine was suddenly on her, trying to get to the door, screaming again. This time, Mari back-fisted the woman across the face and put her down. She rose up on her toes again.

"Keys!" she shouted through the bars at the bald guard. "Where are they?"

He twisted her way. "In the desk!"

Mari dropped to her feet. The place was so dark that even her eyes saw little more than black shapes. She sidestepped, and some of the ghost's light spilled through the bars, striking a desk nearby in the outer chamber.

She ran for it, ripping out drawers and dumping what they held onto the floor. Hearing a clatter of metal in the third drawer, she grabbed a ring with three thick keys.

Someone else stepped to the door, blocking the ghost-light.

A snarl built in Mari's throat, and this time she'd make Sabine stay down. But it wasn't Sabine at the cell door. Someone taller there turned upon hearing her with the keys. Two white pinprick lights for eyes in a pale face focused on her.

To Tris's left, Sabine was struggling up again.

"Get in there," Mari shouted at him, and chucked the key ring.

He caught it, but spun away from the door and called to Sabine. "Move back!"

The white glow through the bars brightened for an instant and then erupted without sound through the iron door. Glowing mist lit the outer chamber and then gathered into that starved ghost hovering between them. It twisted like vapor, but it didn't flee this time, and fixed on Tris.

Mari froze, not knowing what she could do.

Tris faced only the spirit, as if nothing else existed for him. Something in his expression changed in the glow of that ghost. He looked calm, maybe coldly emotionless. He backstepped twice and dropped the keys.

What was he doing?

He continued retreating, and it looked like he was going to run. Why? Drawing the ghost out was what he'd planned—what he'd wanted. She looked to the keys lying near the cell door as the ghost drifted after him in slow shifts toward the passage out.

Then Mari knew what Tris was doing.

The ghost had shifted its attention to him after whatever it'd done to Bródy. This would be what Tris wanted. He was drawing it clear of everyone and kept backing toward the way she—and he—had entered.

Mari took two careful steps, halted, and then two more. Nearly to the cell door, she glanced the other way. Sabine was curled up and shuddering next to the wall. At least she'd shut up. Mari watched down the passage, and Tris suddenly moved out of sight.

He was going for the door out.

The ghost vanished straight through the passage wall in the same direction.

Mari almost bolted down the passage. Instead, she turned, grabbed up the keys, and shoved the first in the lock. That didn't work, but the second one did.

Tris was out there alone.

Why should that matter to her now?

"Get up!" she ordered Sabine as she shoved the cell door open. "Get them out of there—*now!*"

Sabine stared at her.

Mari didn't have time to wait and ran for the passage out.

Tris had barely stepped out in the cold night when the spirit reappeared four strides back and out of the stable wall. This was what he had wanted—to move it out of reach of anyone else and make it come for him. He had feared finding it only to lose it, for another ploy like this would not work again. It had not worked as planned in the first place.

The spirit now fixed only upon him, its rage plain on its transparent face, still gaunt with starvation, even in death. By its present form, it had not relinquished the horror of its final moments before death.

Tris had seen this many times before. Such anguish was often the cause for a spirit to linger among the living. Those who died in peace, happiness, or even simple sorrows were rarely seen again.

What mattered first was that this one would do no more harm to anyone. Second, no one else, including Mari, should be near it when the portal opened. This spirit especially would not go willingly, peacefully, or even alone.

Tris backed farther away from the stable—away from the door—and the spirit rushed him. As in the last time, its mouth gaped. Its lower jaw dropped impossibly low, as if broken loose somehow before death. He slipped one foot back in a half step to brace as the spirit's right hand shot for his face.

Spirits feared him, sensing him as abnormal, but sometimes, those like this one did not care. None knew until too late what he could do to them.

Tris snatched the spirit's wrist as if it were solid. Force from the ghost's rush made his boots slide an inch on frozen ground. He quickly grabbed for its neck below the dangling jaw.

The spirit's sunken eyes widened more in shock and then fear as its rage faltered.

Tris closed his hands more tightly, though it felt like trying to grip slick mud. His focus sharpened under that *feel* of death, and what he gripped became more solid. He pushed back, and saw terror grow in the spirit's eyes.

Shock was always short-lived, quickly replaced by maniacal panic.

The half-starved specter thrashed and then lashed at Tris's face with its other hand. His boots slid again, and he faltered this time. His arm, with his hand braced at its throat, began to buckle. The dead refugee's face leaned in at his until even his own eyes began to grow chill under its close, cold presence.

Tris saw every detail—bone beneath shriveled skin, broken teeth in the right side of its hanging jaw, and the lines around its wide mouth. Those hollow eyes filled up with frenzied hatred.

It stopped pushing and thrashed backward suddenly to break free.

Tris held fast and forgot everything—the world, the night, his life. He heard voices shouting, but they were so far away. Then any scant light in the darkness beyond the spirit vanished as something blacker than night appeared.

Tris held on as the blackness beyond his adversary began to turn . . . to swirl.

Mari ran out of the stable, looked both ways, and spotted Tris beyond— *through*—the ghost. Again, he'd somehow gripped a spirit as if it had flesh, though it still glimmered, transparent enough to see how close it was to his face.

Between him and her, night air grew darker, began turning and rippling inward, like thinned black ink dripped into a whirlpool's edge. It spun inward toward the center, until that whirl in the air began to blacken, shadowing Tris and the ghost.

Mari barely remembered what she'd seen the night he'd banished Brianne's spirit, but she saw everything this time. Would he finally expose himself for what he had to be? Would those other spirits, those wisps that killed her family, appear again?

Would he become the black thing again?

"By the gods!" someone exhaled.

Mari twisted, ready to lunge.

Stàsiuo and several guards came trotting toward her, though all eyes looked beyond her. Lavich was among them, and Farrell. Had they heard the screaming?

The captain's mouth hung half-open at what he saw, expression shifting between disbelief and something like revulsion. When Mari turned back, Tris was farther away, driving the spirit ahead of himself. She heard someone behind her drawing steel.

That strangely panicked her.

These men couldn't do anything. She couldn't do anything. Instead, she ran toward the captain. Until it was over, she'd let no one get in the way.

Tris's strength drained as he fought to push the spirit toward the portal. He had expected a difficult battle, but why was this one so much harder to banish than others? Behind it, the night swirled around a spot so dark he saw nothing within it. And then came the whispers.

... *my Tris . . . me Tris . . . I Tris . . . not you . . . Tris . . .*

Fear twisted the dead refugee's white features. It screeched and thrashed, wrenched its wrist free, and slashed at Tris's face. He ducked his head aside, still gripping its neck with one hand. On its backswing he caught its forearm and shoved with both legs.

The spirit inched closer to the portal but not close enough. Fear mounted in its eyes, though it quickly fed into rage on that elongated face, more so as the whispers came again out of the portal behind it.

... *I Tris . . . not you . . . Tris . . .*

"No!" Mari shouted.

Not knowing if she wanted Tris to succeed or just to finally expose what he was, Mari stepped into Stàsiuo's path as she reached for her dagger's hilt.

"Move, woman!" he barked at her.

Farrell lunged in on the captain's right. "Please, Miss Mari, get behind us."

"Get back, both of you!" she warned, drawing the dagger in a backstep. "You can't help—if you tried, you'd end up dead. Or worse, you'd finish *him*."

Stàsiuo's eyes shifted once, looking beyond her.

"It's already gotten to Bródy," Mari added.

The captain's gaze returned to her. "What?"

"*He* is the only one who can touch it," she said, pulling her dagger. "Stay out of the way—understand?"

The captain still stalled, and she took a quick glance back toward Tris. She saw only his feet, for the rest of him was blocked by that whirling mass of darkness. But she heard his harsh breaths in the dark, gasping and straining.

Farrell took a step.

Mari flashed her blade at his face.

Tris's strength began to falter.

Why was it so difficult this time?

Perhaps because of that other *him*? The time of its next true appearance—by Heil's calculations—was nearing.

Tris fought on with sheer determination. This thing in his grip did not belong in the world of the living. Perhaps he did not belong here either.

He forgot all this, looked to the spirit, through it into that whirling black void.

Then he shoved with all he had left.

As always, he neither heard nor felt anything. He did not even know he had advanced far enough until the spirit went into a frenzy, clawing at him more wildly.

It began to shred apart.

The whirling darkness beyond it appeared to spread all around.

After so many times, Tris knew he was within a breath and a hairbreadth of the end. More and more of the spirit unraveled, until even the wrist and neck he held came apart in his grips.

He saw its long face begin to break up. He felt an instant of relief as exhaustion took him.

A black hand shot out through the spirit's distended mouth.

Tris lurched back as his throat closed up, choking off his breath. The spirit's last shreds ripped apart in the vortex of darkness—around black fingers clutching and clawing at air.

. . . my Tris . . . not you . . . Tris . . .

Tris stumbled, tripped, and fell, rolling away and up again on one knee. He clamped his hands over his ears. That did not stop the whispers coming out of the void.

. . . my Tris . . . me Tris . . . my life . . . not yours . . .

Always before, the other him had simply appeared. No part of it had ever come out of the portal. It had never touched him. It was growing stronger.

Still on his knees, Tris shut his eyes, focusing on closing the portal. This time, he did not watch as the void twisted inward and drained out of the night.

"Tris? Tris!"

Mari stood over him, watched him flinch as his eyes opened. When he looked up, for an instant it seemed like he didn't recognize her. Then the others came rushing in around her and him.

He'd done it again. This time she'd seen him do it—for the most part. The ghost was gone somehow, and when that black whirlpool drained away, there he was, only him. Down on one knee, he'd had his hands over his ears and his eyes crushed shut, as if shutting out some noise she hadn't heard.

What had happened while she couldn't see him through that spinning blackness?

He'd vanquished a murdering ghost and hadn't called for any help. So what was wrong with him? She couldn't bring herself to touch him, to help him up, but now he was panting.

Was that from effort or something else?

Mari crouched down. "Stop fighting for air," she ordered, and then softer, "Just breathe . . . breathe."

Stàsiuo was towering over her. She glanced up to see his face was drawn and pale.

"It *was* a spirit, a ghost," he half whispered, and then nearly shouted, "I saw it!"

Mari bit down her first words, and instead answered, "Yes, and it's gone now, for good."

"Where?" Farrell asked. "It was there before that black whirl came and then . . . what did he do and how?"

Mari couldn't answer that. She had no idea how Tris did what he did any more than why he could. Still on the ground, he hadn't said a word. Someone's steps pulled her attention up and over.

The guard with the shaved head from inside the cell stepped out of the stable's back door.

"Captain," he said quietly. "You'd better come. It's Bródy."

Stàsiuo hesitated only an instant, and with one more glance down at Tris, he went off to follow that guard into the stable's back side.

Mari hovered beside Tris, trying to decide what to do next. She finally stood straight, for he still wouldn't look at her.

"Farrell, stay with him, in case he needs something," she said. "I'll be back."

Mari walked off with one more look back at Tris. He was still completely withdrawn. She hadn't seen how things had happened with

Brianne, and so she didn't know if this change in him was just the way he normally reacted after banishing a spirit.

What was it like to grapple the dead to a second death?

She wasn't going to get that from him, not now, so she wanted to see what the captain found inside. When she reached that first area with the desk, the head-shaved guard had brought a lantern from somewhere. Maybe it had been in the cell, and the ghost-light had overwhelmed that other light.

Stàsiuo stood in the opened cell door, and Mari stepped close on his right to peek in.

Sabine knelt on the floor with the iron key ring beside her. She looked almost as pale as that ghost but broken, sickly. She stared at the back wall rather than the body, whispering over and over, "It's all right, my love. I'm here. I'm here now."

Bródy's body lay in front of her.

His skin looked stretched over his face. His arms were sticklike and shriveled. Eyes and mouth were locked open, as if in a scream. His expression was frozen in an instant of last horror.

Stàsiuo just stood there looking down at the body, as did Mari.

Not long after, Mari settled Tris by the fire in the common room's hearth. Not that she'd had to do more than push him the other way when he'd tried to go for their room instead. She knew—guessed—he'd prefer privacy, to lie on the bed even with her present and sink into himself.

She wasn't going to let him do that. After what he'd been through tonight in the cold, he needed heat. So did she, and there was no heat source in their room.

After so many years hunting her prey, she'd finally, clearly seen what she knew Tris could do. He had power over spirits of the dead, even to send them to a second death. He was what she'd expected—hunted—but the look of him now brought back doubts that made no sense.

Mari's head began to ache under the strain.

Farrell stepped near and leaned down. "What can I do for him?"

He'd apparently forgiven her for slashing her blade in front of his face.

"Get him some tea?" she asked.

"Yes . . . yes, of course."

He went off in a hurry.

A dozen or more refugees were still in the common room, sitting about the tables, sipping drinks or pulling apart bread to soak in late-night soup. Some—most—looked over at her or just at Tris. By now, they might've heard second- or thirdhand about what'd happened. She could see fear in their eyes, though after what they'd been through, it was a lesser fear.

Mari turned back to Tris. A few more guards entered, maybe whispered something she didn't bother to hear, and went to a table. The portly cook carried in a tray with mugs and a pitcher. After he'd set those down, one of the men began to pour dark ale.

Tris ignored everything, and Mari's agitation only grew.

She'd seen him this time—or partly—though no other white wisps had appeared. His face was nearly that pale, and in the darkness, he'd looked darker than night, maybe as black as that swirl in the air that'd hidden him in the last of it.

Was he really the one, or was she wrong?

Quick, heavy steps sounded as the captain entered through the front door and went straight to the table with the other guards to pour himself an ale. He took two large swallows, and all his men looked between him and Tris.

One guard Mari didn't know walked toward her.

"Farrell says there's a spirit among us . . . or was," he started. "Says it's what killed the colonel and the others. Is that true?"

Mari never had a chance to answer.

"Attention, and listen up," Stàsiuo said loudly, looking about the room with the mug still in hand. "The killer among us was a spirit, and it took Bródy this night."

Everyone probably already knew that by now, but the room went silent except for the captain.

"His death will be the last," Stàsiuo continued, and then he motioned to Tris. "Our visiting lord took care of that. For any who doubt it, some of us bore witness, including myself."

Mari felt suddenly self-conscious, for not every peek, glance, or stare throughout the room was aimed at only Tris.

"I am correct, am I not?" Stàsiuo asked, this time in Stravinan, before turning his gaze on Tris's back.

For a moment, Tris didn't answer, didn't even appear to have heard.

"Yes," he said finally, eyes still fixed on the hearth's flames. "As you have said."

The captain addressed the room again, attempting a wry smile. "We're safe once more, at least from murderous ghosts. Of course there are still Warlands soldiers, smugglers, bandits in the crags and hills . . . and the sharp tongues of your wives."

The attempt at humor surprised Mari. But he knew his men better than she did. Farrell returned with a cup of tea, almost offered it to Tris, but appeared to think better and handed it to Mari.

Farrell raised his own mug. "To our lord, the Dead's Man."

Tris flinched slightly. Why would such praise bother him? She knew how it might've bothered her, but not him.

Many guards in the room raised a mug and repeated Farrell's words, though none among the refugees.

Long past the mid of night, Mari lay awake in her bunk, unable to sleep.

Part of this was probably due to having slept through the afternoon, but even so, she was weary after the events of tonight and longed for the oblivion of sleep. Her mind would not stop turning.

Now what?

Tris had rid this place of its unnatural plague, and in all likelihood, he would pack up and start back for home tomorrow, if he had enough strength back. Where did that leave her? She could hardly go with him, and yet her questions were still unanswered. She was still torn in indecision over whether he was the one she sought, whether he was the one to suffer from her revenge.

Turning her head, she let a bit of her other form rise up, enough that she could see his outline. He was lost in deep sleep. She could tell by the rhythm of his breathing. In the night, he did look like a dark silhouette stretched out there.

She almost envied his exhaustion. Closing her eyes, she tried to force herself to sleep.

A scream rang out, loud and filled with chilling terror. Another followed, this one from a different voice.

Without thinking, Mari sprang from her bed and ran out the door of the room. Shouts, cries, and screams exploded in the night, but she saw nothing. The door to the first bunk room smashed open, and several guards came running out. She ran past them, to the doorway, and absorbed the scene before her. Her heart slowed.

Other guards remained, and a few had drawn swords, swinging at white visages in the air.

There were four spirits in the room, floating over bunks, whooshing up the center, or pursuing fleeing men. The ghosts were all stark white and transparent, but their forms were crystal clear. They appeared half-starved, and wearing tattered clothing . . .

A man with a jagged hole in his back.

A woman with a bashed-in skull.

A boy and a girl with broken bones and covered in wounds on their heads and backs as if they'd been trampled by horses.

Guardsman Lavich was on the floor, on his knees, gagging.

The ghost of the little girl floated down directly in front of him. With a cold smile, she drove her hand through his throat, and he screamed.

Mari's mind went back to that night when her parents died. She could not stop seeing white forms flitting about, driving their hands and limbs through the living, causing them agony.

Suddenly she felt herself jerked out of the way.

Before she could strike out at whoever had grabbed her, she realized it was Tris. He looked into the bunk room, and all four spirits turned to see him.

The woman with the head wound was nearest to him, and he rushed for her, but she was halfway inside the room, and she vanished before he reached her. The man vanished, and then the boy.

The little girl was still near Lavich by the far door.

Before vanishing, she offered the same cold smile to Tris. Then she was gone.

Captain Stàsiuo came running in the far door, looking down at Lavich, whose features were twisted in pain as he gagged.

"What in the name of the gods . . . ?" Stàsiuo began.

Mari shuddered. "There is more than one."

Tris was numb.

He watched Mari try to assist as Lavich was carried out of the bunk room. The man was still alive, but his skin was beginning to stretch, and his body mass was beginning to shrink. He groaned and choked as if trying to breathe.

Mari's words kept echoing.

There is more than one.

Some of the guards were beginning to return, staring at him accusingly. He knew their blame wasn't fair, and yet he could not fault them.

Stàsiuo strode toward him through the bunks.

"You said we were safe!"

Tris had no response. He had rid the barracks of a vengeful spirit, only to learn there were more.

"I don't care who your father is," Stàsiuo went on. "Give me one reason not to throw you out tonight!"

"Because I am still the only one who can fight them," he answered quietly. But how was he to both lure and fight four in succession? He could not do this alone.

Coming to a decision, he looked to Stàsiuo, and said, "I will require assistance, and I need to send for someone. I have a few ideas how to protect your men at risk until help arrives."

The anger slowly drained from Stàsiuo's face, replaced by sorrow and resignation. Tris may have failed him, but he was well aware that he was the captain's only option.

"What do you need from me?" Stàsiuo asked.

"I'll need paper, ink, and a quill. Then you'll need to assign your fastest rider to make a run to Strîbrov."

The captain took two long breaths and then nodded. "Come with me."

CHAPTER
TWELVE

Heilman "Heil" Tavakovich paced his apothecary shop at the far end of Stríbrov. It was a short pace at best. A few patrons had come by, more than usual for a small, out-of-the-way town hidden in the southwestern forests of Stravina. But a lack of distractions today still got to him.

Not that he wasn't usually annoyed about something.

He hated feeling—acting—like a mother hen. The peasant boy who'd come looking for the ex-baronet hadn't told a tall enough tale for him to tag along to another grimy village. Tris could handle that on his own.

It was just a ghost, for hell's sake, and Jesenik was only a three-day walk.

Now it was almost nine days since Tris had left, and the next appearance of his "shadow" wasn't that far off.

Heil cast about his outer shop, pacing along the sturdy back counter running the length of the place. The back wall was lined with shelves filled with clay pots, glass jars, and crocks, along with wooden boxes of herbs and roots. A wooden table in the corner was overloaded with ac-coutrements, a pestle and mortar, brass scales, marble bowls, tinder and flint with a brazier.

Oh, he was sick and tired of waiting to hear something!

Snatching up the flint and tinder, he went for the pocket hearth in the south wall, started to set a fire, and then just gave up. There were a number of things he *could* work on, but it was too early to sneak off to his sanctum beneath the building.

Any alchemist who'd lived as long as he had always had something "cooking," but he was somewhat bored with all of that. Perhaps he should work on something else. Heading behind the counter, he lifted out a supply of honey and a large urn filled with rose petals, both delivered yesterday. The next batch of cough syrup was past due, and he had to keep up appearances, regardless that no one took notice that any apoth-ecary in this town wouldn't make enough profit for what he offered in remedies.

One more tedious task in another tedious day.

Maybe a bit of simple ghost hunting would've been better.

He went back to set the fire, and once that was proper, he boiled water and poured it into the urn of rose petals. Then he endured more waiting as it steeped. He would drain it, boil it, drain it, boil it . . .

Gods' guts, could life get any more boring than this?

By nightfall, the water would be saturated with the properties of the petals, and then he'd mix in the honey along with some lesser-known ingredients. The result was a good tonic for a cough. In fact, it was the best in the region. Villagers came for it from as far as they could walk.

He hung an iron kettle on a blackened iron hook-arm and swung that in over the hearth's flame. Then he just stood there—again—looking about the shop. This was the only place he'd ever called home, ever felt at home. He'd inherited it from a man who was not his father, and someday, he'd leave it likewise to Tris.

And now, thinking on this, his mind wandered back along the way that brought him here . . .

Heil's mother, Gabrielle Tavakovich, had been the daughter of a wealthy wool merchant. They'd lived a fine life in a fine, three-story stone manor near Enêmûsk in Droevinka along with a small squad of servants. Though Gabrielle was the third daughter, she was the most beautiful, and her father expected a great marriage for her, perhaps connecting the family to nobility.

Her sisters were obviously jealous—and cruel—because of this. Or at least, that was what Heil remembered of the tale.

When all three sisters were still young, an elderly Móndyalítko woman, who'd lost the lust of wandering, settled with the family to watch over the children. She'd had a great influence on Heil's mother.

At seventeen, Gabrielle met a handsome but penniless man. For love of him, everyone else vanished for her. The man presented his case to her father, claiming he was eager to better himself. If allowed to marry Gabrielle, he would gladly work in the family wool business.

At first, her father refused, calling this suitor a shiftless mountebank, but Gabrielle begged and pleaded. When her father wouldn't relent, she refused to eat until he did. And of course, he gave in.

"You will weep bitter tears over this man," her father warned. "He is a trickster and will abandon you once he has what he wants."

Gabrielle was too happy to listen. A large dowry had been placed aside for her wedding day. For a few moons after that day, she was gloriously happy. Then her new husband announced that the wool business wasn't for him. Investing in wine was more appealing and profitable. He wanted to travel to Stravina with her dowry to buy partnership in a vineyard.

"And I'll come back for you," he promised.

As his wife, Gabrielle had little say in the matter but insisted on accompanying him. Something about being left behind frightened her. When they reached the first small town in Stravina, he lodged her at an inn, took the dowry, and left to go purchase his partnership, saying he would be back before dinner.

She never saw him again.

Though she had not told him, Gabrielle was with child. She had chosen to wait and surprise him when he returned.

She couldn't bring herself to go back to her family. For she was proud, and her father's taunts still rang in her ears. Nothing could have induced her to crawl home to him, abandoned and pregnant, and let him crow over her foolish choice. No man of wealth or position would have her now, and to go home would mean spending the rest of her life under her father's scorn—not to mention her sisters' triumph.

Again, this was the story Heil had been told, though she never told him his father's name. She used her own family name of Tavakovich.

She'd hidden a ruby necklace in her bags and sold this for a quarter of its value. Then she bought herself a shack on the edge of town—with a bit of coin left over. There were moons of weeping and tearing of clothing as she spent the last of the money, but during this time, she thought over and over of stories told her by the Móndyalítko woman who had looked after her as a girl.

These traveling women earned a living for themselves. She remembered the old woman grasping her hand as if reading the days ahead in her palm.

Gabrielle had no wish, or means, to travel, but she was lovely and charming and cultured. She spoke Belaskian with a Droevinkan accent, and this made her even more exotic. She set up shop in her shack as a "seer."

Of course she had no real gift for prophecy.

It was simply a matter of telling people what they wanted or needed to hear.

After a few moons, villagers came from as far as ten leagues to visit—and to pay—for the sight of the "seer" called simply "Gabrielle."

And then Heil was born, and his mother had his keeping as well as her own.

This was the childhood that Heil knew, watching from behind a curtain as his mother touched people's hands, spun tales of their aching dreams, and finally took their coins. She told him the story of her life over and over, of the beautiful home of her youth, of her heartless father and jealous sisters, and the one man she'd ever loved and let betray her.

As a child, he believed every word.

She'd been wronged by so many that he forgave her every sharp word, calling him her "burden" when at her worst, or forgetting to feed him when she sank into past sorrows. He loved her no matter all of this, in the beginning.

By the time he was eleven, he began to see her more clearly.

She was still astonishingly beautiful with smooth skin, green eyes, and long, thick blond hair. She was also selfish, saw herself as the victim in all things, and never wondered at the part she may have played in her own fate. She spoke several languages, and he learned Droevinkan in multiple dialects as well as the "old" Stravinan of the noble classes.

About this time in Heil's life, suddenly fewer and fewer people began coming to see her. He was never certain why. Maybe her novelty had worn off after a decade. No one came looking for an exotic blond "seer" anymore. So she started looking for ways to enhance her allure and her perceived abilities.

The Móndyalítko woman of her youth had told her of enchanted objects.

Gabrielle bought a donkey and hauled Heil off on a journey. At first, he had no idea what they were doing, but it was still an adventure waiting to happen. Upon reaching a town in northern Belaski, she took him to a small house in the middle of the night.

"A woman here possesses a velvet choker with a stone that allows her to speak in other voices, both male and female."

At eleven years old, Heil had no idea where she'd learned of such a thing or why she told him.

"You must crawl through that window and steal it," she said.

Frightened at the prospect, he found he couldn't refuse upon looking in her desperate eyes. His stomach knotted, but he still did as she asked. Once through the window, he sneaked past a sleeping elderly woman and began searching her home. It took a while to find the choker inside a wooden box in a big chest in a back room. As he'd never done anything like this before, he was in too much of a hurry and made noise getting back out of that house. By sheer luck, he wasn't caught.

"Oh, my darling," Mother whispered before kissing both of his cheeks. "How clever you are!"

He did not feel clever. He felt like a thief.

Upon returning home, his mother began using the choker. The number of voices that came out of her was astonishing, more so to those who believed she spoke for dead loved ones, ancient spirits with secrets, or even obscure oracles and demigods. More and more people heard the rumors; more and more coin was dropped in her palm. And over the

next two years, by the secrets she tricked out of others, she asked Heil
to repeat his thievery again and again.

Whenever she learned of some desirable object, another journey
would follow and another night of sneaking through a house or shop,
seeking her next obsession.

He came to hate his life even more each passing season.

When he was thirteen, she brought him to a small town called
Strîbrov in southwest Stravina. At its far end was a three-story building
with a shop on the main floor.

"Inside that shop is a crystal globe resting in an iron pedestal shaped
like a claw," she said. "Within the globe are mists that change colors by
the movement of a hand. A silly toy but can dazzle those who don't know
its truth."

Heil hesitated. Before now, most of what she had made him steal
came from those who had little chance to track what they had lost or
had other reasons not to report what was taken. This shop looked different, a respectable place, small as it was in this wilderness town. And
what his mother described sounded somewhat valuable unto itself and
not just for what she could do with it.

"What are you waiting for?" she asked. "Go on! Find a way in."

Stealing for her was all he had to contribute to their lives, and experience had made him much better at it. She'd even purchased a small
set of lockpicks for him. He never asked her where she'd bought them,
but he'd learned to use them.

After sneaking around back, he picked the back door's lock, and
crept inside.

He made his way down a dark, narrow passage through the building
and rightward toward a curtained entrance that led into the shop. Once

he'd brushed past the curtain, he could see better as front windows allowed light to stream in from street lanterns outside.

Jars, urns, bottles, pestles and mortars, brass scales, and wooden bowls were everywhere. What kind of shop was this? Then he spotted a small table near the back, and sitting atop it, in plain sight, was a clear globe in an iron claw stand.

Crossing over to see it more closely, he knew he should grab it and run, but he hesitated. This was too easy.

The globe was about the size of his two fists. The iron claw stand was elegantly crafted. Remembering what his mother had said about the globe, he waved a hand before and over it. Nothing happened.

"It will not work for you, young thief," said a calm voice. "So there is no point in taking it."

Heil whirled around, ready to run, but a man about fifty years old stood before the curtained doorway. Short of stature with a slightly bulging belly and thinning hair, he was unimpressive overall, though he stood there, as if nothing were wrong.

Heil had not heard the shopkeeper enter, but Heil didn't run. Instead, he couldn't help blurting out, "Why won't it work?"

The man assessed him in mild surprise. "Most such creations function only for those who created them." He paused. "Care to see?"

Heil should've run—could have run—right past that older man. Instead, he nodded.

This brought a smile to the face of the pudgy man, who walked over, closed his eyes as he paused, and then waved a hand like a whip along one side of the globe. A glowing green mist appeared and roiled inside the crystal ball.

Heil drew in a breath.

The man passed his other hand over the ball's top, and a sapphire blue bled through the mists turning in the glass. Another wave of the first hand brought red and then yellow.

"What else does it do?" Heil asked, still watching the crystal globe. "Do?"

And then Heil looked. "I mean, why did you make it?"

The man smiled openly this time. "For the enjoyment of it. It does nothing more and it's harmless, so I leave it out in view to entertain visitors."

Suddenly Heil grew anxious and took a quick glance to see how he might get around and reach the curtained door. The front door was in sight toward the left corner of the shop, but that was probably locked.

"How does it work?" he asked as a possible distraction.

The man's smile faded.

Heil didn't like the way that man appeared to study him.

"Don't you believe in magic?" the shopkeeper asked flatly.

Heil stalled at this. Was that a real question to be answered?

"You made this?" he asked instead. "How?"

"That is a bit . . . complicated. Would you care to learn?"

Heil was suddenly desperate to know, but his mother was waiting outside in the dark.

"What is your name, boy?"

Heil hesitated, and then surprised himself by answering, "Heilman Tavakovich."

"I am Römhild." The man walked off to the front door and opened it. "Come and see me again, at a more appropriate time."

A strange, sad desperation took Heil in that moment. He knew he'd never see this Römhild again. But what else could he do? He eyed the curtain doorway, thinking to run off the way he'd sneaked in. Certainly, his mother had seen the front door open.

Römhild merely smiled with another wave of his hand and ushered

Heil out into the night. By the time Heil was halfway along the next building, his mother appeared.

"What are you doing?" she whispered. "Why the front door?" When she saw his empty hands, her expression hardened. "Where is it?"

How could he explain? She would never believe the globe would not work for her.

"I was caught," he answered.

She slapped him.

She'd never done that before.

But he barely thought on her harsh reaction. His thoughts were too busy with the globe itself, with Römhild, with the colored clouds inside the glass. And the longer this went on, the more unhappy he was in not knowing more about such things.

He felt trapped in his life. Sooner or later, someone would hear of a "seer" using a power—or an item—familiar to them or to someone they knew.

Ten days following the visit to Strîbrov, a knock came at the door of the little house Heil shared with his mother. She didn't get up, so he opened the door.

Römhild stood on the other side, tipped his felt cap, and nodded.

He carried the globe and claw pedestal in one hand, and his other hand held a small pouch.

"May I come in?" Römhild asked.

Trying to slow his breaths, Heil nodded. The shopkeeper entered and took off his cap. At the sounds, Heil's mother came into the front room. She stopped when she saw what their visitor carried in his hands.

"Have no fear," Römhild assured. "I came to see if we might strike a bargain."

Her gaze flitted to the globe. "What bargain?"

He set his burdens on the table out front that she used in serving her "clients" and held up the pouch.

"I will give you the globe and twenty silver pennies for the boy."

Her eyes narrowed and flew up to Römhild's face.

"As an apprentice," Römhild added quickly. "Though it's more usual for parents to purchase such and not the other way around. You can come see him as you wish, and I will train him to make such things as that."

He gestured to the globe, and the room appeared to spin before Heil's eyes, all around that globe so still and empty at the moment. He never heard nor remembered what was said next by anyone.

In the end, Römhild and not his mother asked, "What is your choice? To stay here or come with me?"

"I'll go with you," Heil answered instantly, but then he turned to his mother. "To learn, just to learn . . . more."

That would keep her satisfied that he hadn't abandoned her. It would leave her believing he might gain something more she could use. Of course, the globe would never work for her—which might be why Römhild also offered a sum of money.

She wanted both, but one was as good as the other to her.

How had Römhild known?

Before midday, Heil was packed and boarded the mule cart the elder shopkeeper had left outside. On the road with his new teacher, as they headed for his new home, it was a while before something more settled upon him.

He was finally free, at least a little, with more to come later.

Over the following years, in addition to learning the skills of an apothecary, came more precious secrets. He came to know the art, craft, and science of alchemy. In more years, he surpassed his beloved teacher, and Römhild found this joyful enough for outright laughter at any time.

As a young man, Heil embarked on some of his own adventures, but he never resided anywhere except the shop. He was always available when his mother came, though eventually she stopped coming when she found she couldn't get anything more from him. Upon Römhild's passing, he learned that the shop—the whole building and all within it—had been left to him.

Heil had never discovered where Römhild had come from, where he'd learned his alchemy, or if anyone else might come looking for his old master. Heil lived there alone in the shop until one night when he'd been called to a town named Ceskú and saw . . .

Fist pounding on the shop's front door broke Heil's reminiscing, and it didn't stop. The door sounded as if it might break inward. Someone was going to regret that. He strode over, jerked the door open, and—

He froze, as did the scowl on his face.

A disheveled soldier in a white tabard and padded armor stood before him. The man wore no helmet, and his hair stood up in the front as if it had been blown in the wind for days. He gripped one side of the doorframe as if needing support to stay on his feet.

Heil leaned aside and saw a sweat-frothed horse three strides off, its head down as it sucked air through its nostrils.

"Are you . . . Heilman . . . Tavakovich?" the soldier panted.

Now puzzled as well as irritated, Heil asked. "What of it?"

The soldier dug inside the wool shirt beneath his tabard and pulled out a folded paper and a small pouch, held out both.

Now what?

Heil grabbed both and snapped open the paper.

I am at the northern barracks of Soladran. This courier bears coin for you to change horses along the way. Bring the disk and the conch and stop for nothing.

—Tris

Heil read the short note again.

This raised even more questions than it answered and left him grinding his teeth. Brevity was a vice rather than a virtue with that brooding ex-baronet.

But Heil moved into action without delay. If Tris had gone so far as to send a Soladran guard with a message, he was in difficulty.

"Come in," he said, stepping aside. "There's a pitcher of water on the counter."

"I need to see to my horse," the guard said.

"In a moment. Let me fetch a few things, and I'll take you to the stable. I need to hire a horse for myself."

He did not stop moving as he spoke. Quickly, he packed a water flask and some food. Then he went to his room and packed the silver disk. Finally, he knelt and lifted a loose floorboard.

Carefully, he lifted out an object he kept hidden there: the brown and white striped conch of a sea snail. Tris had rarely asked him to use this particular weapon, as it was unpredictable and they had rarely needed it. Heil wrapped it in cloth and packed it.

After crouching there for a moment, he decided to pack one more object from among his alchemical possessions—just in case. This one was also wrapped in cloth. Without unwrapping it, he stowed it in his satchel.

Jogging back out, he found the soldier gulping water. The man had clearly ridden hard.

"Come," Heil said. "We'll settle your horse, and then I'll direct you to the inn before I ride out. You should eat supper and spend the night before starting back. I'll pay."

At first, he thought he might face an argument, but the man had done his duty. He'd gotten the message to Heil. With a weary nod, he followed.

Lying in a bunk, just before dawn, Tris was so tired it was difficult for him to think. Three days had passed since he had sent the note to Heil, and they had been a long three days . . . and nights.

Guardsman Lavich had died the morning after his attack. His body was skeletal.

Though Stàsiuo could barely bring himself to speak with Tris, they had managed to work together to a point. At Tris's suggestion, the captain changed the guard rotation. Any man who had ever by action or intentional inaction refused to assist one of the escaping refugees was pulled off night duty. These men were all packed into a single barracks room as soon as the sun set and remained until dawn broke. They even used chamber pots to relieve themselves, as they were not allowed to leave the bunk room.

Tris slept in there with them.

This was the only way he could think to protect them.

Mari slept on the bunk just above. He didn't like the idea of her staying in here with a pack of men, but it was better than the alternative. He could not leave her alone and unprotected in their room all night.

None of the men involved liked the arrangement. The bunk room was overcrowded, and it stank by morning. None of them wanted to be sleeping in the same room with the Dead's Man. These same men who had raised their ale mugs to him now blamed him for Lavich's death, almost as if he had brought the quartet of ghosts down upon them.

But neither did they protest his presence or his plan. In three nights, there had not been a single attack or a single death.

For Tris, this arrangement was torture, and spending every darkened hour in a room filled with people was beginning to take its toll. He was not sleeping, and in the wee hours, he'd begun counting the moments until dawn.

This morning was no different, but today, at least he could feel a glimmer of hope. If the rider Stàsiuo had sent was as fast as his reputation, he could have made the run to Stríbrov in a day and a half. For an aging man, Heil was skilled on a horse, and he could make it back in almost equal time.

Barring anything unforeseen, he would arrive before darkness fell again.

To Tris's relief, dawn broke with a hint of light coming through the window.

Above, he heard Mari stirring and knew she was awake as well, but she did not speak to him yet.

Rising, he sat up in his bunk and saw movement across from him. Guardsman Kreenan sat up as well. On the first night, Tris had been surprised to see him among the men chosen for this curfew. Kreenan had not struck him as the type of man who would side with the colonel in regard to the refugees.

Kreenan's eyes were bleak. Perhaps he had not slept either.

"What is your duty assignment today?" Tris asked quietly.

"I'm on the front gate."

The thought of the front gate brought Tris another hint of hope. "Keep your eyes out for a man with longish silver hair and a silver ring in his ear. His name is Heilman Tavakovich."

Kreenan nodded but did not appear to be truly listening.

A part of Tris wanted to offer a word of reassurance, but he didn't know how. His own task took up all his efforts. He needed to make sure there were no more killings before help arrived.

Then he would make sure those four spirits died forever.

Heil approached Soladran's front gate in the midafternoon. He stopped urging his horse, and the beast slowed in exhaustion. It was the third horse he'd worn out in a night and more than half a day.

Tris hadn't ever sent for him while on the hunt, not even once.

Ahead, guards framing the great stone gate didn't stop or question anyone. All wore the same white tabards and padded armor as the messenger who'd come to Stríbrov, but these also wore fur-trimmed helmets. There was something odd about the way they eyed all comers and goers, but more so the road and land all around, as if they were watching for something.

Soladran was a vast, walled city, home to thousands, and he'd visited it only a few times in his life. Whatever was happening here, he didn't like not knowing.

He had a few choice words for Tris about that short, cryptic note.

Reaching the arch, he dismounted, approached a guardsman to ask the quickest way to the northern barracks.

"Sir?" someone called.

Heil frowned to see another guardsman hurrying toward him. It was a young man with a brown ponytail hanging over his left shoulder from out of his helmet.

"Are you Master Tavakovich?" the guard asked. There were dark circles under his eyes.

Heil was exhausted and impatient. "Who's asking and why?"

The guard appeared to take that as a yes and exhaled in relief. He called over one shoulder. "Jacques! Take my place." Then he turned back to Heil. "Sir, I'll bring you to the barracks. The Dead's . . . Baronet Vishal is waiting for you. Please come with me."

Heil grumbled under his breath; Tris hated that title, but it obviously had its uses.

"All right, lead on."

Mari stood outside the common room on the frozen ground, leaning back against the worn doorframe and watching Tris pace before the barracks. At every turn back the other way, he peered toward the court-yard's entrance. The last three days had been tough on him, but they had also been hard on her.

They were stuck, unable to do anything, until Tris's "landlord" arrived. Or that was all that he'd told her. She was curious. Learning whoever this Heil Tavakovich was, and whatever he could do to help, might also offer Mari another way to track the truth about the Dead's Man.

Tris never talked much about anyone in his life except Heil. Apparently, this person had concocted the powder Tris had stuck in her mouth back in Jesenik.

But Tris had barely spoken at all these past three days. He hardly ate and spent the long nights in that bunk room, which meant she had to as well. She hadn't slept much in keeping an eye on him; she did sleep sometimes, but she wasn't sure he ever did.

Why did she worry about that?

The bunk room was the last place she'd wanted to be, after what she'd seen upon following a scream in that first night. The guards in there had drawn swords, swinging uselessly at white wisps flying at anything that moved.

All those ghosts looked half-starved and tattered, like the one he had dispatched earlier that first night. The cries in that near-dark room drove Mari back to where she started—frozen in fear, a little girl hiding in the Wicker Woods as she watched her family die.

And there was nothing she could do about it—not like *him*.

Everything he could do told her that he was the Dead's Man, the one she'd been hunting. But everything else about him . . .

She couldn't stop thinking about that night in the field, across the stream from the northern gate. He'd just sat there, alone in the dark, with a small knife in his hand.

Why'd he gone out there like that? If not to raise another host of spirits, then for what?

And now he just kept pacing.

"Stop, *please*," she whispered without thinking, like a child who'd suffered too long.

Tris stopped pacing and looked at her.

"What?" he said, just barely loud enough to hear. "What did you say?"

The air was cold and growing colder as the afternoon waned.

Mari couldn't stop anger from rising. "Will you stop this? Pacing out here won't bring him any faster. Get in by the fire, before you freeze us both!"

He didn't answer, frowned at her, and started pacing again.

She should have just gone in herself and left him to freeze, but she didn't. She couldn't let him out of her sight.

Tris stopped again.

"Finally," she sighed.

Straightening, he stood there and looked out into the city.

"What now?" she asked.

A door behind her opened.

When she turned, Stàsiuo stepped out—again—as he'd done throughout the day, more times than she'd counted, to ask her if Tris's "associate" had arrived yet. The last time, she'd simply jutted her chin toward Tris going back and forth in the courtyard.

Stàsiuo didn't ask anything this time when he spotted Tris hesitantly walking through the courtyard toward the city.

Mari stepped out halfway behind Tris. She easily recognized one of the two men coming toward them: Guardsman Kreenan. The other man led a sweating, almost staggering horse. She remembered him from the night she'd first reached Strîbrov.

He was maybe around fifty years, with long silver hair that framed his eyes of the same color above a stubbled long jaw and chin. Now and then, a thick silver ring in his left earlobe showed when his hair swung out of the way. He was dressed in canvas pants, a dark leather jerkin, and a cloak with the hood thrown back. The closer he came, the more speed he picked up as he walked straight to Tris.

Tris quick-stepped out of the gate to meet the older man.

"Heil," he breathed. "Finally."

Mari was taken aback by the relief in Tris's voice.

"Well, you look awful," Heil quipped back. "What have you been doing to yourself this time?"

The two men didn't shake hands, but the obvious connection between them left Mari feeling uncomfortable. For some reason, standing there beside the captain, she felt like an outsider watching Tris and Heil.

Kreenan approached the captain, looking hesitantly hopeful. Like everyone here lately, he stank of fear to Mari. Stàsiuo dismissed Kreenan and walked out toward Tris and the newcomer. Mari caught up.

As they approached, Heil looked their way.

He studied the captain first, briefly, before his gaze fixed on Mari. Her own steps faltered once when he frowned at her and she heard a sharp exhalation through his nose. His expression was intense, almost as if he recognized her.

Other than the night she'd seen him open the shop's door at the pounding of a peasant boy, she'd never met him.

"Captain Stàsiuo," Tris said, "this is Master Heilman Tavakovich. Perhaps we should retire to privacy before speaking further."

Mari glanced up and found Stàsiuo studying Heil.

"The common room is too busy now," Stàsiuo answered. "Follow me to my office. We can talk there."

It seemed Tris wasn't going to introduce Mari. She didn't do so for herself, especially not for the way Heil kept looking at her, narrow-eyed and almost suspicious—of what? She found herself liking him even less. He stepped up to walk with the captain as she followed beside Tris.

"Captain," Heil said, "perhaps you should excuse your girl."

"My girl?" Stàsiuo slowed in his steps. "She came with the baronet, as his translator."

Heil stopped completely, turned to fix on Mari, and snorted. "His translator?"

Mari flushed hot at that, clenching her jaws.

Heil's sharp eyes shifted away from her. "Tris?"

Tris shook his head. "Not here; in private."

Heil's frown turned to a scowl, and he assessed Mari again. Then he turned onward with the captain, and Mari followed, still watching his exposed back.

Maybe this older man wasn't a soft way to learn more about Tris.

CHAPTER
THIRTEEN

Not long after, Tris stood in the captain's small, sparse office, too relieved by Heil's arrival to be embarrassed. All that bothered him now was that the elder alchemist seemed irritated—possibly concerned—by Mari's presence. In turn, she watched him with puzzling intensity. What was her sudden interest in him?

When Heil asked about her again in a hushed voice, Tris only whispered, "Not now."

That did not please Heil, and Tris had no intention of explaining later. What could he possibly explain?

Stàsiuo closed the office door, and Mari shifted uncomfortably in the tight space. She continued watching Heil.

Tris did not care for the close quarters either, but important issues needed to be addressed if anyone in the barracks was to survive another attack. And he had not forgotten that black hand coming at his throat several nights before.

Thankfully, as all four people in this room could speak Old Stravinan, this spared Tris another of Heil's dry comments over his "inadequacies."

"So, what are we dealing with?" Heil asked as the captain settled behind his small desk.

Tris began recounting deaths and causes, starting with what had been learned of events before arriving at the barracks. With several interruptions by the captain, he explained Mari and Bródy's first sighting, the conflict at the stream, the initial trap, the vanquishing, and Bródy's death. He ended with the final attack by the four spirits in the bunk room.

He did not mention his own flight from the city and the night he spent across the stream, alone in the field.

Stàsiuo braced both elbows on the desktop. "What's next?"

Tris hesitated, as he had been thinking this same question.

"Four ghosts, all at once?" Heil whispered, stalling Tris again. "Makes me wonder about a vengeance in common."

Heil would know there was more that Tris had not mentioned. He also knew that the next scheduled appearance of Tris's other half was not far off.

"Have you ever dealt with so many at the same time?" the captain asked.

Yes, such as on the night Tris had first met Heil, but this was different.

Had Black Tris found a way to gather and command spirits from beyond the living world?

"It can be done," Heil answered the captain.

"Did you bring the disk and the conch?" Tris asked without thinking—and regretted this.

This slip earned him an angry glance. Heil disliked such mentions in front of outsiders about his pursuits in alchemy or artificing.

"Of course," Heil growled at him.

Captain Stàsiuo's focus shifted between them. "What disk? What conch?"

At this, Tris balked, wondering how much to say, but to make proper arrangements, they would need the captain, and therefore, he would need to understand the details of any plan.

"This disk can ward off a spirit," Tris answered. "Sometimes disperse it temporarily. If we are dealing with four that might appear together, I can banish only one at a time."

At this, Tris stopped and waited. Heil's jaw muscles clenched.

"Where is it?" the captain asked.

With no choice, Heil knelt to dig in his pack. He withdrew the flat disk resembling a plate with strange, engraved markings lining its outer edge. This diverted both Mari and the captain. Heil still hesitated in placing the disk on the forward edge of the captain's desk.

"And the conch," Tris said. "They will see it soon enough anyway."

Glowering, Heil reached back into the pack and withdrew an object wrapped in cloth. This device was harder to explain. Heil unwrapped it carefully, exposing the brown and white striped shell.

It was an experiment gone wrong.

Before meeting Tris, Heil had created objects to drive off spirits, though he could not truly banish them, as Tris did. Desperation and obsession seeded the idea of a way to trap the essence of a ghost within a natural substance, thereby to use its properties against others of its kind. And an object that could transmit energies trapped within it might be a more active repellent against other spirits.

Spirits did not normally group together.

Heil chose the conch of a sea snail as the vessel. It was now etched with tiny symbols and coated in a concoction that kept the material's original glossy sheen. The spiral cone's tip had been ground off, allowing one to blow into it like a horn.

Then it had to be tested.

Hearing of parents plagued by their daughter's dead spirit, Heil traveled to their village. The girl had been a singer in life, performing for nearby nobles and gentry to earn a living with her voice. But when ample coin began to come her way, the parents limited her, also requiring charitable performances for the sick and the poor.

After one such event, she caught a fever and died within days.

A spiteful spirit rose the following night, seeking vengeance upon the parents.

When Heil faced her in the family's home, he had brought both disk and conch. He did not tell the parents all that he intended. Using the disk, he taunted the daughter's spirit by dashing about, flashing the disk before her and not allowing her to leave. He had been younger and faster then, and whipped up her anger. In her fury, she rushed him.

He dropped the disk and held out the conch.

She passed through the shell and his right arm, shrieking as he cried out in pain, and then she vanished.

If not for his mineral and herb concoctions—alchemical and otherwise—Heil would have died. It had still been a long recovery, though he thought it worthwhile. Part of the girl's spirit was forever trapped within the conch.

Only later, when he tried to use it, did he realize it did not work as planned. Upon attempting to repel another spirit, he'd blown long and hard into the shell, and a lovely sound came out, like a note of music hanging in the air. But as opposed to repelling the spirit, the sound had the opposite reaction and worked as a lure, calling the ghost directly to Heil.

He'd escaped only by dropping the shell and grabbing his disk.

After that, the conch had little use to Heil until he met Tris, and the two of them had used it a few times. The results could be unpredictable, though. Sometimes the shell worked. Sometimes it didn't. Once, it had called more than one spirit, and the result caught Tris off guard.

Tris normally preferred his own methods for setting traps. He preferred depending on his own abilities as opposed to Heil's devices.

Now, however, he needed to use everything at his disposal.

"What does it do?" Stàsiuo asked.

"By blowing into it," Tris answered simply, "Heil can call spirits. They are lured by the sound."

He decided this was enough of an explanation. It was time to make a plan.

Turning to Stàsiuo, he said, "This disk will help, but we'll need more. We'll need to set a trap, with bait, like before."

The captain's expression darkened. "Last time, the spirit didn't go for the bait you set. It went for Bródy."

"This time, we'll use several tactics, including gathering a number of the men you singled out as targets. I suggest we place them inside the stable. There is room in there, but it's a contained area."

"And how will you protect them from four spirits?" Stàsiuo challenged.

This was a fair question, and Tris looked to Heil. "I'm thinking once we gather the men inside the stable, I'll hide myself and you call for the spirits. When they come, I'll call up the portal and vanquish one of them as quickly as I can and go for another. My hope is that once they have arrived, the men they seek to punish will work as a temptation and so will the conch if you continue to use it. If a spirit tries to flee or kill one of the guards, you can use the disk to deter it."

Mari was listening closely, and she looked to Stàsiuo. "In a true pinch, Tris can punch through a ghost and shatter it as well. I've seen him do it. It doesn't vanquish the spirit, but it works in the short term."

Heil stiffened, and his consternation grew.

"I'd rather not," Tris said to Mari. "I want to keep their manifestations whole long enough for me to send as many as possible through the portal."

"Can you do that?" she asked. "Banish more than one in a night? I mean . . . just taking out one of them seems to make you so tired. You can barely walk afterward."

Heil's expression shifted to alarm. "How long have you two been—?"

Tris waved him off. "Not now."

Stàsiuo was watching and listening. "Most of this makes sense to me, or as much sense as all this madness can make, but I don't see how one element is going to work."

"Which one?" Tris asked.

"If your friend here, Heilman, is manning the conch, using it to continue calling the spirits, how will he be able to dodge around with the disk at the same time?"

Tris tensed, running this scenario through his mind and realizing the captain had a point.

"I can use the disk," Mari said quietly.

"No!" Tris answered without thinking. There would be too much risk of a ghost flying through her. In truth, he didn't even want her in the stable. He wouldn't be able to protect her.

"It should be me," she insisted. "Using the disk will take speed. I'm fastest, and you know it."

Heil said nothing, but by the expression on his face, he was wildly searching for other options and failing.

"Will the disk function for her," Tris asked him, "even though you created it?"

Heil was silent for a long moment, and Tris feared he might not even answer. Then with an angry nod he said without commitment, "It works for any user."

"I'm risking my men," Stàsiuo said. "Is Mari as fast as she claims?"

"Yes," Tris answered tightly.

"Then she's right. It should be her."

"Settled, then," Mari said. She looked to Stàsiuo. "I won't let your men be hurt."

Tris struggled for an argument and found none. If they wanted the captain's agreement, Mari would be the one using the disk.

Then Tris closed his eyes. In a short while, he'd be doing battle on a scale he'd never tried before. He couldn't let anything interfere with his focus. He would have to trust Heil and Mari—even if they clearly did not trust each other.

Opening his eyes, he spoke to the captain. "All right. You decide which men to send, or let them volunteer. I'd like at least four. That will offer enough targets without giving us too many to protect. Have them gather in the stable after supper."

In resignation, Stàsiuo sagged and put one hand on the desk. "I'll ask them now. Volunteers would be better."

Straightening, he walked out the door. Mari followed, and Tris walked a few paces after her.

A few steps out, Heil caught up to him and touched his arm. "Wait! Tris . . . who is this girl?"

Tris could not explain Mari's presence here, nor why he allowed her to remain with him, not even to Heil.

"Leave it," he said, walking away.

That night's dinner was quiet and somber, not that Mari had much appetite anyway. Whatever was going to happen tonight, too much of it seemed to depend on Heil. He was not exactly the right kind of companion or friend for Tris, though she'd never thought about this before.

Until now, she'd not given thought to how anyone who knew Tris would view her connection to him. Not that it mattered.

How much influence did this Heil have over *him*?

Could the old man talk Tris into sending her away? Or into sneaking away without a word to her? That wouldn't have worked, but still, it was risky, an extra snarl in all this mess.

She couldn't sit still any longer.

Leaving Tris—and Heil—at a table, she went to the hearth, where most of the refugees sat to eat. From what she understood, Stàsiuo hadn't mentioned anything or insisted they leave. A few days of food and warmth had done them good.

She crouched by the young woman who had lost someone named Tichen. The woman's sling was gone, and her arm seemed better. She also appeared to have taken on the boy Mari saved, and was feeding him dinner. Mari didn't know either of their names.

"How are you?" she asked.

The woman was a little wary. Maybe that was just the life she'd lived and had nothing to do with Mari, herself.

"Well enough, I think," the woman answered. "I found some scullery work at a nearby public house. There's a small room for me, for us." She looked at the boy. "It'll be warm enough, near the kitchen, and I can keep an eye on him, even when working."

Mari wasn't certain what to say. "Sounds good . . . a good start."

While struggling to find something else to say, she spotted Tris getting up to leave, though Heil didn't follow him.

"I'll look for you again later," she told the woman, and hurried off.

Down the short entryway, Tris stepped out the barracks front door.

Mari followed. He wasn't dressed for the cold—no cloak—and he was heading for the stable. She caught up quickly, making enough noise that she didn't startle him once she did.

He looked back upon hearing her.

"Your friend doesn't like me," she said.

"He does not know you," Tris answered, stepping onward as if that ended the matter.

Mari couldn't help thinking, *Neither do you*, and wouldn't let it go.

"He doesn't trust me. I can see it in his face."

At this, Tris stopped again near the stable's front bay doors.

"Heil always enjoys the company of women," Tris said.

Mari snorted. He was obviously trying to avoid the reason for Heil's dislike for her.

"But he is mistrustful of strangers," Tris went on, "and by his own experiences, something in his past, I think, he seems to find women to be . . . self-serving."

Mari raised an eyebrow. "I'd say the same about him."

"You do not know him, any more than he knows you."

"You don't know me either."

After this, Tris was quiet so long that she started to regret her words. Had she just given herself away? Why had she said that?

"No, I suppose I do not," he answered softly. "But I saw you rush into that stream to help those trying to cross the border. I know you a little."

She stood there with no idea what to say. Though shadowed from the full moon by the stable and the city wall, she could still see his eyes in the dark. They were nearly colorless in a face far paler than her dusky skin. He looked so helpless.

Mari pushed that thought away; he was far from helpless.

"Once this starts, what do I do?" she asked. "What's the best way to use the disk?"

In truth, she still didn't believe such an object could do what Tris claimed. She'd wanted only an excuse to be present at the banishing.

"Just do whatever Heil tells you, and if need be . . . use it to protect yourself first."

He started to raise a hand, slowly, maybe to reach for her for some reason. She inched back, half a step. Then he turned away and headed into the stable before she could say anything.

Tris went straight into the stable and toward its rear to get out of sight in one of the far stalls. All horses had been removed, and a few lanterns were already lit around the main space. He did not hear Mari's footfalls, though he had grown accustomed to this and knew she followed.

"Wait for the others," he said.

Not looking back, he slipped into the last empty stall, closed his eyes, and took several deep breaths. A moment alone was necessary to prepare for what would come. The truth was that he did not know if he could banish four spirits, one after another. And would one continuous portal give that other *him* a greater chance of stepping through?

It was a tenuous plan at best. All he could do was focus on catching a spirit and seizing the next—and the next—as quickly as possible. Hopefully, Heil could keep them contained and Mari would do as instructed in the moment. Hearing voices, he peered over the stall's gate and around it with one eye.

In the stable's open area, Mari had picked up one lantern on a crate. She strung it up on a center post to spread its light as the men began arriving. Guardsman Kreenan came first with three others. Tris knew them by sight if not name, for they had all spent the last three nights in the same bunk room. One of them was called Jacques.

All were volunteers from what Tris could guess, and none of them supposed cowards like Bródy. These few were willing to risk themselves to help rather than to leave him to deal with everything.

Heil entered last. He went straight at Mari, and their mutual dislike was obvious. She still listened intently to what he told her. Then the alchemist hesitantly held out the disk to Mari.

Tris clenched his hand on the top of the stall's gate.

By Heil's pointed gestures and expression, he was reluctant to let Mari handle his "spirit shield." Whether she could do so was another matter. Such devices were never simple to wield, regardless of assumptions. Using one—at all, let alone effectively—required more than simply knowing what it could do.

There was no other choice; Heil needed both hands to use the conch. Even then, he might be running and dodging for his life, if it even worked. Mari would have to handle the disk, at least until Heil could retrieve it and use it more effectively.

Tris wished all of this were otherwise. Sending her out of harm's way would have been better, for she had already done far more than should have been asked of her.

Now that everyone was gathered, he wanted this over and done.

Heil stepped back from Mari, looked about the stable, and, upon spotting Tris, nodded once. Then he crouched to dig in his pack.

As he rose, all others fixed on the conch he held. It was big enough to have filled a third of the pack, and it was unpredictable, but there was no other way to draw all the spirits in for Tris.

Heil stepped to the stable's center, lifted the conch's sheared end to his lips, and blew.

The sound from it was like nothing found in nature. Like a human voice pulled tight by sorrow, the long note from the shell carried pure and mournful into the rafters.

All four guards, and even Mari, backed away. None could take their eyes off Heil, as if waiting for that note to stop and another to begin.

The dead were not the only ones the conch could affect.

Mari blinked, shuddered, blinked again, and backed away as she looked about, finally raising the disk in her hands as if awaking to potential threat. The long note faded in echoes within the rafters, and Heil blew again.

The boy appeared first, translucent, white, and phosphorescent. One of his arms dangled as if broken and a crescent gash in his forehead looked as if it had come from a horse's shod hoof.

Mari retreated at first, as did the guards, though no one ran as yet. She then sidestepped toward Heil, never taking her eyes off the boy.

The girl materialized just above Heil.

Ghost-light increased subtly inside the stable. She would have been no more than ten or eleven when she died. Her left leg was crushed and twisted with its calf shredded off. She floated overhead, mesmerized as Heil blew again into the shell.

Both children, near Heil, were halfway between Tris and the stable's front doors—a good distance away from Tris. This was the risk in having to remain hidden until all the spirits gathered.

The woman appeared next. Half of her skull was caved in, and her head was crooked rightward on her neck. Mari spun toward her, startled, and held out the disk with both hands. Guards backed away in all directions, some reflexively reaching for swords.

The woman was closest to Tris, but he would still have to make a run to grasp her.

Then the man appeared about five paces from him. With that spirit's back turned, Tris could see the jagged hole between the man's shoulder blades. This spirit fixed upon Heil as a fourth tone bellowed from the conch.

Tris slammed the stall's gate open and charged. As the male spirit twisted toward him, he grabbed its upper arms. As always, his fingers sank in slightly at first, until his focus sharpened.

Cold crept into Tris.

The spirit pitched forward at him with an echoing shriek and began fighting and writhing to get free of a grip it had not expected. Tris held on as his feet slid.

Beyond the spirit of the male refugee, the stable began to darken, with light being sucked into a point hidden just beyond the ghost's back. All darkness there began to turn, sucking into a hole in the living world.

Mari bent at the knees, ready to act, when a stall's gate slammed open, and Tris rushed the ghost nearest to him. White sparks burned in his eyes again as he grabbed the ghost man. And the big seashell's tone came again. The other three spirits twisted away from Heil. Not a one seemed to hear that last tone.

The woman was distracted when she spotted Kreenan. Then the stable started to darken.

Mari saw something happening around the ghost Tris had grabbed, as if darkness was gathering. It was the same turning of the air that she'd seen when he'd gripped the ghost that killed Bródy. A screech in the stable felt like it was piercing her skull.

Mari spotted the girl ghost with the shredded leg. That smaller one swirled toward the stable's west wall. Shaken to awareness, Mari bolted past two shocked guards toward the west wall, not even knowing what she could do.

She didn't trust anything that old man told her.

But she wasn't letting Tris out of her sight.

And he was already tangled up with one ghost.

Mari neared the wall at a full run and shoved the disk out. Its metal scraped the wallboards. She felt splinters pierce the back of her hand as the disk slid in, right in front of the girl.

The girl struck the disk, face-first.

Mari felt a chill spread from the disk into her hand and down her arm. It took her breath away for an instant, but then it faded.

The girl ghost blew apart like a splash of flour in the air—and then re-collected into the small form again.

Even though she'd volunteered to do this, Mari was relieved, and shocked, the disk had worked.

The girl ghost shrieked in fear, fury, or both, and veered off, flying like a white wisp toward the boy. Heil's shell-horn sounded again, but as Mari cast about, the noise didn't seem to work this time.

The woman with the bashed head was still focused on Kreenan and dove at him.

Mari shook off fright and uncertainty and ran to get between them. If she lived through the night, having taken part in this would still be the stupidest thing she'd ever done.

Tris shoved with all his strength, and the spirit struggled to escape. It pitched forward into his face, thrashed, and heaved backward, trying to break his grips. He gained momentum in the last of its struggle and drove it toward the portal.

As all others before, the dead refugee's form began to shred as it touched that inky swirl in the air. Vaporous white pieces spun in that pitch-black whirlpool.

. . . my Tris . . . me Tris . . . I Tris . . . not you . . . Tris . . .

Tris panicked, released the ghost, and lurched back. For an instant, the refugee's ghost appeared to struggle out of the portal. And then it tore apart and whirled away to nothing. Tris stumbled, and then he saw Mari block the girl spirit with the disk to keep it from fleeing. As it coalesced, it raced off toward the boy.

Tris ran in, trying to catch the girl by her mangled leg.

Mari raced after the woman ghost. It veered toward Kreenan, who lurched back and away to the left. That was just what she needed.

As the woman ghost sailed toward Kreenan, Mari cut it off, thrusting out the disk. This spirit did not collide with the device, but veered away.

. . . my Tris . . . me Tris . . . I Tris . . . not you . . . Tris . . .

A voice echoed through the stable.

What did that mean?

Where had it come from?

Mari whirled around, searching for the woman's spirit.

And there was Tris, snatching the little girl by her mangled leg. Then Mari saw it clearly—that swirling black hole in the air—like the last time he'd banished a ghost. He pulled and wrenched the little glowing girl in the air, as if she were solid though floating.

More whispers tore at her ears to scratch in her head.

. . . my Tris . . . me Tris . . . my life . . . not yours . . .

Mari retreated a step—those whispers came from the portal. If it was always how he got rid of a ghost, then why hadn't she heard anything the last time he'd banished one?

Or hadn't it happened before?

What was in there?

All four of the guards were panicked. Two pressed against a stall gate, their eyes wide. Jacques ducked and scrambled behind Heil and the big shell. Kreenan's face was so pale, she'd have thought him dead on his feet, until he twisted about and looked toward the stable's far bay doors.

"Don't!" Mari shouted at him. "Don't run!"

Heil blew again into the conch, but she wasn't sure it had any effect now. A hollow shriek caused her to turn around.

Tris was dragging the girl toward the swirling black portal. The small spirit began to shred like threadbare cloth. Tris's features tightened in desperation around those pinprick glimmers of white in his eyes.

For an instant, the sight of this made Mari's stomach lurch.

The boy ghost stopped in the air above. Tris turned and saw it. The portal swirled inward.

With fear dawning on his transparent face, the boy flashed away like vapor in the air.

He was fleeing.

"No!" Tris cried.

Mari followed the boy's vapors and saw the woman ghost. Her translucent features stretched as her mouth gaped in a silent wail. Kreenan's terror broke loose, and he charged away for the stable doors.

"Don't run!" Mari called again, but it was too late.

As Kreenan bolted out into the night, Mari shot after him. If that ghost touched him, he'd die like the others, wasted away in the space of one night. Mari ran after them, and the last thing she heard over another fading peal from the shell was an anguished shout, from *him*.

"Mari!"

CHAPTER
FOURTEEN

O utside the stable, Mari ran after Kreenan—or rather the woman's ghost. She barely glimpsed Kreenan ahead as he cut right away from the barracks and toward the city wall.

Maybe he'd thought of someplace to hide, not that this would work, not against a ghost. Then she spotted where he was headed, to the half tower with the stairs leading up to the wall's top. He'd be trapped in there trying to get up those curving stairs.

Kreenan glanced back just before reaching the half tower's bottom opening. He saw the ghost coming for him, suddenly dropped, hit the ground, and rolled.

The woman's wisp shot over him. A trail of vapor shaped into a hand and lashed at his face. He rolled away, and the wisp curled up, roiling to turn on him.

"Stay down!" Mari shouted at Kreenan, and she slapped the disk through the wisp.

The metal suddenly chilled her fingers to the bone, and that glowing white mist fanned, swirled, and billowed in the night. She almost dropped the disk and quickly grabbed it with her other hand.

Kreenan rolled to his feet, his expression flat and stunned.

A wave of panic flooded Mari; he was numbed with terror, and she saw no reason left in his eyes. This brief assessment cost her as he rushed at her and grabbed the disk out of her hands before she could jerk it away. Stumbling backward, he looked up. The woman ghost had fully formed again. As she hovered there, a grating moan rolled out of her, and her head swiveled toward Mari.

Mari's mind blanked and then raced for what to do. Rush Kreenan for the disk? Turn and run? Try to shift fast enough, even with Kreenan watching and her clothes restraining her?

Soundless now, the woman dove at her.

Mari dropped, and rolled, and somehow wasn't touched. When she came to her feet again, Kreenan turned and ran for the entrance of the half tower in the wall.

The ghost didn't even look at him. It shot downward.

Mari dove aside, rolled again, and lunged the other way. She came up to see the woman rise out of the ground where she'd been an instant before. Mari couldn't keep this up all night, and she circled to the right, trying to get near the wall.

The woman rose fully out of the ground, floating a forearm's length above it. Her face was twisted up in madness, from rage or anguish or both. She rushed in, level with the ground, and Mari didn't know which way to go. Maybe if she waited for the last instant, the ghost might slip through the wall behind her. It might lose awareness long enough for her to run.

The spirit suddenly lurched to a stop, as if jerked backward. Two white sparks showed through her translucent form.

Mari knew those eyes.

Tris felt cold sinking deeper into his flesh, stripping away his strength. It was nearly as bad as the icy waters of the stream. He had never tried to banish so many spirits so quickly, one after another. He wrenched on the woman's leg, released his grip, and lashed his arms around her torso.

Cold sank into him—his chest, his arms—and he felt it on his face. All his body heat was draining away, but he could not let go. Not with so many lives so close—with Mari so close.

The white woman thrashed and then screamed. The sound vibrated through him into his bones, magnifying the cold. He fought to drag her back into the clear.

He could feel the portal already opening.

There it was in the dark, beginning to turn and blacken, like a hole in the night.

The woman kicked backward with her feet, driving the cold into his thighs and knees. Of the three he had fought this night, she was the strongest. She twisted on him.

Her hand raked across his right cheekbone.

He shoved as she tried again to claw at him.

Her head struck the vortex and began coming apart—hair swirling, flesh and eyes shredding, until bones beneath them fractured into white dust sucked into the swirl. Her screams echoed back, fainter and fainter out of the void, and she was gone.

Tris stood shuddering and fighting for breath as he waited for the portal to collapse. He heard Mari's rapid footfalls coming beyond it, but the vortex still hung there before him. Something in that blackness moved the wrong way—or did not move as if it resisted the current. That null point spun in the center, held, and began to expand. A bulge protruded outward like black oil with a sheen of light upon it.

Black Tris was coming.

Mari watched as that swirling, turning portal appeared, cutting off sight of Tris and the woman ghost. She charged wide around the portal and saw only him. The woman was gone.

Why hadn't that portal closed like before?

Tris didn't look her way and only stared, unblinking, at that turning black hole in the world. When he backstepped away from the portal, she rushed wide around its edge to see.

Something was coming *out* of it.

Out of that black darker than night around her, something bulged at its center. She wasn't certain what, or what to do about it, and stood frozen. First an arm and a hand; then a shoulder followed. Was that a face coming next?

All black with no detail of features, it leaned into the world, struggling to break free, but it gained no more ground and didn't step out. Features began to form. She saw the long straight nose in its pure black profile, and then the silhouette of cropped hair on its head.

Mari stopped breathing, not thinking anything as her eyes twitched away to *him*.

Tris backed away another step.

Everything about that pitch-black form was a mirror image of him. What was that *thing*? *What was he?*

Tris retreated another step. He wanted to close his eyes but could not and struggled to think of any way to stop this. Movement made his eyes twitch left. He felt ill and cold inside.

Mari was here within reach of the other him.

. . . not you . . . I Tris . . . now . . .

"No!"

That one word came out of him in a scream as he rushed the portal. There would be no more deaths, not anyone, not her, because of him. He could not allow himself to be taken. He could not allow himself to be replaced in this world. Wildly, he fumbled for the knife he had again hidden in his belt beneath the front of his pullover.

But the portal whirled inward, sucking the other *him* with it, and vanished. Tris stood there, not moving, as he saw nothing before him in the night.

"What was that?"

He shuddered, turning his head toward that hissing voice. There stood Mari, staring where the portal had vanished. Had she seen the other *him* trying to come through?

"What did you do?" she whispered.

How could he answer her here and now or ever? He had not done anything to cause any of this except to be born . . . dead.

No one would ever believe him. No one ever had. Even Heil was doubtful of the cause of his other self, and Tris had told him far more than anyone else.

"It looked like you," Mari bit off, as though the words hurt. "Was it you? Is that *thing* you?"

Each question sharpened the chill inside Tris so that it spread outward on his skin.

"That thing, that . . . *you*," she whispered, inching in toward him, "slaughtered my whole family!"

Tris was uncertain what she meant—or perhaps he did not want to be certain. She glanced again toward where the portal had vanished.

"All in one night," she said, "in the Wicker Woods."

Those last two words made Tris nearly retch, but he had not eaten anything to come up. He knew that night. Standing upon the hill, he had watched three Móndyalítko wagons roll into those trees. At thirteen, he had fled the slaughter inside that main hall, as white wisps dove through servants and guards, all dying in horror.

His mother was still somewhere inside the manor.

He had to lead those spirits to where no one else would go, and the dead always followed wherever he went. As he hit the front doors and shoved one wide-open, he hesitated and looked back. That was a mistake.

Down the passage behind him, a black form walked through the hallway's dusky shadows—but it never made a sound, not even a footfall.

Slender, perhaps frail, the same height, with the silhouette of dangling hair like his own. It was like him. Did it stall after so many steps, like he did, so often uncertain or second-guessing where he could go to be alone?

Unable to move, he still waited to hear even one footfall—or any noise to tell him it was someone else coming up the dim passage.

No sound came except the screams of the dying echoing out of the far hall. And still, his mother was somewhere inside; the only person who never looked at him in fear.

Tris turned and ran out of the manor. He remembered that black form in his childhood bedroom among the wisps of white circling around him and the other *him*.

Running blindly down the main road, he looked back once and saw the form in the shape of himself pause at the road's crest.

Spirits roiled out into the night around the other *him*.

Tris ran until a stitch in his side took away his breath. Panting, he stood in the dark, looking all ways. Where could he go that no one else would ever go? Then it came to him.

No one ever dared the Wicker Woods anymore.

He ran for the trees.

Gasping again, as branches whipped at his arms and face, he stopped to look back. All he saw was the black silhouettes of trees in the night.

The first scream rolled through the Wicker Woods.

Another scream, then shouts, and he turned back, stumbling more than running while looking for the source of those voices. Another scream and another came and cut off too quickly.

Tris stopped, gasping for breath. Turning back would not save anyone anymore; he could only hope those spirits might come after him. He turned and ran—and ran—until his legs gave out.

He crashed upon the wet earth, skidding over rotting leaves and twigs. The world went dark. Nothing more disturbed him. He could barely open his eyes after dawn, too late.

Rising took effort. Braced against the bare trunk of an ancient oak, he listened but heard little more than tree branches and leaves chittering in an early breeze. Longer still, and he stumbled back the way he had come, or so he thought. When he broke through brush into a clearing, he could go no farther.

There were bodies everywhere. Mouths open in a last cry, eyes wide in the moment of death, they were so pale he would never have known them as Móndyalítko except for the wagons.

Tris backed away, stumbled wide around, and never entered the clearing.

He had saved no one. He had only brought death with him.

Tris stared at Mari, still inching toward him. Why had he never thought of that night after she had saved him when he'd left Strîbrov? He stared at her, studied her face. He had never realized it was her.

A little girl with chocolate brown hair had sat on the lead wagon's bench between a large man and a pretty woman in a head scarf.

His stomach clenched again.

"It was you," she said.

Too much became clear.

. . . her hateful but doubtful glares, as if she was uncertain about something, about him.

. . . puzzlement—no, obsession—over spirits and what he could do to them.

. . . questions that no one else wanted or dared to ask.

. . . and she would not leave, even if—when—he told her to do so.

She saw that other *him* as him, one and the same. She was neither right nor wrong.

"You have been hunting me," he said, numb now.

Not a question, for he did not need her answer, and she did not need his excuses. He had led his other self straight to her and hers.

How many more had died in his passing after that night, or beyond the plagued village of Yan'vul or elsewhere? He had not asked to be born this way. It had happened; that was all. But wherever he went, no matter the restless dead he banished, more death had followed him.

There was a blade in Mari's hand.

Long and narrow, that dagger was so much more suitable than the small eating knife tucked into his belt beneath his pullover, long enough to go straight into his heart.

Black Tris would have no flesh in which to walk among the living.

Mari closed in, watching for him to run or do anything. He only stood there looking tired, as if he had given up. He knew about that night in the Wicker Woods, because he'd gone there, bringing that night-shadow death that was *him*.

She'd seen him banish more spirits, and that black whirlpool he called every time he did so, but this time he'd tried to call back something else.

Like him, though separate, it was still *him*. That was enough—wasn't it? So why hesitate? Years of caged anguish surged up, and she felt her bones begin to shift.

No! She wanted him to see her—her face—when he died.

Mari charged with that hard-won dagger, finally ready to bloody it.

Tris stood motionless and emotionless. Relief would finally come.

He understood why some spirits rose in seeking a need left unresolved, a need that would not let them rest. What if a life itself could not be resolved? What if that unresolved life cost the lives of too many others? What of the endless grief he left in his passing?

He could not bear that any longer. And perhaps she gained a resolution for what he had done to her in ignorance.

Black Tris would be trapped forever.

Would he meet that other *him* in death? It did not matter, so long as no one else ever met it again in life.

Tris stood still as Mari came for him.

Something flew in from the left and struck her shoulder.

He flinched as the conch spun upward on impact and careened off her head. She went down—stayed down.

Tris hurried toward her.

"Bad kitty," someone growled.

Stumbling to a stop, Tris looked for that voice.

Heil stalked out of the dark from the stable, glaring ahead. He headed straight toward Mari. When Tris looked the other way, Mari had started to push herself up. He took two more steps to reach her first, and a fist struck the side of his face.

Tris's head whipped aside, the night spun, and he stumbled away as a burning sting rose in his left cheek and temple. He barely regained his feet when . . .

"You get that damn death wish out of your head! You hear?"

Tris straightened up, dizzy in shock, and met Heil's angry gray eyes.

"We've got enough trouble without your self-pity," Heil snapped, and then he turned on Mari. "And you, you little *stray*, what's with you?"

Mari was on her hands and knees as her eyes fixed on Heil. They narrowed, and it seemed they were brighter, more amber than before.

"Some bone to pick with him?" Heil went on. "You think you're the first to blame him afterward for putting the restless dead to rest? Maybe a lover or just a relative?"

"That is enough!" Tris shouted.

Heil turned on him but said nothing. At a slight movement, Tris saw Mári's glittering eyes twitch toward the dagger on the ground halfway between her and him. Heil turned back on her.

"Really?" Heil asked her. "Are you that stupid . . . or inbred?"

In a single movement, he reached one hand behind his back, up under his pullover, and ripped it back out. Even in the dark, Tris saw the disk in Heil's hand.

"Where?" Tris started. "You gave that to her."

Heil groaned. "You think I'd give anyone, let alone *her*, my only one? How stupid would that be?"

"Then where did—"

"I started making another the day after you showed up at my shop."

Tris was still too lost and unsettled. Mari's eyes shifted again and again between him and Heil. She looked to the long, narrow blade.

"Care for a nap?" Heil asked her. "You think ghosts are all I can affect with *this*?"

He flipped the disk, catching its other edge without looking, and Mari inched back.

"Now, where's my other spirit shield?" he demanded.

Tris looked to Mari but did not see the first disk. Had she put it away somewhere in her clothing?

"A guard took it," she answered, breathy and quick. "Grabbed it when I went down . . . protecting him."

Again, Tris wished he had dismissed, abandoned, or never encountered her. He had destroyed her life in childhood. She did not deserve to lose it because of him or to be treated this way.

Heil stepped on the dagger. With a backward scrape of his boot, he sent the blade skidding across the ground, away from Mari. Tris looked down on where the dagger stopped, only two paces before him.

"Don't get stupid," Heil warned Mari, "or you will get a nap. Now, how many have you banished?"

Tris looked up, saw Mari watching him, and glanced toward Heil. "Three."

"Then there's one left before we—you—get out of here. Sooner the better."

Tris took a long, shaky breath. "Then the conch should—"

"It's not working anymore," Heil interrupted. "And we won't need it. The last one will be coming for you, after what you did to the others. Kitty there's not the only one looking for some misplaced revenge."

Heil was wrong. It was not misplaced.

Mari regained her feet, though she neither ran nor charged. She watched both of them, and Tris could not tell which she would go at now.

"What is that thing?" she asked angrily. "That black one that tried—"

"Not now!" Heil barked at her.

Tris looked to Mari, wanting to try to answer her.

"Not you either," Heil warned.

Tris bit down against a retort, for his mentor was correct. Until the last spirit was banished, and they fled this place, that other *him* was too close. Even so, another portal would need to appear, and now it was so close to the next time on Heil's calculated schedule.

That was why *he* had nearly breached the portal—that and too many deaths in Tris's presence. He glanced toward Mari and quickly away when he found her watching him again.

"Where's the guard who took my shield?" Heil asked.

"Don't know," Mari answered reluctantly. "Off along the wall, somewhere."

"Then go get it. We might need both shields," he ordered. "Sniff him out if you have to."

Her eyes widened slightly, as did Tris's.

"Ah, grief and guts!" Heil scoffed. "Like I couldn't spot one of your kind, *shifter*. Now get moving!"

How did Heil know what she was?

Mari sidestepped wide around the alchemist, more than once looking at Tris. She turned suddenly and bolted off, and Heil sighed as if relieved.

Tris watched Mari fade in the darkness.

If he was fortunate, she would not return until everything was done.

Mari raced through the night along the city wall. She let her other form rise enough to see clearly in the dark—and to smell anything that had passed this way.

She didn't like letting Tris out of her sight, but something wasn't right in all she'd seen and heard. That black thing trying to get out of the portal had to be him or a part of him. Still, that wasn't all there was to it.

The old man knew something more, seemed to know *him* more than anyone. And what he'd said—or hadn't—about Tris needled her doubts again. Why hadn't either of them just tried to run her off or kill her?

Sooner or later, she'd make Heil talk.

But right now, regaining one of his toys would be an advantage.

Picking up that coward Kreenan's trail ate up too much time for her patience. When fear's stench grew, filling her nostrils, she followed the scent all the way to the turn in the outer wall. Another small tower was half-embedded in the city wall's joint. She looked up to where it rose above the walkway high overhead.

Mari ducked into the opening at the tower's base and climbed the spiraling stone steps. She crouched before approaching the top, stepping up only enough to peek level with the walkway's stone.

Kreenan cowered down on the wall's outside corner below its protrusions. His head down, one arm wrapped over it, in the other dangling hand was the first disk.

"Kreenan," she whispered.

He clenched all over as his neck straightened. His head cracked against the wall's inward corner as both hands gripped and thrust out the disk.

She crept one more step. "Give me the disk, you coward."

He spotted her inside the deeper darkness of the tower's exit. "No! It's all I have against them. You can't have it!"

Mari's impatience turned frantic. What if that Heil took Tris and ran while she was gone?

"Kreenan!" she growled, fury rising.

He scooted back tighter into the corner.

Instinct forced pain through Mari's flesh and bones.

She held it back. A half shift was worse than a full change, so painful, and that made fury grow. She lunged out at him in a crouch. In the disk's polished surface, she glimpsed a reflection.

Half animal, eyes burning amber, pitch-black pupils, fur half-sprouted from cheeks, forehead, chin, and with ears and teeth elongated, and fangs . . .

"Give it to me!" Her voice grated like a cat.

Kreenan screamed, and she grabbed the disk with one hand, her claws squealing on metal. She raised the other hand to slash him.

Kreenan convulsed, his eyes rolled up under fluttering eyelids, and he slumped into stillness.

Mari froze, sniffed once. She shook her head, snorted to clear the stench of urine from her muzzle as she backed away. Disgusted and still in pain, she raced back into the tower and down through its darkness.

Once Mari was gone, Tris looked sidelong at Heil. His mentor did not understand what it was truly like to live this way. The fear and guilt had become too much. He had grown too tired of trying to survive until next time.

Black Tris would always come again—sooner and sooner, by Heil's calculations.

"It's coming," Heil said quietly.

"What?" Tris whispered. "Now?"

"Yes, now," Heil said. "You think that fourth ghost just wandered off?"

Tris calmed for the moment. He did not ask how the alchemist knew this. If he let go of all else, he would have known as well. A cold quiet inside would warn him, but now he looked down.

Within two steps lay the long, narrow dagger.

White vapor rose and collected in the night air right in front of him.

The boy spirit's transparent face twisted—little lips curled back, exposing teeth over shrunken gums. It looked only at Tris, and he remembered . . .

Bródy had said the first ghost looked at him and then turned on Brianne. For vengeance—for its own suffering—it went after someone it thought for whom he cared. It wanted the one it hated to suffer loss before death.

Tris did nothing in watching that phosphorescent spirit. He did not need to do anything.

The spirit dove straight for Heil.

Tris snatched up the dagger and slipped it up his sleeve.

Mari raced back along the city wall, wanting to finish her pain, tear off her clothes, and change flesh completely. But she'd have to drop the disk if she did, and carry it in her teeth after that, and she couldn't use it that way. She'd need it for what was coming, and maybe use it in dealing with that Heil.

What about him? How did he know she'd come back?

Of course she would, and he knew.

The pain dulled along the way, replaced by the strain of flight. She knew her other flesh had faded completely when her breaths turned ragged with every stride.

Tris tensed, even knowing what would come, as it always had before.

Heil whipped the disk out, and the boy collided with the metal, face-first, and splashed into vapor.

Tris saw within that curling mist what other eyes would not have at first. The small spirit coalesced. The instant one small leg materialized, he grabbed it. He did not need to look beyond the spirit to know the portal was already forming.

It happened whenever he gripped death as if it had flesh.

Night began to turn and twist beyond the boy, warping sight of anything beyond that swirl. Darkness bled inward, draining to its center. The little spirit shrieked, looking behind itself at what was there.

"Finish this, now!" Heil shouted at him. "And shut that damn hole!"

The spirit twisted back and screeched into Tris's face.

He grabbed one of its arms and shoved it toward the black swirl. Its free leg caught in the turning current and began coming apart. This time was easier than the last three.

"Ah, no," Heil moaned, and then whispered, "Damn it!"

The last of the boy shredded in the black portal. As Tris was about to look for Heil, something glimmering and white shot past in the air.

And then another.

Mari heard a shriek in the night. She still hadn't reached the barracks' stable. It was another dozen hard gasps before she did, and another before she saw that first wisp of white in the dark. Another pant, and three more swirled downward beyond the stable's far end.

White vapors raced by her face as she ran. Terror choked her as she rounded the stable and stumbled to a halt. There were so many—too many—everywhere, as in that night within the Wicker Woods.

She had waited and watched to see *him* call them up and prove his guilt, and now she knew that he'd been there. Out in the path before the barracks, Tris and Heil were surrounded, white wisps diving everywhere.

But only there.

They weren't going for any other living thing. Not like they had with her family.

Heil swatted off one after another with the disk, as Tris tried to shred others out of the air with his hands. He was not a silhouette so black that nothing showed of it, even in movement. He was just himself except those pinprick lights in his eyes.

A wisp shot like an arrow at the alchemist.

Heil bashed it into vapor with his second disk. Another passed too close to Tris, and he swung at it.

Spirits rushed, and the sight dragged Mari back to that night where loss swallowed her whole life. She was ten years old again and lost in fear, until fury came and ate it.

A wisp rushed at her. She ducked and dodged, forgetting she held the first disk.

Beyond Tris, a black whirlpool hung sideways in the night.

Another ghost came straight in for Mari's stomach. This time, she struck down with the disk, and it exploded silently into powder. And then she hesitated again.

This wasn't what she'd wanted.

A clean, certain kill—that was what she'd needed to end the pain.

Heil suddenly bolted away from Tris's side. Ghosts veered after him. What was he doing?

Tris had said Heil knew what he was doing. Then she saw Tris stumble. His eyes closed as he turned toward the black whirlpool in the air.

Was he trying to close it? How—why? There were so many spirits all around, and they couldn't hurt him, from what she'd seen since finding him. What was he doing now?

Something caught in the corner of her sight. She barely dropped and rolled as a wisp passed just above her face. She swiped the next one into vapor with the disk and rolled to her feet.

Inside the whirling blackness before Tris, something moved—something blacker than that swirl. A hand and then a head pushed outward. Not even the glimmer of the ghosts reflected upon it, like its form swallowed any light.

That hand reached out for Tris, but he just stood there.

Mari froze and was almost struck. She barely swatted aside the next ghost coming at her with the disk. When she looked again . . .

That black hand gripped Tris by the throat. He still did nothing.

Mari's flesh and bones began to ache.

Tris raised a hand, but not to grab the black hand on his throat. And that grip on him began to spread, like it flowed into his flesh. In his own hand he held her dagger.

With a gasp, Mari charged.

. . . *us Tris . . . we Tris . . . me Tris . . .*

Tris heard the other *him*. A swirl of desires overwhelmed him—its and his own. He longed to live a normal life that would never come. He longed for no more death because of whatever he was.

In the touch of that other *him*, he felt a powerful hunger for life. That nearly took him whole, made him want to live at any cost to anyone. Nothing had ever terrified him so much as it tried to become *him*.

"Stop him!" someone shouted.

Tris flipped the dagger in his hand, blade inward to ram into his heart.

Mari lost all reason as her other form surged up. She fell, skidded, dropped the disk; clothing tore and ripped as bone and flesh changed. She was shuddering in both panic and pain as she thrashed free of her shredded clothes.

"Stop him!" Heil shouted from somewhere.

Mari saw Tris turn her dagger blade down in his grip. The blackness of that other *him* bled across his throat, wrapped around his neck, and began to bleed upward into his face.

If that thing touching him touched her, would she die?

Did she screech like the animal as she leaped?

She'd never know the latter; there was only instinct within a fury that now fed fear.

Mari slammed into Tris at the peak of her leap.

. . . I Tris . . . not you Tris . . . now . . .

Those words whispered inside of Tris's thoughts. They were a chill in his mind to match the one spreading from his throat into his head and chest. What if that chill reached his heart before he died?

Something came at him from the corner of his sight. Startled, he rammed the dagger toward his heart, and then his head wrenched at an impact.

The blade's tip ripped through his pullover and shirt, tore skin from the right side of his sternum and outward. He slammed down too hard on his other side, and another weight crushed breath out of him. He heard its harsh, rumbling breaths panting near his ear, but he did not care.

Tris craned his head back along the ground. There was the dagger within reach.

The lynx struggled to regain footing, paws shifting over its downed prey.

Mari pushed up off Tris, didn't care about white wisps whirling all around, and twisted her head back for that other *him*.

That black man-thing stepped toward her, though maybe too slowly. Its footfalls made no sound that her tall ears could hear. Her jowls pulled back, exposing teeth and fangs in a threat for it. After one hiss at that black thing, a screeching yowl smothered any other sound.

It didn't stop; it stepped closer.

Someone ran by behind her, but she didn't take her eyes off her enemy. She curled all the way around to face her enemy.

Her true *prey*.

His black hand reached out. She peeled back her jowls, spreading her jaws to snap on it and tear it off.

"No!"

Something struck her head hard, making her flinch away. The impact rang metallic in her ears, startling her even more.

She twisted back, fury faltering.

Heil swiped at that black shape, again and again, striking its hands as it tried to grasp him. Though the metal rang with each impact, those hands didn't turn to vapor like a ghost. Then she saw the wisps of white.

Those were spirits all around her—Mari.

"Put him down, now!"

She stiffened at Heil shouting at her. He dodged a slow—too slow—swipe of the black one's hand. In turn, he pounded that hand down with the disk. The clang of impact barely came before he slapped the other disk against its head.

Another clang woke Mari to full awareness.

He had both disks now? Why was that thing moving so slow?

"Knock Tris out!" Heil shouted.

Mari twisted the other way. There was Tris struggling to reach out for the dagger that had fallen beyond his head. He looked dazed, hurt, half-aware.

"Do it, or we're all dead!"

She didn't know what was happening. She didn't trust that old man. But Tris still struggled—slowly—to get one hand on her dagger.

He had tried to kill himself.

Mari leaped on him and pinned him, flat on his back. At her weight, his face twisted in pain, but when his eyes opened, he wasn't afraid of her. She couldn't strike, not as she was, or she might kill him.

"Get off . . . please."

His words came hushed with too little breath. All thoughts of vengeance fled from Mari at the sight of agony on Tris's face. When she didn't move, his eyes widened and his jaw clenched. He punched her.

The blow barely whipped her head, and she struck back.

The first strike of her paw dazed him.

"Again, damn you!" Heil shouted.

The next strike wasn't as much paw, more of a fist, and she punched him hard.

Mari whimpered in the pain of her other flesh leaving her.

Tris's head lolled on the ground, and his eyes rolled up before they closed. Thin lines torn through the hair at his temple started to bleed. Blood seeped from thin lines of claw marks down across his cheekbone.

Everything became suddenly too quiet, even to her ears, and she heard her own whimpers.

What had she done?

In pain and exhaustion, she collapsed.

Mari lay naked and panting atop Tris. All her fur gone, the cold of night began to chill her from outside. It didn't match the cold inside of her. Someone dropped to the ground too close, and she twisted, ready to lunge.

Heil sat there near enough to strike, but he was gasping for breath and sweat glistened on his old face. He dropped one disk with a dull thud on the ground.

Mari quickly looked back—and saw nothing. No black *him*, no whirl of black in the air, no spirits racing about, and everything too quiet, except for Heil's gasps and her own.

"How?" she got out without real voice.

Heil barely turned his hanging head enough to glare at her.

"How did . . . you . . . know?" she tried again.

"'Cause I know him better than anyone," Heil panted. "Including you!"

That wasn't what she'd really asked, but when she looked at Tris, she panicked again. She rose off him on all fours, leaned forward, sniffed him, then heard him still breathing.

His breaths were shallow but steady.

Mari almost collapsed atop him again. She stopped herself and backed up on all fours. She stopped halfway at the dark stain over his right side. Rising up to see more clearly, she found his blood smeared all over her belly as well.

She started to breathe too fast again.

"It's not that bad," Heil said.

Still worried, she reached to peel back split clothing, and a hand grabbed her wrist, stopping her. When she looked, Heil stripped off his own charcoal pullover. He held it out.

"Put this on before you freeze," he commanded. "Then we get him inside."

Mari stared at Heil. "Why did you tell me to put him down?"

That scowl rose on the alchemist's face. "Because I've had to do it."

Mari was still lost.

"That thing can only come when he's awake," Heil said. "On nights it can come on its own—sooner and sooner every time—without him even giving it a way to do so. Once it's gone, the wisps all vanish."

That still wasn't enough. It didn't answer every question she had, especially the ones that kept her from facing what she'd almost done. After so many years in pain, guilt, and fury, she'd hunted and nearly killed the wrong prey.

Mari looked all around in the night; there was no right prey left for her.

CHAPTER
FIFTEEN

L ater that same night, Mari headed for the common room. She knew
the guards would be desperate to know all that had happened.

Tris was in bed in their room, bandaged up though not asleep. When
it was clear that Heil wouldn't leave him and didn't give a "crow's crap"
about the guards, Mari said she'd go to the captain herself.

All heads turned her way as she entered the common room. The
border guards—especially Stàsiuo, the four volunteers, even that coward
Kreenan—deserved something.

Familiar faces were all about the room, including those of Kreenan,
Farrell, Orlov, Rafferty, and the three guards who'd come to the stable.
Kreenan's head was bandaged. Some refugees were gathered at the hearth,
but not as many as before. And since the four volunteers were present, likely
Stàsiuo had already heard something about this night. The captain rose up
at his table and waved her over, so she joined him.

"Are they gone?" he asked. "All of them?"

"Yes."

"It's over? All of it?" he pressed.

"Yes," she said again, though she wasn't certain about that last part. What else could she say?

No one would believe too much of what'd happened. Thinking on that, she fixed Kreenan with a stare. He dropped his gaze and looked away. He wouldn't tell anybody about her, at least not for a while. By then, she'd be gone, and it wouldn't matter how much others believed. And Kreenan would have explaining to do about what he'd done, if he said anything at all.

Men like the captain were interested only in results; the rest didn't matter as much.

When Stàsiuo nodded once at Mari, low murmurs of relief rose around the room. The night was a success as far as everyone here was concerned. They'd lost no more of their own.

Stàsiuo ran a hand down his face and asked, "Is the . . . baronet all right? What happened to him?"

She couldn't answer either question—wouldn't answer the second.

"He'll be better soon," she said.

To his credit, the captain frowned in concern but didn't press for more. "Can we do anything for him?"

Mari thought about that. "I'll let you know." And she left.

Halfway down the back passage, she slowed, wanting to look in on Tris, but uncertain if she should or could. In that empty passage, and more than halfway through that night, she slowed to a stop.

She still smelled Tris's blood on herself, as she stood there too long in the dark.

Two days later, outside Soladran's main gate, she stopped again on the road.

Tris walked on, not noticing, and Heil was strides ahead.

In the daylight, she was still in the dark.

She watched Tris's back as he walked slowly, with some effort. It would be a long journey for him back to Stríbrov. He'd said almost nothing about what had happened in the street two nights ago.

He'd said only one thing when she'd finally returned to the room that night.

"Thank you for being there."

Could he have said anything else that would have made her feel worse?

She'd spent more than half a lifetime since the morning she'd awoken on her dead father's chest. She'd been hunting Tris so long, and this had been the only thing that kept the pain, guilt, and anguish held down. Now she didn't have that.

He wasn't the one who'd done this to her.

She'd never get the one who did.

That one was already something dead and beyond her reach.

Tris hobbled along, holding his rebandaged side. How many times had Heil—or Mari—changed that bandage in the past two days? Too often, both of them worried somehow in their different ways. And anyone else would—should—have been relieved to be alive.

In part, he was. Another part wondered whether she should have stopped him.

His other half, his shadow, would come again; Black Tris would always come again.

Tris slowed a bit more, though Heil was already too far ahead. His mentor had said nothing about the walk back to Stríbrov, but Tris knew that without horses Heil was going to be in a foul mood by the time they reached home.

Something else brought Tris to a halt. He heard only Heil's footfalls ahead and looked back. His breath caught.

Mari stood still in the road a short ways behind. Vacant of expression, she stared down at the road, maybe not at anything at all. She might have been lost in a passing thought of her own, if not for the tears running down her blank face.

"Mari?"

She flinched, looked up to meet his eyes, and quickly lowered hers again. He knew.

He was not the only one who lived with guilt. He should have sent her away before, even before going to Soladran. Why had he not done so? He could not now, though he could not see how she would ever want to go anywhere near him.

"Are you coming?"

She did not look at him. She had not been wrong in hunting him; if not for him, Black Tris would not exist, her family would not have died, and they would never have met.

Why did the last part now bother him so much?

Tris lowered his eyes. "You can come . . . come with me."

A loud scoff carried from up the road.

"Guts and grief!" Heil griped. "Just get a puppy or something!"

Tris risked looking up. Mari's wild, frightened eyes stared at him. He began to turn, hesitated, and whispered, "You should come . . . please."

He stepped onward, slowly at first. He stalled more than once, listening, but heard only his own quick breaths. Then he heard something more—soft footfalls reached his ears.

Soon she was right beside him.